Praise for *Her Last Words*

'Opens with a te
and ch[...]

'A truly gripping plot'
Sinéad Crowley

'Tense, claustrophobic and absolutely absorbing'
Sam Blake

'Compelling, clever and chilling'
Michèle Forbes

'Breathtakingly paced . . . frighteningly plausible'
S. A. Dunphy

'A stunning writer'
Elske Rahill

'Truly surprising . . . original'
Emily Hourican

'A chilling, magical read'
Patricia Gibney

'Spellbinding . . . Kelly had me in the palm of her
hand for every single page'
Irish Examiner

'Tautly wrought . . . the twisting plot leads the reader
on a surprising journey'
Dermot Bolger

HER LAST WORDS

E. V. Kelly holds a PhD in sociology from UCD. Her short stories have been broadcast on RTÉ and published in *Crannóg*, while her winning stories have appeared in *The Irish Times*, an anthology and online. She has been shortlisted for various awards including the Francis MacManus Short Story Award, the Hennessy Literary Awards and the SBP/Penguin Ireland Award. She was nominated for The Pushcart Prize 2021. *Her Last Words* is her first novel.

E.V. KELLY

HER
LAST
WORDS

QUERCUS

First published in Great Britain in 2022 by Quercus
This paperback edition published in 2023 by

QUERCUS

Quercus Editions Ltd
Carmelite House
50 Victoria Embankment
London EC4Y 0DZ

An Hachette UK company

A CIP catalogue record for this book is available
from the British Library

PB ISBN 978 1 52941 719 7
EB ISBN 978 1 52941 718 0

10 9 8 7 6 5 4 3 2 1

Typeset by Jouve (UK), Milton Keynes

Printed and bound in Great Britain by Clays Ltd, Elcograf S.p.A.

MIX
Paper from
responsible sources
FSC® C104740

Papers used by Quercus are from well-managed forests and other responsible sources.

For Emmet
and our children
Charlie, Daniel, Leo, Myles and Felix

TUESDAY

CASSANDRA

It's a cold, crisp April morning, not long after sunrise. We are parked above the beach, looking out across the expansive bay with its cushioning arms either end. Dalkey Island to the left and Bray Head to the right, holding the deep blue in front of us. This is our version of the Amalfi coast, and it's every bit as stunning on a good day. In the distance, Sorrento Terrace brightens and winks at us, welcoming the day. A smattering of slate grey and pink-tinged cloud interrupts the sky.

Ted climbs into the front seat beside me and he looks out through his yellow binoculars. Ten steps below us and off down at the shore, Jeff prepares for his daily ritual swim, folding his clothes and leaving them on top of his shoes. Red swim shorts today. He hobbles to the water's edge, crunching through damp cold stones and he keeps going, straight in, as if he doesn't feel the sting of it. He walks out to his midriff, makes a triangle with his arms and dives under. Jeff's the only swimmer. It's too early even for the dog walkers. He emerges, shaking his head to remove the hair from his eyes, droplets spraying in a halo around him. He cuts a strong front crawl and then swivels, stops for a breath and takes off again on his back. On the days that I wait, it's this bit that I like to watch most of all. His face up to the sky and his arms shooting straight up out of the water, then pivoting back behind him. He stops to float. The relief he must feel. His bad leg buoyant, supported by the sea. Right now he looks just the same as anyone else. What does he think about as he lies back looking up at the clouds? I like to guess. Today I decide that he's thinking about how we will celebrate the third edition of his *Critical Introduction to Film Theory*. He's disappointed not to have found a publisher for his latest book and doesn't feel like making a fuss about a revised edition of a much older book coming out. I told him we're doing it anyway. It's a super achievement to have written this seminal text. Important for Ted too, I argued, to see us celebrating this. Role modelling. A lesson in resilience and not succumbing to disappointment. That's what turned it for him. Anything for Ted.

A burst of hailstones pummels off the windscreen and for a moment Jeff is obliterated.

'Can I get out? I want to feel them, Mum.' Ted has the door open and is out before I can answer. He stands beside the car, arms outstretched like a scarecrow, laughing as the hail hits him, stinging his face. I turn the key in the ignition and set the wipers to work. As they clear the screen, I see Jeff swimming towards the shore. Ted jumps back in behind me. I turn to look at him. His thick, wavy hair is sodden, darkening the blond to a dull brown. His navy puffer jacket glistens with the wet.

'They were huge,' he says, his eyes gleaming with delight.

'You're very brave. There's no way I would've got out in that.'

I turn back and watch the hail melt away, the sun shining down as if the shower never happened. Jeff hobbles out of the sea to his pile of clothes and his stick. He's cut the swim short. I watch as he pulls his black towel around him. He stands there, looking out across the bay and as he does, I have that thought again. If it wasn't for the stick, he'd pass for a fit man, not yet forty. He snaps his head suddenly to the right and turns to look down the beach. He raises his stick up. The windscreen begins to fog. I open my window a little to let it clear.

'Wrap the picnic rug around you to dry off and warm up,' I say to Ted, and I turn to look at him putting the red tartan rug around his head first and then wrapping it around the rest of himself.

'Snug as a bug in a rug,' I say to him and he giggles. I pick up his binoculars from the seat beside me and use them to look back down at Jeff. He has turned to face the length of the beach, towards Bray Head. He's dropped his towel and he's no longer getting dressed. He seems to be shivering. I look to my right to see what has stopped him in his tracks. A girl runs towards him, removing her white shirt, throwing it off. I look back at Jeff. He doesn't move. He knows her.

'Can I get in the front again, Mum?'

'No, sweetheart. Have a little lie down there, you seem tired,' I say as I watch her speed up, her turquoise skirt flapping in the wind. When she reaches Jeff, she leaps up on him. He doesn't falter. He lets go of his stick.

'Please, Mum.' I flick my head to check. He's lying down.

'No. Stay where you are, good boy.' I put the binoculars back up and look down at the beach. The girl's legs are wrapped around Jeff's waist, her arms around his neck, skin to skin. Her head tilts backwards and her long, curly hair dances in the wind. She's laughing.

'But I love sitting in the front waiting for Dad.'

'I know. But today why don't we surprise him instead. You hide there. Down on the floor would be even better. Then when he gets back you can jump up and give him a big fright.'

Jeff puts his hands on her tiny waist and his head moves from side to side.

'Yeuch,' Ted calls out. He must be sitting up now, watching too. My mouth goes dry. There's nothing I can do.

Jeff's left hand goes up to greet hers around his neck and his right arm cups her back. Her hold loosens and their hands move down together. They stay for a moment like this, hands grasped just underneath her small right breast, her left arm around his back now.

'There's a rotten apple core under your seat, Mum. I'll throw it out the window.'

He hasn't seen.

'No, leave it. Just lie there, very still. Otherwise he won't get a fright.'

4

She's talking a lot, but I can't hear what she's saying. I fiddle with the focus knob on the binoculars, turning it until I can see a little more clearly. Both of his hands are back on her waist. He's lifting her down. She stands on the stones looking up at him, talking still, but then her chatter changes into something else, a groan which accelerates quickly into something louder. Like a caterwaul.

'What's that?' Ted calls out.

'Just another swimmer screaming about the cold water.'

'Dad never does that.'

'No.'

I watch Jeff put his right hand over her face, and his left hand holds her head which is tilted back slightly. Her arms rise up towards his, but then flail down by her side. He's talking to her. The binoculars begin to cloud with my breath. I wipe them quickly on my top.

'Dad's brave like me,' Ted calls from behind.

I put the binoculars back up and see her fall to her knees and then keel onto her side. I focus in further. She's completely still. I stare at her chest. It's not moving. Something glints at me, caught in the sun. I focus again and catch it. Jeff steps backwards. He's backing away from her.

'Remember the time he trod on the fish hook, and it was stuck in his foot and he didn't even cry?'

'I do.'

I turn to check he's still lying on the floor. I look back down on the beach.

Jeff throws his clothes on and steps into his shoes without

bothering with his socks. He doesn't tie the shoelaces either. He's coming towards us, more quickly than I'd think he was able to. I put the binoculars under my seat and close the window. Within seconds he's up the steps and back in the car beside me.

'Boo,' Ted shouts out, jumping up from the floor.

'Quiet now,' Jeff says. He doesn't turn to look at Ted and he doesn't look at me. His head tilts to the left instead, staring out at Sorrento Terrace. I can feel Ted's disappointment as I hear his seat belt click. I can't look at him either. I turn the keys in the ignition, press on the clutch, slip the gears into reverse and turn the car around as fast as I can.

I glance in the rear-view mirror. She is still there, a crumpled heap on the stones. Her long, curly hair straggles beside her, blending her in with the russet and black seaweed that surrounds her. The waves crash inches from her and then retreat leaving a frothy residue for a moment before that too disappears. She is alone. Her white shirt which she shed just minutes ago is being buffeted away from her. A seagull circles above her, shrieking into the wind.

In the car nobody says a word.

A steep exit tunnel takes us up and away from the beach. In the darkness the shock of it kicks in and I hold onto my scream. A train clatters overhead. Out of the tunnel, blinking into the sudden strong light I drive straight onto the road. A cyclist swerves to avoid being struck. I slam on the brakes and the cyclist mouths something at me. I wave an apology.

'Bloody cyclists, what's he doing out so early anyway?' Jeff says, looking straight ahead.

'Bad word, Dad.'

'Sorry, Ted.'

I don't know if he knows that I saw. He's not looking at me. Not catching my eye. But that's pretty normal for him. This is all so normal. We do this every morning. His doctors prescribed swimming to strengthen the nerve damage. He's no longer supposed to drive himself. Some days we drop him off and collect him when he's finished. Other days we wait. Next we go home and have breakfast. Then I drive Ted to school and Jeff into college and come back to prepare for my appointments.

What the hell just happened? I want to shout out, but I can't. Not with Ted in the car.

I squeeze my grip tighter on the wheel.

'Did you bring the flask of tea?' Jeff asks as we snake around Vico Road.

This is what I do every day. Give him his tea after the swim. Warm him back up.

'It was ice cold today,' he says, clutching the top of his walking stick. His knuckles have a blueish tinge to them. Seawater patches seep through his cream chinos. He hasn't dried off properly.

I point to the glove compartment. Normally I get the flask out as he comes back up the steps and hand it straight to him when he gets into the car.

He fidgets with the lid and takes a slurp.

'Ah, lovely,' he says, as he does each morning, and keeps drinking, as if everything is just the same. If Ted wasn't with us, would he tell me? Would I want him to tell me? If he says anything, I'll have to react. Join him in whatever this is. If he says nothing . . .

'I'm going to drive you straight in to college and then bring Ted to school,' I say. He screws the lid back onto the flask so tight that it squeaks.

'Shouldn't we have some breakfast first, like we usually do?' Usually.

He's telling me to carry on as if nothing just happened.

'No. I haven't time this morning. My mother needs a few groceries so I'll do that before my first appointment.'

He stares out the window. The lush green verge is peppered with pink valerian, catching his eye.

'The glories of springtime,' he says, and when I look to search his face for something, some little hint that he's unsettled, I don't see it. His bottom lip curls into a smile.

'Freezing hailstones you mean?' Ted joins in, laughing. 'Did they hurt you?'

'No, little man, not at all. I love getting caught in hailstones as a matter of fact. They wake me up.'

'They hurt me. Well, just my face and hands really.'

'What, you were here for them?' He says this quickly, slightly high pitched.

'Yep,' Ted says, sounding proud of himself.

'And you got out in them? You mad thing,' Jeff says and he looks behind him, at Ted in his seat.

8

I keep my eyes on the road. We're so high up. A little veer could have us plunging into the sea. One of my nightmares. My worst nightmare, until now. What would I do if we were plunged into the sea? Open the door or the window? Who would I try to save first? What the hell would I do?

'Did you see the waves and the spray today?' Jeff asks, unravelling his socks. Tiny pebbles fall out of them onto his lap. He bends forwards to pull the socks on. He wants to know if I saw.

'No, I was sending emails. My caseload is mental at the moment.'

'Pity,' he says slowly, tying his laces, pulling them tight. 'They were spectacular.'

A shiver runs through me.

Spectacular?

I saw something spectacular all right, I want to roar.

'I forgot to learn my six-plus tables for homework,' Ted says from behind me.

'Don't worry about it, pal. All that learn-by-rote stuff. It's no good for you,' Jeff says.

'But there's a classroom game we play. King of the tables, and I'm always coming last.'

'You see what it's doing to him, Cass?' Jeff whispers to me. 'How it's skewing him, turning him into a little automaton. Making him feel inadequate. Is this really what you want for him?'

'I'm never quick enough,' Ted says.

'See?'

'Six plus four?' I ask, tired of this argument and not quite believing that he's doing this right now. How? How could he do this right now?

'Ten.'

'Great boy. Six plus seven?'

Ted counts out loud, using his fingers. I quiz him all the way into the campus. Stops me from having to talk to Jeff. I pull into the admin car park. Jeff opens the door and gets out slowly, stick first, tiny beach pebbles left scattered on the seat behind him.

'Hang on a minute, what about my briefcase?' he says, leaning back into the car.

I forgot about that. It's in the cottage. He gets it each morning after breakfast.

'You'll have to do without it for today,' I say and he presses his lips together in the way that he does when he's thinking. As if he's spreading lipstick evenly around them. He hobbles off, his bad foot slapping the paving. When he turns around and waves his stick at us I don't wave back.

'Bye, Dad,' Ted calls after him.

I drop my head onto the steering wheel for a moment. Then I accelerate off, jerking Ted sideways.

'Sorry, sweetheart.'

'Go, Mum! Go, Mum! Go, Mum!' Ted chants, as if it's a race we're in. Which is exactly how it feels. The smell of cold sea from Jeff's togs is nauseating me. I open the window and let the air rush through.

Back along the dual carriageway what I witnessed at the

beach flashes before me, as if I'm fast forwarding a film to get to certain bits. Then pausing on them. On one in particular. The image of her left breast in close focus. The dark brown areola ring on a small, firm handful of translucent white flesh. On what's missing from it. Like an iris without a pupil. To what's there instead. A barbell piercing, glinting in the cold morning sun.

OCTOBER

NINA

It's close to dawn and Nina silences her alarm before it has a chance to get going. She crawls out of bed and makes her way to the kitchenette. Flicking the kettle on, she sends coffee granules tinkling into the bottom of a glass cup and she reaches for the folder in her bag. She feels a dizzying emptiness like she used to on exam mornings. A hunger accompanied by an inability to eat, while knowing that eating is all important to get through it. For now a cup of black coffee will have to do. She sips at it, the sharp bitterness jolting her towards the task ahead.

Running through the copy of her proposal she decides that Professor Hogan will have no time for it. A month and a half of work has gone into it, but it looks mediocre in front of her now. The work of an undergraduate who doesn't deserve to be enrolled for a PhD. Derivative. Not fresh enough. He'll see straight through it. Big flaws will wave at him and when he points them out to her today at ten o'clock she will nod and smile and she will accept that she has been punching above her weight. The dream of landing Professor Hogan as a supervisor will be over.

She packs the proposal back in her bag and runs a bath. It's not about to get any better by staring at it and a bath might just help her carry off a detached look when he tears her work to shreds. She tips lime salts into the bath and climbs in, sinking herself under, immersing her head, even though she has run it too hot. Under here she holds her breath and visualizes the moment when Professor Hogan tells her she'd be better off with another supervisor. Or better off taking time out and travelling for a year. She'll go for the latter option, she decides now. Spend a year in Positano with her Nonna, work in the café, binge watch Fellini boxsets, hone her topic. Then she'll resurrect herself and hit him hard with an excellent proposal. Something that will resonate deeply with him. Some angle he has not managed to probe for himself.

She lures herself out of the water and is thankful that the mirrors have steamed up. There is nothing worse than catching sight of her child-like asymmetrical body, reddened. Tipping her head forwards she wraps a towel into a turban around her hair. She slips into her dressing gown and ties the belt tighter than usual, to remind herself. This is the day where she is to remain taut, no matter what is said. This is the day that will decide her future.

Nina plucks a pomegranate from her stash. Early October is her favourite time of the year, when they appear in the shops again. She would like to be able to eat fresh pomegranate all year round. She splices her sharp knife into the tough outer layer, cutting the fruit and releasing its blood-red jewels. Halved, this one looks to her like the four chambers of a heart, and she stares at it for a moment before digging a teaspoon into one chamber and dropping the little gems into her mouth. She bites down on them and sucks hard as they release their juice into her. This will be enough to get her through the meeting. She plucks and picks away at the rest of the beads and puts them into a freezer bag, as she did yesterday. For each half fruit eaten the other half is stored. This is her way of stretching out the pomegranate season.

She has chosen her clothes for the meeting. A black polo neck over faded Diesel jeans and silver Converse runners. The jacket worries her though. The biker's marine-blue leather or the cream linen one? She tries both. The biker's gives off a nonchalance that she likes but fears she won't carry off. The linen is more the thing, more capable-looking somehow. The rumpled material gives off a respectful casualness. Before leaving the flat she tips the freezer bag to her mouth and chomps hard on the half-frozen pomegranate beads. She is ready to face Professor Hogan now.

TUESDAY

CASSANDRA

I dump Jeff's togs and towel in the washing machine, heap the powder into the drawer and turn on a sixty-degree cycle. For whites, even though they're not. I think that by washing them extra hot it will help somehow. I watch the water rise up around the red and black items, huddled together, alone. I watch them churn. The foam forms quickly, subsuming them. They disappear into the suds. Good.

The groan that came from the girl. A low-pitched guttural wave at first, building and building. Then the silence. I've no way to interpret it. I've never heard anything like it. It spins in me and spins in me as I watch the foam swirl round and round. I run to the loo and throw up.

My phone rings in my bag. Jeff's tone but it sounds different.

I can't answer it.

I'm not ready to speak to him.

If I speak to him now, without Ted in earshot to buffer us, I'll just come straight out with it. Who the hell was the girl on the beach? What in god's name did you do to her?

There's no going back then. No matter what he says. Once I ask him, I am part of it.

'Do I have to go to school today, Mum?' Ted is in the kitchen with me now, dressed in his green gym gear. He's a little pale.

'Yes. I'll put some toast on for you.'

'But I'm so tired.'

'You had a little rest when we were at the beach.'

'Not really.'

'No? Who was that curled up under the picnic rug, then?'

'Not me.'

'Ah, it must've been the dog. But I didn't think we brought Tuppence with us today.' Ted giggles. His little world is still the same. I want to keep it just like this.

'Can we walk this morning and bring her with us?' Ted asks.

'I thought you were tired, you scamp.' His chocolate eyes twinkle with his smile.

'Yes, of course we can bring her with us.'

Anything that'll make you happy little man.

Before.

After.

We are still at before.

Before everything changes.

Before you know your world has been shattered.

I need to hold onto this.

The toast pops up, the noise of it startling me, and a small gasp escapes.

'I'm not hungry, Mum. I'll just have the orange juice.'

He's unsettled this morning. He's like that sometimes. Otherwise I'd be worried that he saw something too. He takes a gulp of the orange juice and his eyes widen. He runs to the sink and spits it out.

'You gave me the one with bits in it.'

I check the bottle. He's right; I've given him Jeff's one. He can only drink the smooth.

'Sorry, sweetheart.'

'That's okay,' he says, and he goes to the back door to get the dog's lead.

We're on our way and Ted is bristling, proud as punch with Tuppence trotting along beside him. A little bit of colour returns to his cheeks as he walks.

I haven't thought it through though.

Tuppence is a magnet.

A Shetland sheepdog.

Cute as hell.

As we get close to the school, hordes of little kids and mothers surround us. Forcing me into inane banter.

Yes, she's lovely.

Four and a half.

A bit neurotic, but hey, who isn't? I'm over-smiling, like some cheerful American. Acing the banter. Until Susie steps forwards, bends down and starts stroking Tuppence.

'How are you?' she says, glancing up at me.

My eyes sting.

'Good, thanks.' My cheeks begin to tingle too.

'Time for a coffee before your first appointment?' she asks, standing again.

I shake my head. My wide smile gone.

'Nine-thirty,' I manage to say.

Her pale blue tranquil eyes lock with mine. Almost calming me. I drop my gaze back down on the dog. Susie Donovan. The most real person I think I've ever met. Congruent. That's the psych term for her. I didn't need to bump into her today.

'How about Thursday?'

'Yes. Yes, Thursday is good,' I say.

'Yeah?'

It's as if she knows already that I'll be cancelling.

'Yes.' I yank the lead to go. Ted walks up the slope towards the main door. He turns to wave. Tuppence lets out a yelp and Ted doubles up. He runs back down to me.

'Forgot your hug,' he says, squeezing my waist.

'See you later, Tups.' He pats the top of her head.

Before.

Walking home I decide what I am to do. For the next hour that is. Before my first appointment. That's how it is going to be. Dividing this day up into little chunks. Continuing as normal for as long as I can. My phone buzzes in my pocket. I wrench it out. Mum. Oh god.

'Cass? Jeff's been on wondering if you're here. He's tried your phone but can't get you. He says you're coming over to me with some groceries?'

'I thought I might, yes. What do you need?' My voice wobbles.

'Nothing, darling – you brought me everything I need yesterday, remember? Come over anyway. I'd love to see you.'

'I think I'd better prepare for my ten o'clock, then. It's a tricky one. A teenage girl, cutting herself. Her mother's at her wits' end, poor thing. Maybe tomorrow.'

'Okay, darling – whatever suits you. I'll be here.'

The tears are backing up now. I smile to bat them away.

'See you.'

'Cass? Is everything all right? Jeff rarely phones me and . . .'

'Everything's fine.' I hang up.

Her world too.

The caterwaul rings in me as I open the front door. It's beginning to remind me of something. The building heave of it. Inside the cottage, alone now, I'm looking around as if it isn't my place. Our place. It feels different. It looks different. I survey it at a remove. The floorboards that I sanded and varnished myself seem to belong to someone else. The burnt-red leather couch that we were sitting on together last night. Wine glasses with dregs left on the mantelpiece. The smell of an old fire. The spiral staircase up to the dual office where the light floods in. The reason we chose this cottage above the others. A sanctuary for Jeff to work in when not in college. A place for me to see my clients. Now I climb that staircase to search his section.

Who is she?

How does she know you?

What have you been doing with her?

Why was she at the beach?

What did you do?

The questions that I should be putting to him. Entering us into that after-space.

Sitting in the middle of his desk is his latest manuscript. *Joycean Influences in Modern Italian Film*. Rejection letters are dotted around it. He's highlighted the punchlines in neon yellow – too theoretical for our list; doesn't live up to the promise of the title; too much Rossellini and Scorsese, while missing the critical influences in Fellini; more literary criticism than necessary for a book such as this; publishing a similar book in September.

Five years of work and here it sits. Just as he said he knew it would. His ticket out of assistant professorship and up to Associate on hold, once more. I rifle through his desk drawers, pull everything out and spread it all in front of me.

Old draft chapters of his book.

His blue marbled fountain pen. He will only write with a Shakespeare fountain pen.

A pink highlighter.

Student thesis proposals written all over in his hand.

But one of them, oddly, has just one word: *Supremo*.

Someone's hammering on the door below. I check the clock. My appointment is here. Shit. I haven't even showered. I'm still in my leggings and runners from first thing this morning. I sweep all Jeff's papers up and plonk them back in the drawer. I run down the stairs. The hammering gets louder.

'Just a second,' I call out and bang into our bedroom to change. The curtains are drawn still, thankfully, otherwise they'd see straight in here. The navy trouser suit and cream blouse I wore yesterday are in a ball on the floor. I throw them on. There's no sign of my shoes.

I go to answer the door and it strikes me.

What if it isn't my appointment? What if the urgent knocking is to do with the beach?

A wave of nausea rises in me.

'Who is it?'

A man's voice booms out. 'Ian Kennedy.'

I'm not expecting a man. I begin to tremble. I don't want to open the door.

'Sheena's dad,' he calls out. Sheena. But she's Sheena Ryan and her mum brings her.

I open the door. Ian Kennedy looks me straight in the eye. My height, broad shoulders, slim. He holds Sheena by the arm, as if he's dragged her here. She won't look at me. Instead, she tilts her head in the direction of our bedroom window. Her long, straight, mousy brown hair hasn't been brushed and it's laced with grease. I haven't seen her like this before. Ian Kennedy puts out his free hand to introduce himself.

'Do I have the wrong time? Alice said it was ten, but we seem to have taken you by surprise.'

'No, no, Alice is right. Sorry about the delay,' I say, without offering any excuse for it. Ian Kennedy does not look like the type of man who would tolerate excuses. His slate-grey eyes are cold. Uncompromising.

'Sheena, can you show your dad where to go, please. I'll be up in a minute.' She doesn't answer but brushes past me, both her arms tucked into the front pouch of her dust-pink hoodie. Ian Kennedy follows, dwarfing the staircase, making it seem toy-like. As I'm sure I do too. I hunt through the sitting room for my shoes. I'm on my knees looking under the couch when I hear a loud roar. Followed by my name. He's calling me.

I sprint up the stairs.

Sheena is sitting in my chair holding Jeff's fountain pen to her wrist. The golden nib sparkles in the light.

'l told you I didn't want to come with you, but you made me,' she says to her father.

'So now you know what I'm going to have to do.' She digs the nib into herself. Little staccato jabs. Ian Kennedy looks imploringly at me. He shakes his head while quiet tears stream down his face.

'Sheena, why do you think your dad has brought you here today?'

She keeps jabbing the nib into her wrist, my question not enough to divert her.

'Don't know. I only like coming with Mum.'

I focus on her face and not at what she's doing with the pen. I don't even mention it.

'But your mother couldn't be here, Sheena, and your father has brought you. Why do you think that is?'

'No clue.'

'Have a guess. Or would you like me to?'

'You.' She casts her gaze towards the skylight, in a prolonged eye roll. She stops jabbing the nib into herself. Black ink spots bleed into one another. It's difficult to see the damage.

'My guess is that your father has brought you here today because he is very concerned about you.' Sheena drops her gaze, settles it at my bare feet, which are cool and clammy now. I feel as if I'm on the verge of shivering. I rub my hands along my trousers to stave it off. Sheena follows the movements.

'You okay?' she asks, not expecting an answer. Clearly glad of the opportunity to take the heat off herself for a moment.

'In fact, he's so concerned about you that it's upsetting him,' I continue.

A grin breaks across her face when she looks up at him.

'Are you *crying*? What would they think of that down at the station?'

I glance his way and take it all in. His navy trousers with a neat crease straight down the middle. His light blue collar with navy tie, half hidden under a beige jumper. His boots. Thick-soled, shiny black toecaps. My heart thuds in my neck. Without the jacket I'd never have guessed.

'And the lowlifes. They'd love to see this.' She's fake laughing now, forcing it out.

'Inspector Kennedy. The big wuss.'

All the air goes out of my lungs and I don't seem to be able to get any back in. I try small, shallow breaths while Sheena offers him a mock snort, underlining her disdain.

He nods in my direction, as if to say cheers. Cheers. Nice one. Now she hates me even more. My cheeks tingle and must be red. He averts his gaze. He thinks he's embarrassed me. If only it were that simple. I need to get this back on track. Get the session over. Get them out of here.

'I'd like my chair back, Sheena, and my pen. You can sit beside your dad.'

She gets up, pulls a tissue from my box and hands me the pen. She waves the tissue at her father. He takes it. Then she walks back to my desk and reefs another one out. She sits down beside him and dabs the tissue on her wrist. Faded black ink soaks into it. There's no sign of red. The nib wasn't sharp enough to draw blood.

'Would you like to tell your daughter what brought you here today?' His eyes narrow slightly. He'd rather not do this, it seems. But then he begins, tripping over his words at first, stopping and starting like an anxious runner, bouncing about, waiting for the sound of the gun to get out of the blocks. He's off now, a smooth stream. I sit back and breathe deeply again. I zone out from this big, vulnerable policeman pouring out his love for his daughter.

Supremo.

That single word scrawled onto the document in the drawer just here.

I've never seen Jeff write just a one-word comment, and in Italian. It's taunting me.

Sheena blows her nose loudly into the tissue, bringing me back into the room. Ian Kennedy slips his hand into his trouser pocket and pulls out a mobile phone. It's vibrating.

'Excuse me for a minute, I need to take this.' He steps outside.

I ask Sheena to tell me what she thinks about what her father has just said, and as she speaks I listen. Not to her. To her father. It's indiscernible. Monosyllabic. Could be anything at all.

'Will do,' he says and pushes the door again.

'Sorry about that.' He doesn't sit back down. 'I'll have to make a move.'

There's an ashen hue to his face now. He's heard something bad.

'We need to finish up first. Sheena can you tell your dad what you were telling me just now?'

'If he sits down I will.'

He perches on the edge of the seat and pretends to listen. She's punishing him for something that I don't know about. He nods. I nod. He presses the home button on his phone, checking the time. He needs to go. I need him to stay now. When she stops I ask him what he thinks about what she has just said. A further stalling. A little finger in the dam.

His brow furrows as he stands back up.

'I hear what you're saying, Sheena, but I really have to get to work. Can we pick this up next time?' He's addressing me, but it's a statement more than a question. A statement that doesn't deserve to be answered. Not that I can answer it anyway. Will there be a next time? If his urgent work call is anything to do with this morning, there won't be.

'What do you think, Sheena?' I say instead.

'I think this is the same bullshit as always. Even with the tears. Nothing's changed. Nothing ever will.' She gets up, flounces past him and hammers down the spiral staircase.

OCTOBER

NINA

Nina takes the cycle lane along the coast road, bypassing the traffic jams, oblivious to the frustrated drivers beeping their horns. Cycling relaxes her, clears her head. Cutting up from Booterstown towards the campus, she becomes aware of all the young students who drive in. She wonders about this. How it's possible for so many of them to have cars. Whether it should be possible. Eighteen-year-olds tootle past her with an indifference which makes her uneasy. On another day she might take this on, allow it to smoulder, and then to build into something else. Not today. She pushes it down as she spins across the bridge and through the college gates, pumping hard on the pedals, passing the cars now as they get clogged up, looking for spaces in which to park. She spins on past the lake, still and glassy in the morning autumnal light, the fountains not yet in motion as they were when she was last here. A handful of students dot the steps to the water. Later on she knows they will be thronged. This is the best part of the day. She locks her bike outside the library and checks the time on her phone. Nine-thirty. She has time to grab a coffee and do some deep breathing before heading up the stairs for her meeting.

At one minute to ten she is outside Professor Hogan's office door on the third floor. Her heart pounds. She raises her hand to his nameplate and is just about to knock when she hears voices in the stairwell. It is his voice, along with a woman's, and then loud laughter at something he has said. Like the bark of a seal. Nina could duck around the corner and reappear in a minute or two, but their voices are upon her, she'd be seen. She stays put, trying to look interested in the noticeboard on the wall.

'Ah, this must be Nina Ruzza,' Professor Hogan's voice rings out, pronouncing her surname beautifully, the perfect rolling R an unexpected treat. He puts out his hand. His warm fingers clasp hers so hard that the long silver spiral ring on her middle finger digs into her knuckle. She feels a mapping start on her neck, under her polo. For six months now she has been getting to know Jeffrey Hogan, in her own way. Six months since she sat for the first time in one of his lectures. Just to watch.

'I knew you'd be here already,' he says, the familiarity in his words a surprise to her. It's as if he's letting her know that he recognizes her.

'Come in, come on in.' He slots his key in the door and waves to the woman who Nina knows is the Head of School from her picture on the website. She's a little older in real life, early sixties perhaps. Nina smiles at her, while twisting the ring around on her finger to relieve the pain. The door opens and it is clear to her that he hasn't been in his room yet today. The venetian blinds are closed. He must've been working late last night. He places his briefcase on his desk and makes over to the window to fiddle with the blind. At the back of his head a patch of black hair, the size of a small hand, stands out among the silver. It's as if a child has dipped their hand in black gloss paint and dabbed it on. The silver hair has a gentle wave to it. The contrasting black patch is straight. Is that part of his head made of something different, or is some separate biological process taking place at the nape of his neck?

'That's better,' he says, turning around as the light tilts into the room through the slanted blinds.

'Sit down, sit down, anywhere at all.'

He motions to the circular table in the middle of the floor with six chairs around it and Nina freezes. She'd prefer to sit at his desk. This is a conference table. Where should she sit? Opposite him? Beside him? Beside him but one? He gives her no indication as to where he will choose, so she plumps for the seat nearest to her, closes her eyes and waits. When she opens them again he is sitting directly across from her, his elbows on her proposal and his fingers laced together, as if in prayer.

'I'm terribly sorry, Nina,' he begins and pauses. She pinches her wrist under the table to keep herself poised. To ready herself for the let-down.

The phone on his desk rings. She watches him rise up to answer it, rolling his eyes to her, saying he'd have to get it.

'I thought it might be you,' he says, his voice low and soft. Melodic.

'No, I'm just with a student at the moment. Ten minutes? Great.'

Ten minutes.

That's all the time he's allowing before he tells her to sling her hook. He makes his way back to her, smiling to himself.

'Now, where were we?' he says, his eyes twinkling after the call. 'Ah, yes, Nina – I'm terribly sorry but I haven't got round to reading your proposal yet. I meant to email you earlier to cancel this, but then I got called to a meeting.' As he speaks he gazes at her mouth. She expects this. She has a little turquoise stud in the centre of her bottom lip.

'Now I'm sure it's excellent, given that you're a First Class Honours student. Just give me another day, will you? We can discuss it properly tomorrow morning at, say, nine? How does that sound?'

Nina hasn't yet uttered a syllable. That she's here with him, at last, rendered her mute in the first place. Now she's not sure what it is that's stopping her from speaking. The fact that he hasn't read it or the fact that he's just complimented her. She must say something, quickly, or Professor Hogan might draw the conclusion that she's not really up to this. When she does speak she finds herself echoing his matter-of-fact tone.

'You know what, Professor Hogan, I'd prefer if you didn't read it yet. I think it needs more work. Another week or so.'

His mouth hangs slightly open and his eyes seem to bulge.

Like a goldfish staring out from a bowl. This encourages Nina to continue with the same tone.

'I'll email the final version to you by, say, Monday, give you plenty of time to read it before we meet, say, next Thursday? How does that sound?'

Nina gets up to leave Professor Hogan's room well within the ten minutes he has allocated her. She is pleased with herself, mimicking him, putting things off as if they don't matter a jot.

'Hang on a second, Nina.' He's pointing his forefinger at her mouth.

'I wasn't sure at first, but now I think you might be bleeding.'

Nina's hand reaches to where he points. She knows what it is. The wretched stain of pomegranate juice.

TUESDAY

CASSANDRA

I give Ian Kennedy an appointment card for next week. Same time, same day, same place. Consistency. That's what they need. What we all need.

'Thank you.' He puts his large right hand out in front of me. I don't want to have to do it. Shaking hands would seal the guilt of what I've seen and what I won't tell. What he's off to face now. I pretend not to notice his hand. I focus on Sheena instead. She stands beside the front door, the light shining through the stained-glass panel refracting red onto her dull hair. The splash of freckles across her nose and cheeks seems more defined today, her skin tighter, with an added pallor. Even though she stormed out, annoyed with her father, she didn't leave altogether. She looks more at ease now than when she arrived. Perhaps something shifted in the session, after all.

'I'm not sure if it'll be myself or Alice next time with her.' His weak smile is at odds with his strong face. They're separated. His wedding ring is stubbornly embedded on his left hand. Alice has shed hers.

'Both of you, if possible,' I say, automatically.

He stops smiling.

'It would be best if you could all attend together.' It's true, to get each person in the system is the most powerful session. But why I'm pushing this now I don't know, especially with him. He's not just a parent, after all.

'Whatever you can manage, though – no worries if you can't make it.'

His brow scrunches for a moment, registering his confusion. He'd like a clearer message.

'I can see Sheena for her one-to-one session as well. I'll send out the appointment to Alice.'

He doesn't respond.

'Yes,' Sheena says. 'Send the appointment out to Mum.' She opens the front door and walks down the path. From behind, her waif-like stature makes her seem younger than her fifteen years. More vulnerable. From behind, she looks more like a ten-year-old kid. Then she glances back around to check if her father is coming and you see it all clearly. The face of a preoccupied teen. Unsure of herself. Unsure of the world. She raises her hand in a half wave to me. He follows her down the path. She opens our little blue gate and holds it for him. Something she wouldn't have done on the way in.

Back inside, I collapse down on the couch. Onto something hard. I reach underneath me and pull out one of my shoes, and then the other. Snippets from last night flash before me. Jeff slipping my shoes off, pulling my legs onto his lap and digging his thumb into the sole of my aching right foot. The log fire crackling and scenting the room. Ted in his Spiderman pyjamas brushing Tuppence. The silence. The Rioja, a Gran Reserva, uncorked, breathing on the mantelpiece, waiting for Ted to go to bed.

A stale smell interrupts my thoughts. I sniff at my underarms. Oniony. Yesterday's suit and polyester blouse. I need to shower and change but I feel leaden. Stuck. Pinned down.

His words from last night swirl in me.

It's nice to be able to do something for you for a change.

He massages my right foot and I sink further down towards him, willing him to go on.

To put his damn book down and use both hands.

To give me his full attention.

But that's something about Jeff that I've learned to live with lately. Not quite having his full attention. Part of his mind is elsewhere. Mulling over some minute academic detail. Inaccessible. He's with me and he's not. A one-handed foot massage is as good as it gets.

He laughs as he reads, his stomach juddering as he tries to keep the laughter in. He could let it out, share it, but he doesn't. I've read it too. *Zeno's Conscience* by Italo Svevo. One of the earliest novels about psychoanalysis. Right up my street. I devoured it. A man's search for his identity. *You see things less clearly when you open your eyes too wide.* Jeff's copy is a second edition in Italian. Mine is a translation. Another little void in our relationship. His love of Italian and Italy since his primary degree. My relative ignorance. He massages and judders and I try to imagine which part he's reading now. I feel absurdly close to him with the sole of my foot in his hand as he reads. I move my left foot in towards his crotch and rub gently waiting for him to react. Nothing.

★

I pull myself towards the bathroom. It's as if I was doing some heavy lifting yesterday and the muscle pain kicks in all over me. I turn the shower on to maximum heat and pressure and step in. As I rotate myself, allowing the heavy pulsing water to get at every bit of me, I decide what to do. For now. For this moment. For this day. I do it right here in the shower. The technique I've taught my clients on occasion. I make myself re-experience it. Every little bit through my own eyes again. The range of confused feelings flood me.

The shock of seeing that he knows her.

That he waves his stick at her in the familiar way he does to me.

She runs towards him.

She beams at him and she's laughing.

I can't see his expression. He is side on to me. But he doesn't move. He doesn't back away.

She pulls at her shirt.

Dizzy. I feel dizzy watching.

She throws her shirt behind her.

She is naked to the waist.

He doesn't flinch.

He looks straight at her.

She is beautiful.

Devastatingly beautiful. Natural. Long, dark ringlets. Wide eyes. Pale skin. Tiny.

Her turquoise skirt flaps in the wind.

She's barefoot. If she was walking out of the sea towards him she would look like a mermaid. But she is not.

She leaps onto him, wrapping her legs around his waist, her arms around his neck.

Nausea. I feel sick.

I feel that I should call out and stop this now. But I do not. I watch. I listen.

He holds her by the waist.

Then one arm on her back.

His hand on hers up at his neck, moving down by her breasts.

He lifts her down.

She is talking but I cannot hear what she says.

She makes a noise. Light at first, a light groan, but it builds and builds, a heaving, gnawing groan, a crescendo, as if she is trying to rid herself of something, and she is shaking, and it gets louder still, and I think that I should run down to them.

But I do not.

He raises his right hand and places it over her face. He holds the back of her head with his left hand. He says something to her.

She looks up at him.

She lifts her arms up towards him but then they flop down.

The noise stops. Her arms dangle now, loose along her body. It seems like forever that they stand there like this.

She falls to her knees.

She keels onto her side.

She is still.

My gaze is drawn to her bare chest. Her left breast. Something screeches inside me.

Now I imagine that I can step back out of that place. That I can see myself observing as if on a screen. It is a film I am watching. I can push what I saw away from me, further and further. It moves into the distance. Off towards the horizon. The colours fade away. Sepia creeps in. The details become a blur.

I push and I push it far, far away.

The shower has run cold. I wash my hair anyway. I dry off quickly and dress myself. Cream linen shirt over black jeggings. My flats. I go up to the office to check my afternoon appointments. Just the one. Ben. A teenager suffering from social anxiety. I phone his mother and cancel. I go back into the bathroom. I scrape my hair up into a ponytail and put on some tinted moisturizer, a dash of copper lipstick, some black mascara. I am ready to go to collect Ted. We are going to have the afternoon of our dreams. Before a line is drawn in the sand.

I park outside the school and stay in the car until the very last second. I watch the other mums and a smattering of

dads. The smiles. The forced banter. The little circles form-
ing. Dads with their arms folded, defensive against the tidal
wave of chattering mothers. It's trickier for them. They seek
one another out. Or they look down, pretending to be distracted by their phones. They cannot be too friendly with
the mothers in case they are deemed to be flirting. They're
not invited on the parents' evenings out because parent
translates as mother. If I had the time, I'd research it. The
school-gate dad. The primary carer, excluded from the
main group. Assumptions made about you; being left out.
Although right now I'd prefer to be one of them. No one
quizzing me about how I am. *Any news?*

I put my sunglasses on to deflect the chit-chat. Then when I
see his class walking towards the slope I leap out of the car and
call his name. He's not expecting me, so I call again, a little
louder, and I break into a run. I'm waving and calling his name
until it comes out suddenly as a piercing holler. Everything
goes quiet. Ted turns around. His little brow crumples into a
quizzical frown. He does not seem thrilled to see me.

'In his own little world there,' one of the dads says, putting me at ease. Not judging.

'He's not expecting me. I've taken the afternoon off so we
can do something nice together.'

'Lucky kid.'

If only.

'I'm supposed to be going to after-school club today,
Mum,' Ted says, his brow softening a little. 'It's Tuesday and
you have your people to see, don't you?'

'They cancelled, sweetheart. I thought I'd pick you up and we can do something. Go somewhere you like.' He looks like Jeff did earlier when he got out of the car without his briefcase. Thrown. Thrown, but resigned too.

'I'll just tell the bus driver that I'm not going today,' he says running off.

'Ted,' I call after him, softly, and he doesn't turn around. If he did, I was going to ask him if he'd like to go to after-school club anyway, as that's what he was expecting. Routines. Consistency. I'm glad that he didn't turn. I don't think I'd be able to hear him say yes. Not today.

OCTOBER

NINA

Nina wakes to the sound of a car alarm bleating outside. The light has dimmed, the best of the day now gone. She reaches for her phone and goes straight to her email, thumbing the screen until she sees it, the little blue dot with Jeffrey Hogan's name in bold beside it. She feels her heartbeat quicken, a dull rhythmic thudding announcing itself in her neck. The email has a time of 10.13 on it. She calculates. It gives him about eight minutes. Eight minutes from the time she left his room to the time he sent this. She pores over the contents.

Dear Nina,
Apologies for earlier today. I've now read your proposal and all I can say is supremo! Please do not work on it any further, it doesn't need any work. The next step in the process will be a Skype interview with the panel – one of the interviewers will most likely be dialling in from Florence. You're a late applicant for this year but there shouldn't be

any problem – I will be strongly recommending you as a
PhD candidate.
Best wishes,
Jeffrey Hogan

She feels like she's back in his room again. Back in that
topsy-turvy space, not knowing what to expect next. If he
had said all of this to her this morning, she would've been on
a high. She would've texted Conor to see if he was free to join
her for a swim at Sandycove before the lunch they had already
arranged. She would've jumped on her bike and taken herself
straight down there to frolic in the water and let her new reality sink in. Instead, she had sent a text to Conor cancelling
lunch, had taken herself back to the flat and crawled under
her duvet for the day. Now it is getting dark outside and her
head is spinning. Professor Hogan purports to have read her
proposal and composed this email in under eight minutes. It
doesn't make any sense. The proposal is nine pages long. So
how does he know if it's any good or not? But if he hasn't read
it, then why email her at all? Sitting here now she wonders if
she has somehow skipped a day. That's the only thing that she
can think of that would explain it. She sends a text to Conor.

Was it today or yesterday we were meant to go for lunch?

She gets up and flicks the kettle on. Her phone pings.
There's never much of a delay with Conor.

Wait, what? Today. You cancelled this morning, remember? You okay??

She doesn't feel up to explaining it all to him. Especially when she can't explain it to herself.

Yep fine, just wrecked
Upset or annoyed wrecked ??😫

She was both of these earlier. But now? Now she doesn't know what she is.

Neither
Want some company?
Yep

Conor arrives within half an hour. When she opens the door and sees him standing there the familiar mix of conflicting thoughts flood her. Why is he here and not off with someone else? Does she deserve this? What will she do when that day comes? From behind his back he springs a packet of Revels and thrusts it at her.

'The doctor ordered me to give you these – apologies if the word doctor sets you off – and told me to take you for two laps of the pier.'

Nina laughs as he pulls his bike into the communal hallway.

'Someone seems in better form?'

'I got an email. He says he's read it and it's great but . . .'

'Hang on, he got back to you already? I thought you were going in again next week?'

'I know, so did I. I don't know what to make of it, really.'

'Show me.'

Nina hands him her phone with the email opened and watches his hazel eyes sparkle as he reads it.

'You're in, Nina Ruzza. What the hell is confusing about that? He wants you, girl. This calls for a celebration. Wetherspoons?'

Nina doesn't feel like celebrating. Not at all. It's been a roller coaster of a day and drinking would only confuse her further.

'How about that walk?' she says, looking up at him. His auburn hair is wild after the cycle over.

'You're the doc. Whatever you say,' and he smiles until the tiny star-like dimple under his left eye deepens. She feels herself loosen slightly.

'But not in that crumpled yoke – you'll need something warmer.' Nina looks down and realizes she has slept in the linen jacket she wore this morning. She dumps it and grabs her biker's jacket. Conor is wearing his too. He winks at her.

'Not that one – anyone looking at us might think we're a couple,' he says, poking her upper arm with the tips of his fingers. His touch is a little sore. Surprisingly so.

'Now that really would be tragic,' she says.

The night time walk clears the fog of Nina's mind to such an extent that she notices a slight tingling euphoria. Or maybe it's the effect that Conor has on her, joking around, pointing out the house along the seafront that they will buy together when they realize that no one else will be able to put up with them. A duck-egg blue mid-terrace Georgian, with no parking and no garden, neither of which they will need, he argues, as they will be annoyingly eco-friendly and never own a car and the beach will be their garden, obviously.

'If we're both still single at thirty,' he had said.

'Forty,' she had interrupted. 'You have to give people a chance.'

Thinking about it now, back in her flat, alone, she hopes that they will always be this close. But he'll be snapped up, sooner rather than later. He's too good to slip through the net. It would be so much simpler if she could feel it too but she can't pretend that she does. Not now that she knows what it's really like. She thinks about how as he bent down to kiss her on the cheek just moments ago, a goodnight kiss, and as he inhaled deeply, as if breathing her in to keep for later, what she felt was not desire but something else. Something akin to being tickled lightly with a feather.

She is so wide awake now, going over the events of the day in her mind in an endless loop, she feels she will not get off to sleep at all tonight. Running a bath for the second time today is perhaps her only chance. She tosses a handful of lavender-infused Epsom salts in. It is as she sinks herself down into the tepid water that she begins to think about it. The very first time she saw Jeffrey Hogan in person when she sat in on one of his lectures back in April. She had been reading him, of course she had, and his stock picture on the staff website and on the jacket of his book had given her a vague sense of what to expect. But it was as he walked down the steps into the lecture theatre, turned to face the scattered audience and began to speak that Nina felt a queasiness envelop her, a dizziness, as if she had crawled to the edge of a cliff and was looking down at waves crashing on the rocks far below. She didn't know what was wrong with her but she did know that she'd have to leave. She threw her A4 pad and biro back in her bag and crouched past two other students sitting in her row, her head bent towards the door so as not to look at him.

'Boring you already?' he called out and she turned, just for a moment, catching his eye, before continuing up the steps apace and out into the safety of the concourse.

TUESDAY

CASSANDRA

'Right, where would you like to go?' I ask Ted. We're looking at one another in the rear-view mirror. He's on his booster seat without the belt on. He's tugging at it.

'Anywhere?' he asks.

'Yes, anywhere.' He raises his eyebrows, his dark eyes widening. Jeff's eyes.

'The Titanic Quarter,' he says, giggling.

'We're not going to Belfast, you scamp. Anywhere within reason, in Dublin preferably.'

'Is Dad coming too?'

'No, sweetheart, he's at work.'

'He might be able to cancel some stuff like you did.'

'I didn't cancel, they did. Dad can't just cancel lectures to come out with us. So what do you think? Where will we go?'

This is beginning to feel like a bad idea.

'Why not? He's a professor. Can't they do anything?'

God. 'No, sweetheart, they cannot. They have duties and responsibilities like everyone else. Like your teacher.'

'But they are smarter than everyone else, that's why they're professors, so they should . . .'

'All right, Ted, enough. They're not smarter than everyone else. They just happen to be very good at their subject. Now would you like to go somewhere with me, or not?'

I'm aware that my voice is getting a little high-pitched. A little brusque. This was a stupid idea.

'You know the café with the huge windows and the balcony and the sea?' he says.

'Starbucks?'

'Yeah, Starbucks. That's where I'd like to go.'

'Why there, of all places?' It's out before I can stop myself. As he speaks, I know exactly what he is going to say. Damn.

'Remember when I was little and Dad and you brought me there all the time and I haven't been there with you for ages . . .'

Great. My escape for the afternoon with Ted will turn into one big reminiscing session.

'Put your belt on,' I say, indicating to pull out onto the road.

I click the radio on to the musical sting of the three o'clock news.

'Shit,' I blurt out, slamming on the brakes instead of clicking it off. The wrong reflex.

'Mu-um,' Ted's voice yells but seems muffled. I glance in the mirror. I can't see him. He's been thrown, off his seat onto the floor. Back to where he was this morning at the beach.

'Jesus, are you okay, Ted?' I pull up the handbrake and turn around as he picks himself up.

'I think so.'

'I told you to put your belt on, what were you thinking not having it on?' I click the radio off.

'I was trying to get it on but it was stuck, Mum, I nearly had it . . .'

The car behind us beeps. We're blocking the road.

'Get it on. I'm not moving until you have it on properly . . .'

The car beeps again. I look in the mirror, check his belt is on and then I wave to the car behind, leaving my middle finger up a little longer than the rest.

Ted is very, very quiet. He is never this quiet. I will do it though. Give him a lovely afternoon. An afternoon to treasure, for both of us.

I glance back at him. He's staring out the window. 'Any homework?' I ask to jog him out of it. If he churns what just happened over too much, it won't be good for him.

'Yeah, we always get homework.'

'Let's not do it today, eh? I can just write a note. Say we had an important family occasion or something.'

'But that would be untruthful and we just made our first confession.'

God. The first confession. If I'd known – if I'd looked into it more, if Jeff had told me more about it, I'd have stopped him before it got too late. The homework then that I was helping him with. Finishing sentences. "I was unkind

when" . . . "I was untruthful when" . . . "I was unfair
when" . . . I remember looking at him and not being able to
think of any examples. Telling him we'd have to make a
few things up.

'But wouldn't that be untruthful?' he had asked, his brow
all furrows.

'There you are, write I was untruthful when I made up
sentences for my first confession homework,' I said and we
both laughed. I told him not to learn the Confiteor Prayer
off either. A little child saying that he has greatly sinned,
in his thoughts and in his words, in what he has done and
in what he has failed to do. It's not right. Not at all. Thinking like that could lead to a lifetime of therapy. Through
my fault, through my fault, through my most grievous
fault . . .

'Unless it really is like a special family occasion?' he asks.

He runs ahead of me and claims our favourite corner.
Purple velvety chairs to sink into with views out across the
sea to Howth Head. It's as if we were here only last week.
But it was his pre-school days. Mornings when both Jeff and
I could stream our work to eke out a bit of special time.

'There's one!' he shouts out.

'One what?'

'A train. Dad and I always count the trains. Whoever
spots them first wins. Dad's not very good at it.' Hours we
used to spend here, high above the railway track, looking
out across the bay at Dublin port to our left. The red and
white twin towers, as Ted likes to call them, twinkling at us

from Ringsend. The Aviva Stadium. Buses pulling into a terminus below us. Ted's idea of heaven.

'Can you remember what I like to eat?' he asks.

'I can, but come up with me and see if there's anything new you might like instead. It's been a while.'

'No thanks, I'll keep our favourite place.'

Up at the counter it feels like a bit of a test. I can't remember exactly what he likes and anyway all the labelling has changed. If I get it wrong, how's he going to be? If I run over to check with him, when I've told him I remember what will that do to our precious afternoon? I'm dithering, letting people go ahead of me when I spot the large golden foil chocolate coins and I remember. All of it. A visual trigger. I'm in no doubt as I grab one of those coins along with a mozzarella pesto and sundried tomato ciabatta and a strawberry smoothie.

The sea is flat calm now, a light grey mirroring the dense cloud cover. If Howth Head wasn't in sight, the sea would blend right into the sky. Ted is looking straight out at a car ferry coming into the port from England. I settle his food in front of him.

'Yes,' he half shouts, punching the air. 'You remembered everything. But what about you?' he asks. I've forgotten to get something for myself.

'I'm not hungry, sweetheart. I'll just get a coffee.' I try to remember if I've eaten anything at all today. Nothing comes to mind. But I know I can't either. I go back up for the coffee. Not my usual Americano. I ask the young barista for a cinnamon roll frappuccino. Whatever that is. But right now cinnamon sounds as if it could do me some good. She asks for my name and scribbles it down. Waiting at the counter I wonder about her name too. If there shouldn't be some sort of exchange, a badge that I could read. Now that she knows my name I'd very much like to know hers. It seems only polite. I decide that she could be a Svetlana. Others join me waiting for our special personalized deliveries. When Svetlana delivers mine she calls out 'Cath', looking unfocused into the crowd. She's forgotten me already. Forgotten me and has my name wrong. I pick it up without saying thanks. It's in a plastic cup and it's cold. It looks as if I've ordered an ice-cream sundae.

'Can we go on a car ferry some day, you, me and Dad, when his leg is better?'

'Of course we can. Where would you like to go?' A train rumbles past as he thinks about it. We both think about it. I think that we will never do anything like that. But for now, for this moment we can still do it all.

'Italy,' he says. 'I want to go on the boat with you and Dad to Italy and then take trains everywhere. To all of Dad's favourite places.'

'It's been so long since we were here,' I say, changing the subject, getting away from dangerous dreamland.

'Not really.'

'You must've been only four the last time – it was before you started school.'

'Nope,' he says, biting into his ciabatta.

'No?' He's very particular with a scarily good memory. Maybe he was five. He's chewing away. I'm glad he doesn't speak until he's finished chewing and swallowing. I'm always terrified that he'll choke.

'Dad brings me here.'

'Does he?'

'Yes. Sometimes when he collects me on Thursday when you have to see your people. Sometimes on Saturday after football too.'

'Really? I didn't know that.' He's never mentioned bringing Ted here without me.

'He brings me here when he's meeting one of his students.'

'He does?'

'Yeah, they have to talk about her work or something.'

There's a ringing in my ears. I can no longer hear all the voices around me.

Ted's still talking but I can only see his mouth opening and closing.

Why didn't I know about this? We discuss our days in detail, always, all of us. There's a reason they didn't tell me. Should I ask him now? Who? Who is this student? What's her name? What does she look like?

'Are you okay, Mum? Mum, your drink . . .' He jumps out of his seat opposite me and comes around the table, picking the tipped-over frappuccino out of my lap.

OCTOBER

NINA

Nina wakes at five and cannot get back off to sleep, even though she knows there's no more she can do now. The flat is spic and span. Her laptop is on the table, plugged in. She has washed and straightened her hair. Ironed a white blouse. In six hours she is being subjected to a Skype interview with the doctoral panel. In four hours she is doing a practice Skype interview with Conor. Even though he tells her it's in the bag. A formality, just like Jeffrey Hogan has said. It does not feel like a formality to Nina. Not a bit.

The piercing sound of a fox fight outside fills her room. That's what it feels like, she thinks now. A livid fox fight. If Jeffrey Hogan has already accepted her proposal, why should she be made to fight on? And why a Skype interview when she could just go in to meet the panel? Now that would feel like a formality. Protocol, apologies, he had emailed back when Nina quizzed the necessity of the Skype interview. We have applicants from all over world and the process has to be equal. Also, at times one of the panel will

53

be in a different location, he had written. This had scared Nina even more. She was sorry she'd asked.

She gets out of bed in a bid to distract herself. She switches on the television and chooses a news channel. This ought to do it. Help put things into perspective. Or send her back off to sleep.

A pioneering study has shown for the first time that the brains of men and women are wired differently, which could explain some of the stereotypical differences in male and female behaviour.

She flicks the kettle on.

Maps of neural circuitry show women's brains to be highly connected across the right and left hemispheres, whereas in men the connections are stronger between the front and back regions.

She pokes her head through the heavy red velvet curtains and looks out onto the street. No sign of the foxes. A brief, vicious sort-out. She wonders if it was between a male and a female. Or two males fighting over a female. Two females fighting over a male.

What does this mean to the ordinary man or woman on the street? the interviewer asks, laughing, as if she's just said something terribly funny. Nina sighs. She hates when people do this. Assume their own wit.

It means that women are better at intuitive thinking. Women are better at remembering things. Men are wired more for perception and co-ordinated actions. The brains of men and women are strikingly different, but strikingly complementary.

Nina pours the steaming kettle water onto a peppermint tea bag. She thinks about Conor. How he seems wired for intuitive thinking and remembering things. More than she is. Jeffrey Hogan. She doesn't know how he is wired. Not yet.

The second time that she went to sit in on one of his lectures she was better prepared. She had plaited her hair down her back in the hope that he wouldn't recognize her, not remember her fleeing the theatre. She put a dusk-pink baseball cap on and pulled the plait through the gap at the back of it. It was early September, the start of the new academic year. There would be many new students bustling around and she would melt on in. She had wanted to test it. To test herself really. If she could sit through a full lecture, listen to him deliver on one of her favourite undergraduate topics, then she would know. Whatever strange physiological event had come over her the last time would not re-emerge. She had plenty of time to consider her options while back in Positano over the summer. This was the one she was plumping for, and she'd know after today whether she was right. She swung the lecture theatre door open and surveyed for the best seat. Back row, edge, just in case. What had she been thinking the last time, plonking herself so near the front? She hooked the copper buttons on her denim jacket closed before taking her place, ten minutes early. As she waited she thought of her Italian Nonna's words to her before she left for Dublin. *Cara, adesso puoi aver coraggio anche tu. Darling, now you can be brave too.* Then what Nina had said back to her. *Non credo che possiamo aver coraggio senza aver provato paura. I don't think we can be brave without first feeling fear.* It had certainly felt like fear in here that last time, back in April. Fear or panic. But she had worked on it over the summer. Throwing herself into things that she was less than happy about. Breathing differently, slowly in through her nose, out through pursed lips, as she served grappa to the men of her village.

As the lecture theatre began to fill with first years, Nina distracted herself with her phone, scrolling through old text messages from Conor. Reading them all in a slew, thumbing the screen in rhythmic downward taps until she found her favourite one.

Twenty-two. This year's for you. Time to shine. Let them all know. Happy birthday babe.

The bustle dimmed and Nina lifted her head slowly, knowing that he had arrived now.

'Good morning, everybody. I'm Jeffrey Hogan and today I will be introducing my first-semester course: *Myths and Masculinities in Ancient Rome*. I hope that I won't bore you,' he said and he raised his eyes to the back corner of the lecture theatre where Nina sat. She breathed slowly in and released her breath back out through her nose while holding his gaze. It was as if she was standing at an electric fence, her fingers placed along it feeling the shocks, dangerous and discomfiting, yet not wholly unpleasant. She listened and watched as he paced up and down on the podium, until watching became too much and she closed her eyes, letting the timbre of his voice wash over her.

Fiddling with the lamp on the shelves behind where she'll be sitting now, she angles it down so that it won't glare off her laptop screen. She puts her white shirt on, buttoning it carefully over her red and blue tartan pyjama bottoms. It's just her face and top that will be visible during the interview. Being comfortable and giving off a relaxed yet competent air is what she's after. She places a glass of water within reach.

When Conor calls for the mock interview, Nina conjures up Jeffrey Hogan's face and attempts to paste it onto Conor's. It's easier than she thinks, Jeffrey's sallow skin seeping easily onto Conor's pallor. The silver and black threaded wavy hair taking the place of auburn. The darker hue of Jeffrey's eyes colouring over Conor's light hazel ones.

'Nina Ruzza, thank you for agreeing to this Skype interview,' Conor begins in a mock-Oxbridge accent, irking Nina. It sounds nothing like Jeffrey.

'Not like that. Use your own voice but drop the tone down a bit, mellow it out. Create a soothing rhythm. Let it rise and fall, rising at the end of a sentence, even if it's not a question.'

'Wow. You've really given this some thought, haven't you?'

'Let's get on with it. It will be a help if you sound a little more like him.'

'Right so. Here goes: my colleagues and I have read your proposal, most interesting, and we'd like to ask you a few questions. Perhaps we can start by you telling us a bit about yourself?'

'Jesus, Conor, they won't ask me about myself,' Nina says. She sucks her bottom lip into her mouth so that her piercing glances off her top teeth. A habit she's got into lately when feeling stressed.

'They'll just want to know about the research, how I intend to carry it out, what funding I might look for, that kind of thing.' Jeffrey's features are fading off Conor's face as he starts to speak now, irritating Nina further.

'They can ask you anything they like, Nina. Just because you seem to know all about them, they don't know you, not really. Why, for example, are you moving from Trinity to UCD for your doctorate? They'll want to know that.'

'It's none of their business.' Nina stares at Conor's face, every trace of Jeffrey Hogan gone now.

'Of course it is. You have brilliant grades from Trinity. Firsts all the way. A first in your master's in film just now even. Why not stay there where you're known?'

'Because Professor Hogan is the best there is in my field. No one else even comes close.'

'But you can't say that, Nina. It sounds like you're sucking up to him.'

'So this was a bad idea. If you can't just ask me about my research proposal for the mock interview, we'd better end the call. I could be practising on my own instead of wasting time.'

Conor rubs his hand on his forehead. They look at one another on their screens.

'Fair enough, whatever you think will work best for you,' Conor says and he ends the call. Which was not what Nina wanted. Now Conor is hurt, and from past experience Nina reckons it'll take about a week before he recovers and gets back in touch. Which is bad timing but the least of her concerns right now. She still has the actual interview to get through.

She goes to the freezer to retrieve a bag of pomegranate beads, pops it in the microwave for a minute and tips them into a bowl. She smothers them with the contents of a tub of plain Greek yogurt and stirs, watching the red juices swirl into the white.

Her phone beeps with a text message.

Just a couple of things. Look directly at your camera, not at their faces, to make good eye contact. You weren't doing that with me. A bit of humour if you can manage it would be good. You looked pretty angry with me there when I asked you a question you didn't feel like answering. That won't work in the real thing.
Good luck.

She spoons the now pink mixture into her mouth. That's Conor. Even when his nose is out of joint he's thinking of others. She wishes she hadn't been so curt with him now. This is always how she seems to end up feeling about him. Guilty because he's so good to her. Annoyed because he's so good to her. It's not going to get either of them anywhere.

Her mouth opens to release a yawn and her eyes water. She's exhausted all of a sudden. She decides to lie down on the couch for a few minutes, to get her energy back up for the real thing.

TUESDAY

CASSANDRA

'Would you like to go to Gran's for the evening?' We're driving back towards home as it hits me. I can't have Ted with me. Not while I try to work out what to do.

'Now?'

'Yes, sweetheart.'

'No. I want to go home and see Tuppence. Then go to collect Dad with you.'

Ted likes his routines. Little changes unsettle him.

'Dad's working late tonight and I'm going to try to see the appointment that cancelled earlier. They said they could be here by five-thirty. It would be best if you went to Gran's.'

I can see him in the mirror. He's looking out the window at the cars flying past us. We're in the wrong lane. Sunlight penetrates his hair, making it look as if he has fresh golden highlights. Wavy, thick hair, just like Jeff's. My colour though. He isn't going to say any more. He knows when the deal is already done.

'The student Dad was helping in Starbucks, what is she like?' There. It's out. Despite myself.

'She's funny.'

'Funny?'

'Yeah, so funny. She makes these funny faces when Dad is talking. He doesn't see.'

'What sort of faces?'

'She scrunches her eyes up as if she's working really hard or is confused, and then she opens them up big and wide and winks at me.'

My hands tighten on the steering wheel.

I know I shouldn't be quizzing him. But I know exactly how to draw him out.

'That sounds funny all right.'

'Yeah and I'm laughing and then Dad looks cross with me, you know when his eyebrows look as if they're just one, and that makes me laugh even more.'

'I know,' I say, laughing now too.

'Yeah, and then she whispers *sorry* and pretends to concentrate very hard again.'

'She sounds really nice.'

'Yeah, and she buys me one of the big gold chocolate coins when Dad is at the loo, and he doesn't even know.'

He's smiling now with the memory.

'She sounds really kind.'

'She is. She thinks Dad's very funny too.'

Why didn't he tell me about this before? Was he asked not to?

I pull over to phone Mum. To let her know I'll be dropping Ted in for a few hours.

'Something's cropped up with a client, Mum. I'll have to see them this evening. It's a bit of an emergency. Can I leave Ted in with you?'

'Of course you can. You know how I love to see him. What time will you be here?' Her voice sounds so normal. Usual, everyday Mum. It throws me, hearing her. I swallow hard. I must do my best to sound normal, everyday too.

'We're just a couple of minutes away,' I say, with an extra chirpiness.

'Oh. Isn't he in after-school club until you go to collect Jeff?'

I hadn't thought of that. The degree to which she knows our routines.

'Not today, Mum. It's all a little different today.' I can hear my voice cracking as I speak. I hand the phone to Ted to give myself a moment.

'Hi, Gran . . . yes . . . yes we went to Starbucks and I don't even have to do my homework coz Mum says she's writing a note and that means we can do anything . . . yes I would . . . yes I'd love that . . . here, Mum . . .'

Ted's handing me the phone back, smiling.

'She says we can make pancakes,' he tells me as I speak into the phone again, saying hello, chirpy as hell, to a dead line as it happens.

'She says she'll see us in a minute,' he says.

I can see her front door, already open, as I drive down the road. She really shouldn't do that. Not even when we are close by. Anyone could nip straight in. I park a few houses away.

'That was a lovely afternoon,' I say, even though it wasn't. Far from it. But I haven't finished yet.

'Yes,' he says, hand on the door, ready to jump out.

'That nice, funny student you were telling me about – what colour hair does she have?'

'I don't know.' He's impatient to get going.

'Oh, you were describing her funny faces so well earlier. I really liked hearing about those. I'm just wondering what she looks like. Maybe I know her too.' I can see him relaxing now. Positive feedback. Curiosity. Tools I use with my clients to keep the conversation open. I've never consciously used them with my own child, until now.

'I don't know how to describe it coz it's not just one colour, but it's really curly and really long. I can stick my fingers up into the curls.'

'You can?' There's a dry, sticky feeling in my mouth as I picture this little intimacy. Do I really want him to go on?

'Yes, she showed me, and she doesn't mind. She says her hair is like a load of springs, like a clown's and she puts on a funny face, but Nina's not like a clown at all because she's very pretty, and she's very clever, Dad says. Do you know her?'

Nina.

'No, sweetheart, I don't think so. It sounds like you get on really well with her though.'

'Look, there's Gran.' She's in her doorway now, waving at us. I can't face her.

'Off you go, then. Tell Gran I'm in a hurry and I'll see her later when I collect you, okay?'

'Ok, see ya,' he says and he jumps out, slams the door shut and runs down the hill. I wave at her before reversing into a driveway and turning the car. It's 4.30. I have an hour and a half before Jeff will be expecting me to pick him up. An hour and a half during which I will absorb all that Ted has told me. And then make myself listen to the news.

OCTOBER

NINA

'I bombed,' Nina says into her phone. It's been a week since the interview. A week during which time she has come to accept the outcome and to refocus her lens. Conor is silent.

'I'm actually okay.'

'Yeah?'

'Yeah.'

'Want to talk about it?'

'Nothing to say, really. I messed up, big time. Fell deeply asleep before it. Couldn't wake up properly during it. Mascara and black eyeliner had smudged around my eyes making me look like a junkie. I jumped up to turn off the lamp, remembering too late that I had my pyjamas on. What else? Oh yeah, I said something along the lines of a change is as good as a rest when the Head asked me why I wanted to do it in UCD. So, you know. It was a bit of a catastrophe.'

'God. Poor you. What about your research proposal though – that must've gone down well with whatshisname loving it?'

'The internet connection failed before we got onto that. Froze on Jeffrey Hogan's face as it happens. He didn't look best pleased,' Nina says, laughing a little now. 'He must be feeling pretty silly, seeing as he put me forward with a strong recommendation. It would've looked as if I didn't give a shit. He probably got his knuckles rapped for wasting their time.'

'Can you request a rerun, seeing as the connection failed?'

'I could I guess, but I've given it a lot of thought. There must be a reason that it went so badly wrong. It's a sign. Now is not the right time for me to do this.'

'And I think you're overthinking it. Circumstances were against you. Simple as. Ask for that rerun. I know how much you want this.'

'I'll see. Let's dump it for tonight and enjoy ourselves.'

'You still want to do this, then?'

'Of course. Try and stop me.'

'Right then.'

'Right. See you in a few.'

Nina kicks her Doc Martens through the piles of leaves on the way to Conor's. The Halloween ritual that they have, taking his twin sisters around the houses, will not be disrupted by her low mood. Fireworks crackle and screech around her. She checks the time: 19.33. She ups her pace. The girls will be growing impatient, ready to go. Two jaggedly cut pumpkins light her way to his porch. She doesn't get the chance to ring the bell – the door is swung open by

Ciara, dressed as a zombie. Conor will have had a hand in this, Nina is sure. No little Halloween princesses allowed in Silchester Crescent.

'You're late,' Ciara says, flashing fury through black-rimmed eyes and blood dripping from her mouth to great effect.

Nina smiles. 'Everyone's entitled to be late once in their lives.' She steps into the porch. A waft of fresh baking greets her. Barmbrack cupcakes. Conor's mother, Caroline. A natural homemaker. It unnerves Nina to come here almost as much as it pleases her. She presses her tongue against her piercing and waits for Conor.

'Nina, sweetheart come on in.' Caroline stands in the hall with a blue oven glove on her right hand.

'He's just putting the finishing touches onto Catherine's face.' She smiles and her eyes sparkle. He has her eyes.

'Will you have something to eat before going around?' she asks, looking at Nina with such kindness that a knot of some unpleasant tension begins to form at the back of her throat. She hasn't eaten properly today, not since the interview when she thinks about it. It will be showing in her face now. Pinched skin and bulging eyes.

'Sure, why not,' she says and she follows Caroline through to the kitchen. The cupcakes she'd smelled sit cooling on the black marble counter. On top of the Aga, steam rises from a pot. On the table, a Tupperware bowl is filled with water and floating small red apples for their favourite Halloween game. Packets of sparklers lie beside it. The sliding doors leading out to the garden are decorated with slimy words, cobwebs, a skeleton. Nina feels a little faint, the room is swimming before her. She reaches out to the counter, grabs a cupcake and crunches down on it, without looking up to catch Caroline's eye. Still warm, it melts in her mouth and she sucks hard, the allspice flavour dripping down the back of her throat, smoothing out the tension. She chews then, juicy cranberries and other fruits, while watching as Caroline lifts the lid on the saucepan and prods something with a fork. Where the hell is Conor, Nina wonders, taking the last bite of her cupcake and then spitting the contents back out onto her hand. Folded greaseproof paper.

'You got the ring,' Caroline says as Catherine bursts into the kitchen, dressed as Hermione. Neat, Nina thinks.

'Nina got the ring,' Catherine calls out as Conor sails in.

'Lucky,' he says. He's dressed all in black for the occasion, a sweatshirt, jeans and runners. Even the soles are black. He winks at Nina.

'Now you two can get married. Finally,' Catherine says and Nina glances up at Caroline, she's not sure why, and something passes between them, some shared knowing. Nina unwraps the ring and instead of the usual gold band, this one is light purple. She slips it onto her left ring finger and it changes colour, now dark green.

'It's a mood ring,' Caroline says.

'So don't worry, no pressure to get married just yet. It changes colour to reflect your mood, so let's see now. Dark green. Jealousy. You're not in the right frame of mind to even be in a relationship,' she says and she smiles at Nina.

'Are you jealous of me?' Catherine asks.

'Absolutely. I want your Hermione costume, and for Conor to do my make-up too.'

'Any time,' Conor says, and for the briefest of moments Nina wishes that it could be as simple as this.

'Let's go, before all the best stuff is gone,' Ciara says, holding the front door ajar.

At the sixth house Ciara and Catherine run ahead up the driveway, lit by an array of pumpkins and candles. Conor and Nina hang back. The girls are nine now, after all. Conor taps Nina's shoulder and points up to the sky, to a spray of colour cascading downwards. Nina is half-looking, distracted, thinking about what Conor has said about a rerun. Out of the corner of her eye she sees it. The tail of Ciara's costume dancing just above a candle flame. A light puff of wind and the flame wavers, licking at the costume. The burst is immediate. It is as if someone has thrown lighter fuel at her and then a match. Nina sprints up the driveway removing her parka as she goes. Catherine screams when she sees Ciara's back alight. Nina throws her coat onto Ciara and then pushes her to the ground and rolls her. It is as if she has prepared for this very moment, as if she has always known it would come. She is utterly calm. Conor kneels beside them both, tears running down his cheeks and he bats his face with the back of his hand saying 'Jesus' over and over.

'It's okay, Ciara, it's out,' Nina says and locks eyes with her, nodding her reassurance into her. Catherine's screams die down and Nina sees that one single tear is resting on Ciara's left cheek on top of the fake blood. It may be her own or it may be Conor's. Her pupils are large and shining.

'You're okay, Ciara,' Nina says. 'Do you hear me? You're okay.'

The front door opens now and a woman holding a baby stands before them, looking down at Ciara. She lets out a short, sharp gasp.

'She's okay, I think we got to her before it had a chance to do any harm,' Nina says and the woman begins to cry, a deep, guttural sob and she's muttering something about knowing it, or how she should have known it, and she's saying sorry time and again until Nina gets up and walks over to her. Conor takes over reassuring Ciara while pressing his mother's number on his phone.

'Is it sore anywhere, baby?' he asks Ciara and Nina doesn't hear the reply because she's talking to the woman in a low, calm voice.

'Try to get a hold of yourself, you're frightening the children.' Then she turns around, bends down and blows out all of the naked flames.

As Caroline runs towards them she catches Nina's eye. 'Thank you,' she mouths. Then she kisses the palm of her hand and blows it towards her.

TUESDAY

CASSANDRA

Driving home from Mum's I can feel it pushing to the forefront again and I let it. This time I let the scream out. It has been trapped inside me since 6.50 this morning. When it comes it is not my usual quick-fright scream. My throat is clenched so tight that what comes out sounds like a pig squealing. A low-pitched squeal that gets higher and higher. I indicate to turn onto our road. An elderly neighbour is standing at the junction, attempting to cross. He looks into the car, at my wide-open screaming mouth, and nods his head. As if this is exactly what he'd expect to see. I motion for him to go, hoping that a little deafness has come his way. That it might've looked as if I was singing along to the radio. What if I'd let myself scream at the beach? Let myself belt out the primal, frightened noise that I'd suppressed. As if our survival depended on stifling it.

Opening the door, I'm greeted by Tuppence, bounding towards me, snuffling and sneezing with excitement.

'You need your dinner, don't you?' She's looking behind

me, sniffing, searching for Ted. She makes a little whining noise when there's no sign of him.

'I know, it's just me and you for now. We have a few things to do,' I say, closing the door. She patters into the kitchen to her bowl, wagging her tail in expectation. I dig a fork into the rabbit jelly sludge, holding my breath to avoid inhaling the rancid smell. I give her the whole tin instead of her usual half. Just in case she gets forgotten in the maelstrom that is coming our way. It must be the girl guide in me. 'Be prepared' – the motto that accompanies me in life. Even now, maybe that's what I'm doing. Trying to prepare. Even as I cannot absorb what I saw this morning, I'm preparing somehow for what is to come. The same as I did when I was little. Even if the preparation came a bit late then.

I go back up to the office, to his drawer. Pull out the document with 'Supremo' scrawled across it in his handwriting. I flick through it, searching for that name. The name that Ted mentioned in Starbucks. A name I've never heard Jeff mention. There's no name on it. Nothing at all to identify who wrote it. It's a proposal for doctoral research and there's a title. *Deconstructing masculinity and demythologizing gender in Fellini's La Strada.* This is something Jeff would love to be involved with. It looks like the work of a male student. The topic. The way it has been put together. The confidence in the words used. *Demythologizing.* Forgetting to put a name on it. I search on through the drawer. Rifling. Of course most of his paperwork will be in his room in college. Or his briefcase. Now I remember his briefcase. He's

left it here, somewhere. Where? I think back to last night, to
how he was reading at one end of the couch. I run down the
stairs at breakneck speed and hurl myself into the sitting
room. It's there, exactly where I expect it to be. Between
the side of the couch and the fireplace. Now that I see it, I'm
no longer sure I want to open it. I've never gone through his
things with any hint of suspicion. He has never given me
the slightest cause to be worried. The drawer in our communal office is one thing. His briefcase is quite another. I
hover in this unsure space. Looking around the room as if it
can prompt me to act, one way or another.

The curtains are still drawn from last night and I leave
them drawn. Enough light seeps through for what I'm about
to do. I catch sight of myself in the large antique framed
mirror over the hearth. A ghastly pale visage stares back at
me. A dithering spectre, unsure of her next move. Below
the mirror a picture of the three of us beams at me, prick-
ling my skin into little goosebumps. We are on a boat out in
the bay. The turquoise water glistens around us. Ted has a
wetsuit on and an orange life jacket over it. His hair is wet
and smooth and he smiles up at Jeff – at the mackerel he's
holding up, while looking back down at Ted. I smile directly into the camera. I'm lightly tanned from our trip to
Florence just before this and my hair is blonder from the sun
too. I never show my teeth when I smile, keen not to expose
the unattended-to slight overlap. Yet there I am, beaming
broadly, teeth on show, happy as hell. It's the look between
Jeff and Ted that catches me most now as I see it afresh. The

trust between them. I look like an outsider. Doing my own thing. While they are together. Thick as thieves.

That was only last summer. Before everything. Before his enforced dependency on me. I think about that now. How I have quite enjoyed him needing me a bit more. Until today.

I lift a wine glass from the mantelpiece, and sniff at the dregs in the bottom. Remembering the conversation. We chat differently when we have a glass of wine. Even that first sip seems to flick a switch as we swallow and the warmth trickles down. The tedium of the day begins to evaporate as we discuss it. Last night it was all about the Head, Margaretta. How she seems to have it in for one of the postgraduate students. But then, Jeff tells me, she has a way of making it all seem perfectly plausible. As if the others in the department are imagining things. He can't make head nor tail of it. How she can flip around so much and then make others feel as if they've done something wrong.

'You must've come across this before,' he says, eyes twinkling at me. 'If you have any insights, please share. Most of my day seems to involve working out how to respond to Margaretta. Unless I escape to give a lecture. Quite the relief that is,' he says, smiling still. We play then at diagnosing her. I quiz him, pretending to take notes, nodding a lot.

'I see. What we've got here is someone with narcissistic personality disorder. Utterly untreatable, I'm afraid,' I say and he laughs.

'I thought as much,' he says, kneading the sole of my left foot, digging his thumb into the heel and circling around, sending spasms of pleasure through me. I try again, as I had done earlier while he was reading, rubbing my right foot along his leg towards his crotch. He shimmies off the couch, standing up to grab the bottle.

'Unless you'd like to suggest to her that she has a chat with me,' I say, diverting my sense of rejection, and he laughs so much that his hand is shaking pouring more wine into my glass, tapping the bottle repeatedly off it, drops splashing onto the coffee table.

I grab the poker now, kneel down on the hearth and get to work. The ash from last night's fire falls through the grate. A few orange embers remain, sparkling still. I can even feel a bit of heat from them. Then I sit at the end of the couch, exactly where he sat last night. I pull his leather briefcase up and put it on my lap. I sit like this for a minute before flicking the golden fasteners open with a ping. I lift the top half and stare at the emptiness inside.

NOVEMBER

NINA

Nina pulls on her purple beanie hat, wraps a black scarf up around her mouth and zips up her parka. It is night-time, crisp and cold. She cycles through Dún Laoghaire main street, under the glow of early Christmas lights. Her legs pump the pedals and she feels the warmth of her blood pulsating. She could've got the bus of course. It's practically door to door. But she likes how she feels after a cycle. Confident, vibrant, as if she is capable of anything. As this is her first meeting with Jeffrey Hogan as her mentor, she wants to give off a good air. Cycling will help. She thinks about the short email arranging this meeting. How she had let out a yelp when she first read it.

Dear Nina,

Thank you for your email indicating that you do not wish for me to seek a rerun of the interview due to the technological difficulties you experienced. It is a shame that this happened, but all is not lost. Having given it some thought since, I have an alternative for you to consider. I could offer you mentorship, informally, for the rest of this academic

year. It might help you to keep some momentum up before going on the books next year. If you think this would work, I suggest we meet to discuss further. I have an evening lecture on Wednesdays at 7.00. Perhaps you could come in this Wednesday after that, about 8.00?
Best,
Jeffrey

She wasn't sure what she was expecting Jeffrey Hogan to suggest. But she wasn't expecting this. As she cycles along the Rock Road, past Booterstown, she feels as if the street lights are pulling her along. They twinkle and wink at her kaleidoscopically, as if she's in a tunnel. She cuts through just before the Tara Towers hotel, and takes the bridge above the dual carriageway, stopping halfway across to read a small stone memorial plaque embedded beneath the railing. *Blithe Spirit*. Nina smiles. *To a Skylark* is a favourite poem of hers. She peers over the railing and whispers the words out, letting the wind carry them.

> Hail to thee, blithe Spirit!
> Bird thou never wert,
> That from Heaven, or near it,
> Pourest thy full heart
> In profuse strains of unpremeditated art.

She walks the rest of the way into the campus, pacing herself as the poem chimes in her still. Feeling no jitters at all, she locks the bike outside the library and makes her way to the stairs that will lead her up to Jeffrey Hogan's office.

She knocks twice gently and hears him call out for her to come on in. It is when she grasps the round silver door handle and turns it clockwise, as if she's well used to it, that she hears the thudding in her neck. It's too late to pause, to gather herself. She pushes the door open and he rises from behind his desk to greet her. The only light in the room comes from an anglepoise lamp, pointing down onto a pile of papers on his desk. He looks different in the darkness. Younger. Larger eyes, not twinkling but bulging slightly as if he's surprised by something. An unwelcome heat creeps into Nina's face. She's glad of the dimly lit room which will hide her flush until it settles.

'Ah Nina, come on in. Take a seat.' He gestures to the chair opposite his desk.

'Thanks.' She pulls the chair further back into the room away from the desk and the lamp.

'Glad you could make it in this evening. It's a good time to get discussions under way without all the nagging daytime distractions.'

Nina hears herself laugh, a nervous twitter, and she wishes she could stop herself but then he laughs too. A loud chortle, drowning her out. Thankfully. The tingling heat in her face begins to subside and she pulls her hat off and unwraps her scarf.

'Tell me, how are you after the unfortunate business of the Skype interview?'

Nina stares at his face, clean shaven and smooth skinned. Boyish even, for what must be his considerable years. Jeff, she thinks, holding his gaze. Not Jeffrey.

'Good. Great, in fact,' she says, unzipping her coat and slipping out of it, folding it onto her knee. She takes in Jeff's bemused smile. He's on the verge of saying something which Nina imagines will be some sort of commiseration. She cuts him off.

'I think there's a reason for it.' She watches Jeff place both hands on the desk and push, as if he's going to get up, but then he doesn't. He tilts his head up instead and the light from the papers on the desk seems to bounce off the under-side of his chin now, reflecting yellow like a buttercup.

'What I mean by that is there's a time for everything and I accept that this is not the right time for me to be registered.'

Jeff leans his upper body into the desk for a moment before sitting further back in his chair, smiling at Nina, as if he'd like her to continue. His left cheek has a deep, long dimple that she hasn't noticed before. She puts a finger into one of her curls and twists it.

'A very mature approach to disappointment. I wish some other students and, indeed, staff could think like that sometimes.'

Nina feels conflicted by the compliment. By the fact that Jeff has not understood what she was saying. The basic premise that he has taken from it is wrong. She is not disap-pointed. Not at all and she is reaching to find a way of saying this that won't sound offensive or ungrateful when Jeff continues.

'I suppose what should I expect from a student who writes with such philosophical maturity? What I've been hoping to clarify, though, is how you came up with the central idea in your proposal and whether anyone else is involved with it?'

Nina runs her tongue against the back of her piercing as she stares across the desk at Jeff. He may as well have just got up, walked over and punched her in the gut. She feels the same way she did when he hadn't bothered to read her proposal. Now she could describe to him what it's actually like to be disappointed. He doesn't believe she can do this, after all. He thinks she's stolen the idea. Or at least that she hasn't come up with it on her own. She stands up, slips back into her coat, pulls her hat on and wraps her scarf twice around her neck.

'Thanks,' she says as Jeff opens his mouth to speak again, a glower of confusion shading his eyes.

'It's not the right time for this either, clearly,' she says with a swell of confidence that startles her a little.

'How do you mean?'

'I mean that I have no desire to be mentored, off the books or otherwise, by someone who thinks I've cogged the idea for my research.'

'But that's not what I meant at all,' Jeff says. He gets up from his desk and walks around to her. His proximity unnerves her. She feels a stab of something unfamiliar. A protective jab that a parent might have for a child who doesn't seem to be able to hit the right chord. She wants to leave the room without saying another word. Until he reaches out and touches her coat sleeve for a brief moment, sending a light shiver through her body. She closes her eyes, as if by doing so she can capture this. Revisit it when she needs to. When she opens her eyes again Jeff begins to speak.

'I'm sorry, Nina, we seem to keep getting off on the wrong foot. What I mean is that the idea is brilliant and I hope that no one is lurking in the background who might wish to lay claim to it.'

She inhales deeply.

Stale coffee and something fresher, tangier, fill her lungs.

She looks up at him. At his eyes, which seem to be all pupil in this half-light.

'No,' she says. 'There's no one.'

TUESDAY

CASSANDRA

I stare into the void. There isn't even a scrap of paper in it. It makes no sense. None. He's been walking around with an empty briefcase. Why did he call back into the car for it this morning? What use can it be to him? I dig my hands down into the pocketed sections. Nothing. It's as if someone, something has entered my world and stripped it bare of what I know and trust. I sniff the felt lining. It's his case all right. The lemon cologne that he splashes on in the mornings lingers in the material. He splashes it onto his hands and then rubs it into his unruly hair, dampening the glistening silver waves. He combs it through then and the waviness diminishes for a while. By the time we reach college it's sprung back and he leaves the scent behind him in the car. I love it. I've always loved it. He's been doing this since he was nineteen. Ever since he set foot in Italy that first time and was introduced to it. The well off and the ordinary men were all at it, he tells me. Splashing, rubbing and wafting their citrus selves around. It's a bit out of place here except when the summer sun makes an appearance. But I love it.

It's him. Steady, consistent him. A knot of nerves clenches my gut. I clip the briefcase closed and slip it back down the side of the couch. I have to get the hell out of here.

I change. Then I run. Out of the cottage. Alone. Winding my way through the village and on to the open stretch along Hyde Road, avoiding the coast for the first half of this five-kilometre loop. I pump up a steep, long incline, before yielding to the relief of a stretch downwards again. I run. Past the People's Park. Mothers pushing toddler sons in swings in the crisp spring air. Like I once should have been. But I was not. It was Jeff. The sea is in front of me. Sage green, beckoning. I jog on the spot at the crossing lights now. Jog and think about how I'd love that time back. Those first two precious years. I'd love that chance again. Because no matter what I do now to try to make up for it, it's still there. Obvious to us all. I jog across with the green man, being careful, as if with Ted now, teaching him to protect himself from sudden dangers. Down past Teddy's ice cream where a queue snakes along the path. Siblings with a parent. Some with two parents. Real families. Squabbling and squawking in the surprise burst of evening sun. A pang of loneliness washes through me. Ted loves it here. He thinks Teddy's ice cream is named after him. Which Jeff says is true, of course it is, they heard your name and thought we must call our ice-cream parlour that, and Ted laughs. It's the ease of it. Their relationship is full of ease. They don't have to try. Not at all.

The wall curves with words. White script on blue. Like

little waves spraying on the sea. I stop to read them, as I always do. Even though I know them off by heart.

The first faint noise of gently moving water broke the silence, low and faint and whispering . . .

I run. Past somebody lying on the path in a blue sleeping bag, paper cup empty beside him, words standing on a triangle of cardboard with various pleas. I do not stop. Nobody stops. On another day this would disturb me. Not today. I'm picking up speed, hoping for that release. My ponytail swishes across my shoulders, beating time to my steps. I fly past the enormous sculptured shell, moonscape stuccoes, with lumps like small breasts and fat nipples. I see his face beaming through the hole in the centre of it. Running ahead and hiding. Then popping up to frighten us. I snap it on my phone. His eyes dancing, baby teeth twinkling, thrilled with his prank. With Jeff holding his heart in mock terror.

I run, inhaling deeply. The air is thick with freshly displayed seaweed from a receding tide. I run. Past the adult exercise park with kids using pedalled walking machines as swings. I step up the pace. I'm running faster than ever, hoping for a hormonal rush to assault me. To clear my head. To tell me what to do next.

Sandycove beach is just ahead, warm yellow sand playing host to the buckets and spades of tinies, patient parents digging holes to fill with water, building forts, as we used to. As Jeff used to. Their very own miniature kingdoms to release their dreams in. I'm the observer. The by-stander with the camera at the ready. A mother by proxy.

I run along the wall, skipping over a picnic basket, down the stone steps onto the glinting sand for a moment before pushing myself up the slope and rounding the white sun-trapped wall when it happens. I stop to catch my breath. My head feels fuzzy, light, empty. A whirring white nothingness. I fall to my knees. A half-naked man runs towards me mouthing something. I cannot hear him. He blurs.

DECEMBER

NINA

Staff and Postgraduate Christmas drinks
December 11th B108
From 6pm
All welcome

The notice is pinned to the corner of the board with a single red thumbtack. Nina mulls it over. It would be a good way to make connections. Show herself off in a general sense, away from the strictures of the interview. When she sets about reapplying for her place next September they will all know her just a little bit. The graduates from UCD have an advantage in this. She knows that she would have strolled into a place, had she wanted it, in Trinity. But this is where she wants to be. Without a doubt. Now though, as the time approaches, she feels just that small bit of nausea rising, a tinge of acid in the back of her throat. She hasn't mentioned to Jeff Hogan that she's thinking of going along.

In the bar, to kill a little time beforehand, Nina orders a vodka-cranberry. She sits on a high stool in front of the barman, her iPhone in her hand as a prop, scrolling down. The drink is put in front of her. Basic, like Ribena and ice. Unadorned with lime as it would have been in the Pavilion in Trinity. She prefers it this way. She glances around briefly, just to be sure. He's not here. The sea of students, unfamiliar and familiar all at once, thrums with a beat of its own. She is safe. She tries to imagine what it would've been like all those years ago. When her mother was here. A teetotaler all her life. Still, she'd like to think that her mother might've had some fun times before she'd left to look after her own mother back in Italy. Nina's grandmother survived the throat cancer and her mother returned to the family chip-shop business in Ireland, some years later, with Nina in tow. She never completed her degree in history of art and archaeology. She takes a keen interest in Nina's academic pursuits instead, as if this somehow lessens the dropout stigma. For Nina, the interest is a little suffocating.

Ed Sheeran's 'Stay With Me' blasts, his modulated lilt pinging all around. Nina thinks about Conor now, how he resembles Ed Sheeran just that little bit. The broad, twinkly smile and the wild, tousled hair. How the hell hasn't he been snapped up already? She thumbs a text.

Hey. Saying hello to some postgrads at a drinks thing. Catch you later?

She doesn't wait for his reply. It's 6.30. She's ready to go. Nina listens at the door until she hears him, his voice clear and mellow over the general din, enticing her in. The door opens, a lecturer Nina hasn't seen before scurries past her, muttering. She catches a glimpse of him, Jeff, standing in the middle of the floor, a glass of red wine glinting in his hand. He raises it to his mouth and quaffs it. Nina glides towards him as if in a trance, just as another student he's obviously been talking to returns to her spot with two fresh glasses of red. Nina forks off to the left, over to the wine table. She takes her time, pouring herself a full glass of white, and she sips it with her back to them. It is as if his is the only voice in the room. Other sounds, the laughter, the chit-chat, even the ringing of 'Fairytale of New York' are muffled to Nina. Eyes closed, she picks his words out and jigsaws them all together, as the physical feeling she gets when she's close to him begins to swell in her. Her body begins to do what it does every time. Static little prods, like a magnet scooping up filings from the surface of her skin. She turns around, and as she does, he turns his head, as if the two actions are connected, a puppeteering act.

'Nina?' Even though there is something in his tone now that is less than appealing, a tinge of annoyance perhaps, Nina delights at him calling her name. She smiles.

'Excuse me for a minute, can you?' Jeff says to the postgraduate student. She glances at Nina and then at Jeff, the harsh light above doing little to disguise her thoughts.

'Sure,' she says and Nina feels something rise in her. A prickle of pride. Jeff has made himself clear. He walks towards her and she counts his steps as he does so, with each one just a small increase in those static little prods, the magnet scooping closer to the surface of her skin, circling down low below her navel. He is smiling too – his mouth at least. Something else radiates from his eyes. A touch of fear that Nina chooses not to see. She takes another gulp of wine, which seems to hit her cheeks instantly. She is glowing.

'How come you're here?' Jeff says, half whispering. Nina hasn't seen him quite like this before, almost timorous, unsure of himself.

'Oh, you know, the notice said *all welcome* so that's how come,' Nina says, and she laughs, feeling the full blast of the alcohol in her words now. Jeff laughs too, though not his real laugh, and as he does so he begins to speak in that half-whisper again, the full effect of both things coursing a giddiness through Nina.

'All these people are registered, Nina, and as you're not, not yet, it's not really a great idea to be here.'

Nina wonders if a lip-reader could make his words out. The lips are barely moving. She focuses on the cleft in his chin, more like a hole. Circular and deep. About the size of the tip of a child's little finger.

'I thought it might be good to get a feel for the other students and staff, you know, before I reapply. Might help with my interview technique. Avert another disaster.'

'Ah, I see. Yes, well, you know they'll be wondering who you are and why you're here and—'

'Jeffrey – who's this you're talking to?' Professor Margaretta

Nolan stands before them. Nina watches as Jeff's eyes deaden in a haze of resignation.

'This is Nina Ruzza, you might remember her? One of our applicants for this year. She'll be reapplying after she's taken a little time off to find her feet. Isn't that so, Nina?' Jeff drums this out as if it's been rehearsed. Confident, loud and calm. Almost booming. Nina feels the warmth in her cheeks rise even further now. She must be beetroot, she thinks. She looks at Margaretta Nolan, who shows no trace of remembering her at all, her brow raised as it was throughout the brief nightmare of the interview. Nina wonders what her face might look like in resting position.

'Precisely,' Nina says.

'And what does finding your feet entail?' Margaretta says, looking around the room, as if on a stage appealing to an audience.

'It entails gazing steadily in the right direction,' Nina says, and she puts her glass behind her on the table, turns her back on Jeff and Margaretta and leaves.

Nina walks along the corridor under dim yellow lights and rounds the corner, far enough away from the party, but within earshot of the room. She'll know if he comes looking for her. She doesn't know whether she'd like him to or not. Not really. She presses her back against the cold stone wall and thinks for a moment. He didn't seem to want her there, his words indicated that at least. But then there were the other things to consider. The way that he had whispered those words, with an intimacy that a couple very close might know. The proximity. He had stood within inches of her face, leaning further in so that she could sniff at him, the lemon musk fragrance of his cologne barely disguising the whiff of sweat on his neck, a smell so powerfully pleasing to Nina that she smiles again now thinking about it. The way that he had stood firm with Margaretta, introducing the certainty that Nina would be here. Then the smile that had crossed his lips after he had spoken – *isn't that so, Nina* – with that touch of asymmetry, as if one half of his face was just that little bit happier than the other. Cute. Nina swallows. She knows now that she will wait.

Outside, the night air is sharp, biting. The blackest sky is interrupted only by an occasional star and a low crescent moon. Nina lies on the wheelchair slope to the car park, and gazes up, thinking about what she will do if he is, actually, drunk. She doesn't want him to know she's here, not exactly. But she's not happy with how she had left him to do battle with Margaretta Nolan either. She just needs to check that he's okay. He's sticking his neck out for her and she'd like him to know that she appreciates it. She turns her head to the side. She'll stay like this until she sees him approach. She'll know by his walk whether she should make herself seen or not. A numbness tingles in her fingertips. She tucks her hands in under her jacket and waits.

She wakes to the sound of his voice, her body juddering with the cold, but she stays as still as she can, listening. One voice only. He's on the phone.

'Oh, you know how these things are. A pain in the neck really, but it has to be done. Tell me, how's the little man?'

She can see him now, walking along the path beside the admin building, briefcase in one hand, phone in the other. He looks different, without his jacket now. He must be frozen. His shirt is hanging outside his trousers. His steps are small and unsure, like a toddler's. As if he doesn't really want to go where he's going.

'And you? How are you feeling?' His words aren't slurred exactly, but not as clear as earlier. The tone too is different. A notch higher. Defensive somehow.

'I know. I know.' He stops and tilts his head backwards to look up at the crescent moon, swaying slightly as he listens. Nina has to fight the urge to get up and run towards him.

'It is.' He begins to walk again, towards the steps. He stands at the top of them, parallel to Nina, and finishes his conversation. 'Fifteen.' He slips the phone back into his trouser pocket and holds onto the railing to descend, tentatively, like a much older person. It is as if he doesn't quite trust himself. On the second-last step he falters. Nina gasps into her sleeve as he steadies himself and continues on, reaching his car, one of only three left now, a modest Mars-red Renault Clio. Nina sits up and watches as he throws his briefcase onto the passenger seat and climbs in. She can't make out whether he's putting his belt on, or what he's doing, but he seems to be waiting for something. She wonders if he has perhaps glimpsed her somehow and if it is her that he's stalling for now. She stands, feeling the full force of the cold, a numbness in her legs. She bends to rub them, keeping her eyes firmly on the car. Then she descends the wheelchair slope into the car park, breathing in deeply to calm herself. His lights go on and the key turns in the ignition, blasting a cloud of black smoke out of the back. He reverses and a rattling sound comes from the engine, like the whirr of helicopter blades. As he drives away she stands there wondering how she has just let him go.

TUESDAY

CASSANDRA

I open my eyes. I'm flat on my back on the cold concrete staring into the furrowed face of a complete stranger. I feel his hands on my breastbone, pressing, pumping me. He looks around, frantically, pressing and pushing hard. Far too hard.

'Thanks,' I whisper and he snaps his head back to look at me. He removes his hands, dangles them by his side and smiles.

'I thought you were a goner there,' he says. Perspiration glistens on his brow.

'You didn't seem to be breathing.' He kneels beside me. The towel covering his lower half is knotted to the side, leaving a pleat of thigh on show. He's shivering.

'I haven't eaten much today. I think I just fainted or something.' His eyes widen. Warm hazel eyes.

'It didn't seem like a faint,' he says. 'You were out. I did CPR.'

'You did?'

'Don't worry about it, I'm trained. An ambulance is on the way.'

'Jesus, I don't need an ambulance. I'm grand.' I sit up now to prove it and feel like lying straight back down again.

'Best to get it checked out.'

'I really can't. I've something important on this evening.'

'Well, you very nearly didn't have anything on.'

Oh god. He thinks he's a hero. There's nothing worse than dealing with the ego of a self-proclaimed hero. He's overstepped the mark. Saved me when I didn't need saving.

'Is there someone I can call for you? Let them know what's happened?'

My phone is back in the cottage.

Jeff will be texting soon to be picked up.

Mum will be ringing to say how Ted is getting on.

I hear the siren.

It's getting close.

'No. There's no one.'

'Would you like me to come with you?'

'Certainly not,' I say, a little sharply. 'You've done every-thing you can and thank you for it.' I soften my tone a little. The psychology of the hero when the saved rejects him. There's a paper on that.

The ambulance crew strap me onto a gurney.

'Are you having chest pain?'

'No, not at all, I'm fine. A little nauseous maybe, but fine.'

'Did you pass out?'

'I did, because I haven't eaten anything all day, you see and then I—'

'How long were you out for?'

'Oh, I don't know, seconds I'd say, if that.'

'Two minutes,' he chimes in.

'Were you with her all the time?' the young paramedic asks.

'Yes.'

'Can you follow us to the hospital then? Help the doctors to piece this together.'

'I can indeed,' he says peering in at me as they strap an oxygen mask to my face. Even though I'm breathing perfectly well. He waves at me. Why the hell is he waving at me? He looks like a little boy, saying goodbye to a parent. I'm no good at guessing a person's age. He could be anything from twenty-five to thirty-five. Plenty of hair, which looks as if it'll be some shade of brown when it dries off. He turns around and heads back towards the wall. He drops his useless towel and pulls his boxers on with a deft hand. This is a man who knows how to hurry.

They have the siren on. Fraying my nerves more than they are already. I think of how I've really been expecting this all day. The sound of sirens bleating close to me, but not this close. It should have been me calling for them. Anonymously. *A girl is lying in a crumpled heap on the beach at Killiney. I saw her from the train overhead. The waves were crashing up close to her. She's half naked.* But I didn't. I couldn't.

I'm wheeled straight in, past a half-full waiting room, to resus. I don't need to be in resus.

'What did you feel like just before you collapsed?' She looks young enough to be my niece. She couldn't be a doctor. Not yet. Despite what her badge says.

'A little dizzy, light-headed maybe. That's all. I haven't eaten, you see, Doctor.' She doesn't flinch. The confidence of it. An intern at best.

'Has this happened to you before?'

'Not for years. I used to faint in my teens though. It felt a bit like that.'

'When you hadn't eaten enough?'

How simplistic. Linear. I could just say yes and put an end to it. A fainter. That's all.

'No. When I started menstruating. Every month. I'd faint.'

'Are you menstruating at the moment?'

She must've gone to the easy-peasy school of medicine.

'No.'

Are you? I feel like saying. The curtain blows towards her as someone whips by.

Then it opens, just a fraction, and he is here. The man from the cove. His hair is now dry and he looks different in his clothes. Younger maybe. He sticks his hand out to the child doctor.

'Sorry for the delay.' He smiles at her. A dimple on the top of his left cheek deepens.

'Next of kin?'

'No, sorry, I thought you were expecting me.' He puts his hand back down by his side.

'I was there, saw what happened and administered CPR.'

'Okay, good,' she says. 'Shoot.'

'I'd had my swim and was about to change at the wall when I saw her running towards me. She was very fast, sprinting really, up a slope, but then she stopped suddenly.' I was right about the hair at least. A full head, reddish-brown, tousled, not combed after the swim.

'Then she just hit the deck,' he says.

'Uh-huh, so she stopped and then fell down?' It's only now that I notice her accent. East Coast America. As if she's here on a student placement.

'That's right.'

She scribbles his words down on pink paper. Her head moves in little nods as she writes. A good student, I'll bet. Conscientious. She looks back up at him to continue. I'm looking at him too. His cheeks redden, just a touch.

'She didn't seem to be breathing. I started CPR, I'm trained in it, and called for the ambulance.'

He has the lips of a woman. Naturally sculpted into a perfect plump heart on top.

'I did this for a minute and a half – thirty compressions followed by two breaths three times. On the third time breathing into her she opened her eyes.' He glances at my trolley, at where my feet are, and then back to the doctor who finishes her notes.

'Lucky,' she says. 'We'll do an ECG to see if you've had a

heart event and you have a gash on your head there at the side. We'll need to do an MRI. You could be here for a while before we know what's going on. If there's someone we can call for you, just let us know.'

She whips the curtain open and then closes it behind her leaving me alone with this stranger.

JANUARY

NINA

Nina sits at the pond on the curved wall and waits. She looks up at the cloudless deep blue winter sky, at the low sun glinting through the bare trees. The swans are taking turns at doing what look like headstands, their long necks submerged and their fluffy bottoms up in the air. Searching for something. All around her the students stream. She remembers it well. The first day of a new academic term as an undergraduate. Nauseating. Although from what she can see, this lot seem pretty relaxed. She has come a long way, she thinks now, this past while. It was good not to be registered. She needed that break. A skateboarder curves past her, and jumps off the wall landing somehow upright on the board, bag still slung across his shoulder. Eighteen she thinks. A pup.

Her eye is drawn to a bronze statue. A female, legs spread and crouching, arms open and outstretched, head bowed. If the head was up, she'd be taking on the world. Ready, willing, strong, able. But the head is bowed. This is often how Nina feels, but not today.

She can hear his car now before she sees it and she makes

her way across to the car park. He's refusing to get that rattle seen to, and she's glad of it, letting her know each time he's close by. If it wasn't for this, the Christmas holidays would've stolen him away completely. No meetings. The occasional email. An arid time. But she had glimpsed him out and about aided by the noise of the car. Once, while she was cycling down along the promenade at dusk she thought she heard it approaching, above on the road. She cut up the grass hill and merged into the stream of traffic, Jeff's tail lights twinkling at her three cars ahead. She followed, keeping her speed and her distance perfectly even. He stopped, parking at the small empty cove, as she guessed he would. The back door opened and a child jumped out, wielding a bucket and spade. He was wearing a navy duffel coat and red wellington boots, and tufts of light hair peeped out from underneath his woolly hat. She watched from a distance as the winter sun dropped out of the sky, down behind the west pier, casting a purple-pink hue to the edge of the scattered clouds. She watched as Jeff knelt on the wet, cold sand, digging fervently, sending the boy to the water's edge with his bucket, time and again. Nina was mesmerized by the activity, and by something else that she couldn't put her finger on. Some sort of pleasure hormone pulsing through her. All she knew was that for as long as they stayed doing this, she would stay also, hanging back and imbibing whatever this was.

Nina sprints across the grass now. She can't afford to miss him. He needs to know. She sees the top of his head first as he climbs the steps. Different somehow. What is it? And then he turns back towards the car park. He stands there, halfway up the steps, as if he's changed his mind and he just wants to go home again. Then he raises his hand. She picks up her pace. Her news will make him want to stay. She's about to call out to him when he turns back around, flanked by Professor Nolan now. Nina can see that he's not happy about it. He's faltering, moving slowly. What a start to the New Year, she thinks. Not even being able to get to his office without the nitpicky politics beginning. She retreats, walking backwards at first, just in case he spots her, which would cheer him up, she knows. This is not the right time though. She can wait a little longer to deliver her news.

She goes back to the little curved wall. All along its edge silver balls protrude. About the size of golf balls, smooth and hard, evenly spaced. A quirky design or perhaps to put the skateboarders off. She sits herself directly onto one of the balls. Did he catch a glimpse of her as she turned to walk, slowly, back to the pond? If he did, he would not have called out, not with Professor Nolan beside him. No. He would wait, just as she is doing now.

She looks back at the crouching statue and then beyond her to the entwined male and female statues, reaching up towards the sky. They stand there, back to back, the glint of the water behind them. The female is clad in a crumpled metallic shoulderless dress. The man is naked, with green slimy, sinewy legs. As if he has walked out of the water to her. Back to back, but together, anything is possible. This is the two of them, Nina thinks. Jeff and Nina. Hands reaching up together, almost touching. She's higher up than he is, elevated, which is how she now feels. She's very up. Very optimistic. This will be her year.

It's time. She removes herself from the ball, a little numb now from the cold pressure. She walks at first, before upping her pace to a trot. She will follow them through the concourse, and then, when Professor Nolan diverges off to her room, she will be right behind Jeff Hogan, ready to surprise him.

TUESDAY

CASSANDRA

'I'm going to get a coffee from the machine out there. Would you like anything? A hot, sweet tea is good for shock,' he says to me. Where to begin? How do I get rid of him?

'I'm not in shock, just annoyed with myself for winding up in here.'

'At least you're in the right place.' Kind. Guileless as hell.

'Maybe, if there was actually something wrong with me. But there isn't. If you hadn't been there I'd have got myself back up and continued with my run.' He smiles. A twinkly, wordless smile. He swishes the curtain open and closes it again without looking back. Thankfully. I could just get up and sneak out now. Say I'm going to the toilet and scarper. I need to get home. There's movement directly outside my cubicle, a shadow on the curtain, which bulges into me now. The child doctor is back, dragging equipment behind her. Great.

'We're just going to do an ECG, see if there's anything unusual going on with your heart.' There's plenty unusual going on with it, I feel like saying. Your machine will find that it's racing. For a start.

'Can you just slip your top and brassiere off there for me while I attach these?'

Brassiere? Really? She hands me a blue paper gown.

'You can cover yourself with this after.'

'How long will this all take?'

'The ECG is just a few minutes. The head scan, well that depends on when you get called for it.'

'I really need to get home,' I say to her.

She's deadpan. Impervious. Clinically detached. 'It all depends on what these tests show.' She slaps sticky circles with wires onto my chest and arms.

'They won't show anything,' I say, aware that my voice has the edge of a defiant teen.

'Maybe. Breathe normally and lie still.' She sashays off to some other cubicle.

Waves of peaks and troughs spring up on the monitor beside me.

Am I breathing normally?

Will it show up that I've been holding my breath for protracted periods throughout the day? Every time the caterwaul rings in me.

Movement through the curtain beside me. Groaning. Mewling. Confusion. This really is a hellhole. I'm stuck. Nobody knows. Which is the only good thing about it. I've disappeared. Out of range. Fallen off the radar. Ted is safe with Mum. Jeff will begin to grow frantic. Let him. Tuppence. She'll be fine for a while. Maybe being here is just as good as running around at home trying to work it all out.

Maybe it's better. I have enough distance to see it all clearly. All the bits that add up to something. Ted sticking his little fingers up into her curls. Jeff allowing this particular intimacy. Why? Ted and Jeff saying nothing at all about it. About her. Sailing home on a Thursday to me with a client, distracted, busy. Did I even ask them what they got up to? I must have, but I can't remember now. Ted's homework, always done. The two of them in great form. Peas in a pod. Taking Tuppence out for her evening walk. Me writing up client files. Absorbed. Then switching to the stove. To some sort of dinner. Resentfully at times. The working-from-home mother without the conviviality of the workplace, steeped in domesticity. Why doesn't he do the dinner every second night? Think about it, plan it, shop for it, execute it. All the little taken-for-granted bits that make an evening hang. This can thrum through my mind as I chop and stir like an automaton. Other times I'm just happy to be doing it. Thinking I have it every which way. Not missing out on raising my child. Working at what I enjoy. In a relationship with the person I love. Making nurturing meals is just like a bonus. Forgetting past trials. Attempting to. An active everyday thing. A muscle that needs to be exercised and it is best exercised here.

What I wouldn't give now to be at that stove, consumed by minor irritations.

The curtain swishes and he's here again. Styrofoam cup in hand.

'I thought you'd gone.' Hoped. I hoped you'd gone.

'Nope.' He hands the cup to me.

'I don't think I'll be allowed to drink it. I'm supposed to lie still and breathe normally. I shouldn't even be talking.'

'I've had an ECG. Don't worry. Talking is not a problem.'

Probably depends on the kind of talk. If he thinks I'm going to ask him why he had an ECG, he's wrong.

'You might be right about the drinking though. It'll be over in a minute. You can have it then.'

I'm beginning to feel like a child again. Who is this guy? Hovering and soothing like an anxious parent.

'I'm sure you must have plenty of places you'd rather be. Hanging around an emergency room with a stranger isn't much fun. Thanks for all that you've done. Please go now. I'm not comfortable holding you up any longer.' Nothing. Not a word out of him. He doesn't even blink.

The curtain swishes again. The child doctor is back.

'All done.' She rips the print from the machine and gazes at it.

'Can you wait outside for a minute?' she says to him. Then I see it. A hint of a blush. Maybe he's here for her instead. Now that would make sense. He obeys her like a little dog.

'Well, you're not having a heart attack and you haven't had one, so far,' she says.

'I could've told you that.'

'Yes.' She's smiling now.

'But the trace is showing an irregular beat. Arrhythmia.

It's not anything to worry about, not immediately. We'll need to do more tests though. It may or may not be related to what happened to you earlier.'

Great.

'Can I get those done as an outpatient? I've a lot on at the moment and I really don't have time for this.'

'You've to go for your MRI head scan in a little while and I'm going to organize for you to get some other tests done while you're here. I can't let you go with the event you've had and what's showing on the trace. Sorry. Would you like me to send your friend back in to you?'

God.

'No. He's heading off now.'

'You were lucky he was there. Would you like me to contact anyone else?'

'Not yet, thanks. I don't need anyone worrying about me.'

'Okay. I'll just take your next-of-kin details.'

Next of kin. It should be automatic. Without delay. Jeff.

'That's my mother, I suppose. Eve. I'll give you her mobile number but I don't want you to use it. She'd get the fright of her life.'

'No problem, it's for our records, just in case.'

She exits again, my poor mother's number on her clipboard. How long do I have before she'll begin to wonder? It must be getting on for six now. I'm currently supposed to be battling with my 5.30 appointment. That gives me until seven before she'll try to contact me. Jeff will be expecting me. Or will he? He can phone all the numbers and eventually he'll phone her. He'll be told I'm with a client and Ted is fine with her for now. If I wasn't stuck in here, would I go and pick him up at the usual time? Would he really be expecting me to today?

The bells of the Angelus chime from outside the curtain letting me know that it's six o'clock now. Each bong in this minute of torture stings my ears and sends a shiver through me. The Six One news is coming. Perhaps I should be praying along for once. Pretend that I believe in something just for today. The signature tune for the news pings with that mixture of merriment and menace – something Jeff and I laugh about: how it manages to capture both a little bit of terror and a little bit of hope. Today the terror rings louder. I could block my ears but I don't.

The headlines are muffled by movement and moans and machines. Did he say Killiney beach? What the hell did he say?

'Excuse me,' I call out. A swish of the curtain.

'Can you leave it open? I'm a bit claustrophobic, thanks.'

The screen is angled in a corner to my right.

The words are muffled still, but I don't need to hear them. There it is.

A white tent covering the spot where we left her this morning.

JANUARY

NINA

Nina watches as they walk, side by side, on the path alongside the administration building. Professor Nolan is in full flow, her breath visible in the cold morning air, plumes of white smoke escaping as she talks with an enthusiasm that seems out of place with her otherwise sombre character. The effect Jeff Hogan has on people, Nina thinks, upping her pace a little. He's doing less than a quarter of the speaking, as far as Nina can make out. He doesn't want to be there at all. She walks briskly, perpendicular to them at first. Jeff looks as if he's lost a little weight since the last time she saw him. There's an extra bagginess to his trousers, from this side view at least, and he seems to be walking pretty slowly. If she keeps this pace up, she'll crash right into them. She stops for a minute and listens to her heart thudding. Then she continues towards the path where they've just been. Their heads are lowering in front of her as they descend the steps. She stands at the top of the steps and watches as they walk towards the Arts block. It's then that she sees it. The slight drag of his left foot. The heavy way that he's putting it down. He's injured himself, she thinks, as she runs down the steps and follows, just a few metres behind. Throngs of people are heading the same way. She checks her phone. Eight-fifty. All dashing to their nine o'clocks. He doesn't have one. Not today. She's made sure. They disappear through the Arts block doors and get lost in the crowds. Nina follows blindly until they emerge again. She hangs back and watches as Jeff walks slowly towards the lift. She's never known him to take the lift. Once they are in it and the doors close silently on them, Nina takes the stairs, two at a time. She waits on his floor until she hears him emerge, muttering to Professor Nolan. Something about the common room. She listens as their voices trail off and she pictures them diverging. Then she rounds the corner and walks swiftly to his door.

She knocks, a little louder than she intends to and the door handle turns immediately. Before she has a chance to work out what she'll say he's standing in front of her. Not smiling, but not unsmiling either. He doesn't say or do a thing.

'What's up with your leg?' Nina says.

Jeff casts his gaze beyond her for a moment, as if he's trying to remember something. 'Come in for a minute,' he says in almost a whisper. Nina walks past him and stands with her arms folded across her chest. She watches him negotiate his way around his desk, leaning his hand on it for support. It's as if he's aged five years in the last month. He sits and a puff of air resounds. He's hit his leather desk chair too hard.

'So, what brings you here?' he asks, his voice flat, as if he's already exhausted by the day. There's a chill in the room and the venetian blinds are closed. He doesn't seem to be bothered about either of these things. 'We didn't have a meeting set up, did we? I've been giving this a bit of thought, as it happens, over the break.'

'Did you have an accident?' Nina interrupts, sitting on the chair opposite him. 'At Christmas. Did you injure your leg?'

Jeff takes his time, looking at Nina and then up at the bookshelves, to the display of black, hardbound, gold-lettered theses that he has supervised. As if the answer might lie somewhere there among the spines.

'No.'

'No? Something's not right with it.'

'It's fine, Nina. I think I've pulled a muscle or something.'

'You should get it checked out.'

A flash of something crosses his face. Nina can't work it out. Wistful almost.

'Maybe I will. Look, enough about me. How have you been getting on?' Jeff glances at his watch.

'Great.' She waits for a moment, expecting his curiosity to pique and for him to probe. It's as if he hasn't heard her at all.

'I worked on it over Christmas. I've got something I want to show you.' The phone on his desk rings.

'Sorry.' He picks up the receiver and listens without speaking for a minute, pressing his lips together, as if he's spreading a balm.

'Will do,' he says and hangs up. 'I've got to go. Can you send me what you've done and we can discuss it properly when we next meet?'

'Which will be when?' she asks, and immediately regrets, as she sees it in his eyes, the registering that her tone is a little off, just that tinge of disappointment verging on aggression in it. He doesn't answer.

'Look, it doesn't matter. Just let me know when you're free to meet. I'll be there,' she says, and she slips out of his room feeling she has somehow just dodged a bullet.

TUESDAY

CASSANDRA

The body of a young woman was found on South County Dublin's Killiney beach by a dog walker early this morning. A post-mortem will be carried out by the Assistant State Pathologist. Gardaí have confirmed that the woman did not drown. They are treating the death as suspicious. They are appealing to anyone who might have been in the vicinity or travelled by train above the beach between 6.30 and 7.30 this morning to contact them. The identity of the woman is not yet known.

So now I know. I'm married to a murderer. She did not get up and walk away as my fantasy would have it. You have not simply been having an affair, your weakness for young, petite women creeping up on us again. Oh you've been having an affair, all right. That much is resoundingly clear. Did I already know that? There must have been signs. I will trawl through my mind for them. I'm surprised by my reaction to seeing it there on the news. This thing I have been dreading all day is a reality now and it is not rage with you that's bubbling up in me. It's something else. Something a lot more familiar.

'We'll bring you along for your scan now,' the child doctor says, smiling her perfect straight, gleaming white teeth at me. She no longer irks me though. Now that I know and I'm here in that after space, my whole world changed for ever, once again. It could've been her, this lovely young doctor, on the beach dying at your hand. She'd be about the right age. The dark, long hair. A nymph. Just as you like them. Liked. All far back in the past. Before us. So I believed. You seemed so real. So loving. So happy with the stability we had. So attentive to Ted. To me, most of the time.

She wheels me directly into the scanning room.

'Judy here will go through everything with you and I'll see you again afterwards.' She puts a light hand on my shoulder, and I shudder at her touch, at the kindness of this small gesture.

Don't go I feel like saying, suddenly vulnerable.

But I do not.

I know better than to show my weakness.

She pushes through the swing door and is gone.

'I've just got some questions to go through first of all,' Judy says. Bobbed grey hair frames an unlined freshly tanned face. She's ready for business. Her matter-of-factness is helping to snap me out of my vulnerability.

'Have you had an MRI or any other scans recently?'

Do I have to tell?

'Just an ultrasound.' I hope this will be enough. I don't want to have to go there. Not now.

'How long ago was the ultrasound and what was it for?'

'It was a few months back, an early pregnancy scan.' I can see her calculating. A flash of acknowledgement dances across her light blue eyes. She nods. I'd still be pregnant. Getting towards my due date. Getting ready to close the circle on the family. Give Ted that much-longed-for sibling. Jeff, getting on now for another blast of fatherhood, but he's so good at it. I'm glad now though. Today I can say I'm glad that I'm not about to have that much-longed-for second child.

'Is there any chance you could be pregnant now?'

I like her. She doesn't commiserate. Just gets on with the practicalities. 'There is no chance, no.'

Which makes perfect sense, now. A post-traumatic drop in libido was what I had put it down to. Not mine. I was primed, every cell in my body aching to be shagged, to be pregnant again.

It's too soon.

That's what you kept saying. Seemingly much more trau-matized than I was. I felt like a whore dressing up in my leather miniskirt and crotchless tights ready to hop on you when I knew I was ovulating again. Raw egg albumen seeping out of me, fertility signs dripping down my legs, crying out for me to sit astride you and make you come deep inside.

It's not too soon, you bloody fool. How many shots do you think we'll get at this at our age?

'You seem to be a little anxious about this. Is there some-one here with you that could stay beside you during the scan?'

'No, I'm alone.'

'Are you claustrophobic at all?'

'Well, yes, a little bit.' Much more today as a matter of fact.

'We can offer you sedation if you like.'

Sedation. Now that does sound appealing.

'Have a think about it for a minute and then I can explain exactly what's going to take place. You'll have to remove your rings there and any other jewellery. Only cotton clothes, I'm afraid, too so we'll give you a gown. Any piercings?'

I slip my engagement and wedding rings off with surprising ease and hand them to her. I rub the groove where they've been. Like tyre marks in the sand.

'No piercings,' I say, with a stabbing pang as I see it again now on the girl, glinting up at me from the beach, taunting. An echo of your past, your botched job on yourself. The scarring a permanent reminder of your life before me.

She hands me a questionnaire. When did I last eat? *Yesterday.* On any medication? *No.* Any implants? *No.* Look at me. A breast reduction is what I need, if anything. Pacemaker? *Not yet.*

'The sedative for claustrophobia, would that put me to sleep?'

'It would be moderate sedation. You wouldn't be knocked out or unconscious, it just makes you drowsy and relaxed. You may go off to sleep and not remember parts of the scan. But you'll wake easily when I talk to you.'

Sounds good.

'Or we can try other things, if you prefer. You'll have a bell and can talk to me at any time. You can listen to music and we could blindfold you so you're less anxious about the confined space. If you opt for sedation, you won't be able to drive for twelve hours, or drink alcohol or make important personal or business decisions.'

Perfect. There's not a decision in the world that I feel capable of making now anyway.

'You might be kept in at this stage for observation overnight, so none of those things would apply. What do you think?'

'I'll go for the sedation. Can you remind me afterwards that I'll need to phone my mother? She has my little son with her and he'll need to stay over now.'

'No problem at all. If you'd just like to go behind the curtain and remove anything that isn't cotton, pop the gown on and we can get you set up for the sedation.' She shimmies off behind a glass wall. A blast of no-nonsense efficiency.

Sedation. Even the word has a lulling effect. I really can't wait.

JANUARY

NINA

Nina sits in his office and waits. She checks her email again, just to be sure.

> I might be a little delayed getting back after my lecture.
> Let yourself in – it won't be locked.

The room, without the distraction of him in it, seems different. She absorbs the details, taking in the traces of him. The faint lemon musk smell. The half-drunk cup of black coffee on his desk. His briefcase, open. As if he was in a hurry. Some student's draft PhD thesis, untouched. She tries to read the title upside down, tilting her head sideways. Something about place and displacement in Beckett. Four years of work, more even, just sitting there, on top of a pile. Eliciting no response.

She thinks about her own work now. About how she won't have a title that's dull enough to be left untouched. The light in the room, fluorescent and faint, neutralizes everything into a bland sameness. The daytime light, when it floods into this corner room through large windows that run in an L shape, picks out colours and words, deciphering Jeff Hogan's world for Nina, highlighting the important stuff. Sitting here now, waiting in this anodyne space, Nina wonders if it isn't a good thing to be able to see him in this different light. Casting a blandness over him, dampening his hold.

She gets up, as if in a trance, and walks over to the grey venetian blinds, pulls on the cord so that the slats open and the dark night seeps in. The fluorescent light hasn't got the same grip on the room now, and, pleased with this Nina feels for the switch on Jeff's desk lamp and presses. An open fountain pen rests on a page. Beside it the number 17 is written large, the only thing on the page. The 1 has a hooded upstroke and the 7 has a dash through the middle. Nina picks up the pen and air traces the numerals above the page, smiling as she does so with this new bit of knowledge about Jeff, the small details and intricacies bringing her ever closer. She places the pen back as she found it and reads the full title of the Beckett PhD thesis. Then the name of the candidate. Paul Kane. Good, she thinks, and moves the head of the lamp so that it shines on the thesis, a prompt for Jeff that he might just need.

She hears a tap outside and looks up to see the silver round door handle rotate. Without time to reclaim her seat she steps towards the window and looks out at the car park, to the beam of headlights. Students going home. She turns when she hears his voice.

'You were right, as it happens,' Jeff says as he closes the

door to his office. He holds up a black-handled walking stick for a moment, staring directly across at Nina. She digs her nails deep into the palm of her left hand, tempering her reaction. She cannot do what she would like to do in this moment. She cannot walk over to him with open arms and hug his vulnerability away. She offers her right hand instead.

'Let me have a look at this beauty.' He walks towards her, using the stick to get there, and as he does so, she takes a deep breath to steady herself, while holding his gaze. He gives the stick to her, and perches on his desk, his bad leg dangling. She twists it in her hand, examining. It has a paisley pattern in red, blue and black.

'Nice one.' She grips the handle to try it out.

'A little big for you, but we can adjust it if you want to give it a proper go,' Jeff says, pointing to a protruding brass button.

'How long will you need this for?' Nina hears the quiver in her voice and she watches this register in Jeff, in the pressing of his lips together and then the slow release of them into a smile. She presses the brass button and reduces the stick to fit her.

'It depends on the cause. For now I'll just do as I'm told. A daily swim to strengthen the surrounding muscles for a start. I'll do whatever it takes to avoid surgery.' Nina hands the stick back to him and he walks to the window to fiddle with the blind. His left foot drags slightly and then comes down hard. It sounds like a seal slapping the water. It's much worse than two weeks ago. Nina feels a stinging at the back of her eyes.

'There, that's better,' he says as the outside world is blocked out once again. 'I thought I had closed those earlier. The old memory must be going now too. So, tell me. How have you been getting on?' Jeff turns back around to face her.

'Can you excuse me for a second?' she asks but doesn't wait for a reply. She leaves his room and makes her way straight to the nearby toilets, locking herself in a cubicle. She begins a google search on her phone, pinning in his symptoms. Foot dragging and slapping. Weight loss. Pallor. She narrows it down to three possibilities. Two are manageable and the other is not. She'll be able to work it out before too long. If other signs begin to kick in, she'll know and she'll be the one to let him know. For now though she chooses to think the best. This is something she can help him to manage.

Returning to his room, and entering without knocking, she finds him thumbing through Paul Kane's thesis, like a puppet on a string, going through the motions. It's time to cheer him up. She opens her bag and pulls out the portable whiteboard, the letters a little smudged but legible still. She puts it on the desk in front of him and closes her eyes so that she can listen to his response undistracted by his face.

FEBRUARY

TED

Mum whispers to me that it's time to get up for school. She puts her hand up inside my pyjama top and rubs my back. It makes me feel like staying in bed for longer and sometimes I do, and then she gives me a day off. Not today. I get up and follow her to the kitchen. Tuppence is in her bed still. I sit down beside her. She licks my hand.

'At least when he was going to play school we could take our time. Now it's all rush, roll calls, sick notes, guilt. He's only seven. It's too much, too soon,' Mum says to Dad, or maybe she's talking to herself because Dad doesn't answer. She's standing at the counter with her back to us, filling my lunch bag. She's still in her purple shiny dressing gown.

'Where's my school bag, Mum?'

'On the chair there.' She gives me my Minions lunch bag to pack and I look for the special card.

'Close your eyes,' I tell her. She does. 'Ta-dah, open.' Mum opens her eyes and I wave the red piece of cardboard at her. She takes it from me, smiling. On the front of the card there's a sunflower and in the middle of the sunflower is a photo of my face. Inside there's a Valentine's Day verse in my best-ever joined writing. She reads it out loud. She's blinking her eyes a lot. She hands it to Dad without saying anything.

'What's this, then?' Dad asks and Mum turns around to the sink.

'Oh god, it's that old day again. Roping the kids into it pretty early, don't you think? Whatever next?'

'Ted, run and get dressed, quickly, I'm dropping you to school today,' Dad says. I stay a bit longer, behind the island, rubbing Tuppence on her belly. I want to know if Mum likes my card or not.

'Absurd really, getting the poor little guys to declare their love for their mothers. Although at least it's not for their fathers, I suppose. What would Freud make of all this, lots of therapy down—'

'Oh shut up, Jeff, will you?' Mum turns back around from the sink. Her face is wet.

'It's the most beautiful card I've ever got so if you could just lay off for a moment.'

She does like it. I knew she would. Her eyes are wide and red. There's a drop on the tip of her nose. She stares over Dad, at the clock on the wall.

'But I thought you hated Valentine's Day.'

'I do. Or I did. But just look at him. It's all going so fast. Slipping away from me. Like everything does. I just wish we could slow it down or go back to the first couple of years or something.'

'Come here,' Dad says and he puts his arms around Mum and rests his head on her shoulder. Mum takes a deep breath and her chest rises up but doesn't fall again. Dad whispers to her and she doesn't whisper back, but she blows her nose into some toilet paper over his head. I slip through the door to get dressed as quick as I can. A minute later Dad calls me and I'm ready. It's the quickest I've ever got dressed. Back in the kitchen, Dad is ready to go, his jacket is on and his stick is in his hand. Mum looks down at my legs and smiles at me. I look down too. I've put my gym trousers on the wrong way around. The padded area is at the back of my knees instead of the front. Mum doesn't tell me to change it. She runs her fingers through my hair and kisses the top of my head.

'Have a good day sweetheart,' she says, and she gives me my bag. I take it into the sitting room and swap my trousers around. I don't want to feel silly in school all day.

Dad's face scrunches up and he closes his eyes tight when he's changing gears on the way to school. Sometimes there's a bad sound too, like he's driving on ice or snow and it's crunching and he looks cross. That doesn't happen when Mum's driving but I don't tell Dad this. He flicks on the radio to the sound of the end of an advert . . . *have a break from Valentine's Day. Have a Kit Kat.* He laughs.

'Why does Mum hate Valentine's Day?'

'Oh, she doesn't, not any more at least. Especially not today since she got your card.'

'But she used to hate it?'

'Well, she used to be funny about it. She'd say it's all about making money and nothing about love. One time, before we were married we went out for a meal on Valentine's Day and she said she felt like a sheep being herded into a pen for something unpleasant to take place. A shearing or a slaughter. All the people following one another, going along with it. Allowing themselves to be fooled and robbed. She said she didn't need to go out for an exorbitantly priced meal in a packed restaurant and have some waiter thrust a rose at her on my behalf. She said she never wanted to do it again.'

'It doesn't sound very funny.'

'Maybe not,' Dad says and he fiddles with the mirror so that he can see me better.

'Listen, I have something to do before I pick you up today but I should be there on time. Just wait if I'm a little late. We'll do something nice afterwards. Don't tell Mum, she has to work, so it's not really fair, okay?'

'Okay.' I jump out of the car at the school gate. Dad drives away. The crunching is louder out of the car than in it and some mums turn and stare. It's rude to stare my mum always tells me, but these mums don't know that. I run up the slope and into my classroom. I'll tell Mum later about the noise the car makes when Dad's driving. I want her to drive me to school instead.

FEBRUARY

NINA

Nina wakes with a thud from the dream in which she is falling. Sitting bolt upright in her bed, she goes over it in her mind. Jeff Hogan has scheduled a meeting at three o'clock. Today. Valentine's Day. She's bristling with excitement, her body taut with anticipation as if she is a child again and it's the early hours of Christmas morning. She looks down at her arms, at how the dark, long hairs are standing proud as she shivers. She dislikes her hairy arms with an intensity that has seen her take a razor to them in the warmer months. Only to discover a thickening thereafter requiring more of a cover up. It doesn't matter for today though. It's too cold, thankfully, for her to bare her arms.

He said he'd chosen Starbucks in Blackrock village for their first scheduled meeting off campus because it was kid friendly. Nina had thought he was joking around, referencing their age difference and she had smiled to herself. It was like something Conor would say. As she pushes the heavy oak door open and surveys the immediate area for him she thinks he must have chosen it for other reasons too. It's the old village post-office building, granite-faced and anonymous. No signage allowed. It still says Post Office in brass letters. There's a golden letterbox embedded in the front. It's a listed building and it suits him, she thinks now. Then the way it draws you in to the back, to the wall of glass looking over the sea. She doesn't know anywhere else like this. She scans around. Laptops dot the place. Mostly men but a smattering of women too, all ages, plugged in and working away. There's no sign of him. She orders herself a small Americano, and while she waits, she reads the poster that has been pinned up for the day over the milk-and-sugar dock. *Post your love messages here.* Pink hearts splash across it, filled with handwritten words. Different shades, different scripts. Public declarations. It seems a little absurd to Nina – why would someone put their feelings there for all to see? But she finds herself scanning it anyway until her name is called. Along with her Americano the barista hands her a single heart-shaped chocolate wrapped in red foil. She slips it into her pocket and makes her way to the back, noticing the balcony now, smokers out there cupping their hands around white mugs for warmth, enjoying the views out across the bay. She might just join them, she thinks. Sit among them, relaxing and breathing in their smoke, like she does in Positano. But that will be afterwards. It's now that she spots him, the back of him, down in the far corner. Opposite him there's a little boy in bottle-green school gym clothes with a yellow shamrock crest emblazoned on the top. He looks different from the little boy she saw playing

with Jeff at the cove. Older without the hat and welling-
tons, perhaps. More like seven than the five she had taken
him for. He's pointing out the window at something, laughing. She can feel the creep of it in her neck, the thudding
that will cause her face to blotch as it does when she's angry.
Why would he do that, bring the child along? What kind of
a meeting could this now be? Before she can work out what
to do he has swung around and is staring straight at her.
Staring at her standing motionless in the middle of the café.

'There you are,' he says, the timbre of his voice laced with
a jollity she hasn't heard before now. He gets up from his
seat to greet her.

'Come on over, we've got the best seats in the house,
haven't we, Ted?' He smiles down at the little boy who is
sitting on a huge plush purple velvet chair.

'Our seats,' the boy says and rubs the fabric with his hands.
He looks at Nina, his dark eyes focusing on her lower lip.

'Who are you?' he says.

Good question, she thinks, not quite sure how to answer.

'This is Nina, Ted. Nina, this is my son, Ted. Nina is a
very clever young woman. She's doing an important project
on Italian film and I'm helping her with it.'

'Why are you helping her here?'

'Well, Nina can't be a student until September, so I'm not
really allowed to help her at work.'

The tingly burn that she's expecting to assault her cheeks
does not happen. Something else though. Yes, watching Jeff
Hogan with his son overtly now, the ease of them together,

the obviousness of it, makes her feel something else. The internal electrical buzzing that she feels when she's close to him has kicked in, but it has been compromised now, dulled somehow. Milky instead of crystal. She knows he has a family. A wife and a son. She doesn't need to know it quite like this. The boy is looking up at her still, with a bemused half smile and she can see it now, in the curl of his mouth. That touch of his father.

'Can she speak?' the boy asks and Jeff lets out a boom of laughter, causing heads to turn in their direction.

'No, I just growl like a tiger, grrr,' Nina says and the little boy cowers away from her in mock fear. Maybe this won't be so bad now, after all, she thinks.

'I need to use the toilet, mind that nice place for me or else I might have to eat you,' she says, hissing and clawing the air and the little boy giggles. She can feel Jeff's eyes on her but she doesn't look his way. She's more than a little annoyed with him, showing up with his child, throwing her like this. She turns away from them in a bid to gather herself. She does not need him to know that she is irked. The toilets are back around the corner by the entrance and as she walks towards them she feels the tingling buzz diminish, as if a switch has been flicked. Closing the toilet lid and sitting down she runs it over in her mind. What she has in her bag for him. How she will not now, under the gaze of his child, be able to slip it to him. Why did he arrange to meet her on Valentine's Day, of all days, and then ruin it? Still, he did arrange to meet her, and he did show up, so maybe, she thinks now, she should be happy about that. In fact, bringing the child might be a sign of something. That he trusts her. That he's inviting her further in.

When she returns she chooses to sit beside the boy, and opposite Jeff. She pulls a leather chair over and sits down. She's higher up than she expected to be. When she looks at Jeff directly in the eye she sees a flicker of disappointment. Or is it confusion? Something anyway is causing his brow to furrow, his beautiful olive skin to crumple into deep tracks. She has to fight the urge to fix it with a smile or, better still, a light touch. How she would love to leap up, run her fingers across his forehead and smooth it back. As she thinks about this, this touching him, his skin, she feels the rush of fullness, pulsing, filling her, pushing against the seam knot in the crotch of her jeans. Then the warm wetness. She moves to the edge of her chair and presses herself onto it, rubbing slightly, imperceptibly.

'Let's begin,' she says.

'Let's,' Jeff says, a faint twinkle dancing in his eyes now as he clicks his briefcase open, and pulls out her latest offering, along with some blank paper and a chunky red crayon.

'This is for you to draw something,' he says to his child.

'But what will I draw?'

Jeff digs into his jacket pocket and pulls out a shell. A fan shell, the size of his hand. Nina gazes at it. She has never seen anything more perfect. The colours. Like a deep orange sun setting over Saharan desert sand. The shape. Heart like. Without the constructed indentation. A natural heart.

'Draw this.' He puts it down on the table in front of Ted.

'Wow, where did you get it?' Ted asks.

'Sandymount strand,' Jeff says, and Nina can see now, as Ted turns it in his hand, a touch of wet grey sand in the cup of it. Today. He's been down on the beach today.

'You went to the beach without me?'

'Yes. Remember I told you I had something to do and that I might be a little late to collect you? But I was lucky and found this quickly.'

'Can I bring it into school for show and tell?'

'Well, it's a gift. Maybe you can bring the picture you draw instead.'

Nina feels a clawing tightening at the back of her throat. If this beautiful gift was for her, he wouldn't have displayed it. It must be for his wife. She starts to cough to clear it but she spasms. It is as if she has a golf ball lodged there. She grabs the little boy's straw drink and swallows, gulping it down.

'Dad?' he calls out. She can hear he's on the verge of tears as she keeps her gaze away from him, focusing on a single sail boat whipping along in the bay. Just one more gulp and the cold strawberry smoothie eases the constriction. She can speak again, just.

'I'm sorry, I'll get you another one,' she says, her voice croaky, old.

'That's okay,' the boy says, and he places his small hand on her black jeans, patting gently, his touch releasing something in her. Some small loosening.

'I'm not feeling very well,' she says to Jeff, abruptly, breaking her own spell.

'Do you mind if we rearrange?'

'Of course,' he says, slowly.

'Same time here next Thursday?' She nods her assent and winks at the little boy who is staring at her, red crayon poised between immaculate little fingers, white-tipped nails.

'Here, let me show you a trick before I go,' she says and puts her hand out for the crayon. She rests her left hand on the shell for a moment, and then pulls it across the table towards her. She places the piece of paper over it, angles the crayon to the side and rubs. As the image of the shell appears perfectly before them, the little boy lets out a squeal of delight. She can feel the full force of Jeff's stare but she does not look at him.

'Should be good enough for show and tell,' she says. Then she gets up, turns her back on them and leaves.

Once outside she reaches into her bag, grabs hold of the envelope and slips it into the defunct golden letterbox.

TUESDAY

CASSANDRA

I'm lying on the bed which will slide me into the cylinder. Like a coffin. I don't know how cancer sufferers do it, this virtual-reality death chamber. I'm stiff with sheer terror. Judy tells me the name of the sedative before I swallow it and then she hands me a bell, just in case. The scan is of the heart and head, she tells me, as she attaches a clip to my finger to monitor my breathing.

'It gets pretty noisy in there, a lot of clunking, all perfectly normal. Just relax and it will be over before you know it.'

My mind is whirring.

'How long?'

'No more than half an hour,' she says.

'No, how long before the sedative kicks in?'

'Oh, you should feel the benefit of that any minute now.'

Good – because it's all starting to make horrible sense and I need a rest from it.

How I didn't twig it with the irregular sex down to nothing at all after the miscarriage. You didn't need it, did you?

It wasn't grief. You'd found a lovely little student instead. Half my age, half my height, with the small breasts that you like. Pierced even. The same side as yours. A bizarre echo of you. *More than a handful is just a waste* you told me you used to think, until you met me. But that is what you really think. I'm surplus to your requirements. She was a nymph, resurrected from your past life of too much booze and too many girls to choose from.

You had left all that behind after the arrest. You admitted it. You accepted a caution in place of a charge. A public humiliation came along with it when it was reported on. This was a turning point. No more. You wanted to progress. To make up for lost time. We met at a conference as you embraced your new phase. I was a keynote speaker. You were a delegate. I liked your vulnerability. You liked my drive, the control I had over my life, the way that I didn't seem to really need you. I didn't care about your past, not really. You were lost. I could forgive you your past. But this? The secrecy. Having our son in on it. And now. Now what have you done. And why? So that I wouldn't know? It's that little bit about you. That little bit that I didn't manage to reach. It's reared up and stripped us of everything. Just like my father.

I press the bell.

'It's not working,' I call out.

'Your breathing is a little rapid there. Try taking a few deep breaths. The sedative will take hold, I promise.'

I breathe in and out to the rhythm of the waves crashing

up to her and retreating, leaving their white residue there with her, as if she's backwash. Part of the landscape.

I can feel it begin to kick in. A tingling runs through my body, my hands, legs, feet. An ebbing of the grip of fear. A different lens filters it.

I can see how you would have fallen for her.

Lithe and vibrant.

The way she jumped up on you.

How you could just hold her there in your arms, effortlessly, even with your bad leg. Your leg which has been aging you.

There was a little reprieve, a glance at your youthful self.

It was, in truth, a beautiful sight.

Bare skin touching in the dazzle of the morning sun.

Is that why I didn't run down to the beach and confront you? Because there was this incredible beauty to it. As well as a sense that I always knew this day would come. That you would revert. Leave me. Leave us. That is what I was seeing. You leaving me. Until you put her down and asphyxiated her.

Even that seems different now.

Perhaps you didn't want to leave us, after all.

'What was that Cassandra? You pressed the bell but I couldn't make out what you were saying, something about someone leaving? Are you okay in there?'

Yes he left us, disappeared, and it was my fault because I saw it and I just had to open my big mouth and tell everyone when it was only a kiss, really, but I didn't know why, why he would choose my bed on the barge when from the canal bank it's easy to see straight in and why it's Josh that's sitting on my bed with him and why he is kissing Josh on the mouth and kissing him and kissing him until Josh's head is bent backwards and why Josh doesn't call out to me or wave when he sees me there looking in because he's my cousin and nothing at all to do with Dad but my mum's nephew and he's gorgeous and fun and bold as brass at sixteen, but he doesn't seem any of those things when he looks at me as if he doesn't know me at all.

'You'll hear the noise of the fan coming on now. It's just so you don't get too hot in there.'

I run. Off along the banks of the canal, past all the other parked barges and straight into the Anchor pub where everyone's enjoying Sunday lunch with real ale and I blurt it out, that Daddy and Josh are kissing and Mum gets up from her seat and walks over to me, takes me by the wrist and squeezes it very hard and smiles her beautiful best smile and says Cassandra, Daddy has not seen Josh for some time now, so they are happy to see one another and it's important in life to show affection and to embrace. Now run along and find Henry and tell him it's time for lunch. And everyone's laughing at me, such a silly girl, but Mum is still squeezing and her cheeks are rosy from the sun and the ale, even though she only ever has a glass and she releases her hand slowly, very slowly and there's a white mark where her thumb has been on the inside of my wrist which days later turns a yucky khaki green.

FEBRUARY

NINA

Nina turns down towards the train station with the words of 'The Fool' in *La Strada* thrumming in her. About how everything in the world has a purpose. Even a pebble.

She thinks about the stunning shell. Its purpose before today. Its everlasting purpose now.

If only she could have nabbed it and slipped it into her bag. The boy would've been distracted by the picture she had traced for him and may not have noticed immediately. However, she had already upset him enough, grabbing his drink and gulping it down. She couldn't risk upsetting him further. So she had left it there for Jeff to put back in his briefcase to hand over this evening to his wife as a symbol of love. She squeezes the little red foil chocolate heart that she was given with her Americano between her fingers until it begins to melt. She should've told the boy to do what she did, place his piece of paper over the shell, angle his crayon to the side and rub across it. So that it was his own thing for show and tell. Then she could've taken her tracing with her as something to hold on to. But she wasn't thinking all that clearly at the time. Her mind was flooded with the signals she had been picking up from Jeff for months. She wonders afresh now. Was the shell really meant for her, but he couldn't say so in front of the kid? Was he thinking of slipping it to her when the meeting was over, much the same as she was going to slip the card to him? But then she went and left abruptly and he didn't get the chance. That would make some sense.

'Sandymount, return,' she says at the ticket booth. On the platform the red digital numbers tell her the next train is in three minutes. Good. She calculates how long ago Jeff would've been down on the beach, hunting. She checks her iPhone for tide times. It's on its way in now, but she has enough time to get there and to scour.

She walks along the promenade, dodging the couples as they amble past, holding hands. All ages, shapes, sizes. Proudly displaying their love. What do all the fighting couples do on a day such as today, she wonders. She descends the rickety steps onto the strand. Hard, ridged sand. Lugworm casts dot the place, and lone men dig for bait, white industrial buckets by their sides.

Nina has something else to find. But first she must scour for traces of him. His distinctive marks in the sand.

He could've gone down onto the strand from any number of points so she starts at the first possible place and begins her hunt. The hard sand is in her favour. His marks won't disappear as easily as they would on softer stuff. There's no sign of him at the first point of entry and she stops for a moment to breathe the salt perfumed air into her lungs. The distinctive air that he would have been breathing in himself not two hours ago. A long-haired golden retriever bounds past her leaving his deep paw marks behind. This will be easier than she had imagined.

As she scours, she considers how Jeff Hogan has, today, cast himself in a new light. A light that Nina suspected was there all along. There have been glimpses of it in their meetings. Glimpses that he seems to think he needs to swiftly veil with a feigned indifference. But today there was no hiding it. Even though he could not give the shell directly to her, Jeff Hogan was letting Nina know that he is deeply romantic. He did not pull in at the shops to purchase some overpriced flowers that will wilt and die. Chocolates that will be devoured and gone. Perfume that will disappear on the wind. No. He put himself to considerable trouble, to get down to this very beach and to search for something real. Something with a purpose, a permanence. Today he displayed to her that his values are so very similar to her own. She has been right about him all along.

As she approaches the second set of steps, and sees what she sees, her heart thumps as if she has been running. The three marks, repeating themselves in their distinctive pattern. The lightly placed right footprint, the slight drag of sand up to the deeper slapped left footprint, the hole from his stick. She takes her iPhone out from her pocket and takes a picture of the pattern. Then she walks in his prints, all the way out to where they come to a halt. There in the sand is the groove from the precious shell. She sits down on the wet sand and places her hand in the groove, feeling his moment of exhilaration when he found it. Then she stands back up and begins to scour the area for the shell's other half.

TUESDAY

CASSANDRA

Someone is in here with me.

I can't open my eyes.

I feel the bell in my hand still, but my hand is limp.

I can't make myself press it.

The noise of the fan. The clunk of the machine. It's still all going on.

I can't hear what the person is doing, but it's not her, I'm pretty sure, because she sashays about with efficiency. Whoever is in here isn't moving much at all.

'You'll need to switch that off,' someone calls out.

There's no reply.

I try to move my head, she'll have to come over to me if I move, isn't that what she said? Just stay very still or else we'll have to start again, but my head isn't responding to my wishes.

I feel my grip slipping. I'm going under again.

The canal lock is full, we need to empty it, make it go down, he lets me help, water gushing, swirling, the squeal of the paddles winding, the boat lowering, snailing on through. Dad at the helm, the gates closing again behind us.

'No, she wasn't expecting anyone to be in here with her, but she was very anxious about the confined space. She'll need someone with her afterwards. Is she very claustrophobic?'

I run along the towpath looking for Henry; the boats are moving at half my pace. There's no sign of him, but he's coming along towards me, my father, calling Cassandra, Cassandra, his arms outstretched, and I turn around and run back towards the Anchor and he's shouting out, 'I'll let you steer, Cassandra, come along, it's your turn now,' and I look back at him, the sun glinting off his half-moon glasses, his forehead shining with sweat, and he is like a little boy, in trouble at school, with a please-don't-tell-my-parents look about his eyes – an image thrown only slightly by what's around his neck.

'Almost done, Cassandra, you're starting to move a little in there, try to stay as still as you can now.'

'I've already told,' I call out to him, and he stands there, frozen to the spot, dropping his arms back down to his sides, a soft breeze rustling the leaves on the trees close to him. He smiles at me, a half, sad sort of smile, nods his head once and turns to walk back towards the boat.

'Who have you told?' Someone is whispering to me.

'They didn't believe me,' I call out after him and he lifts his hand and waves it in the air without turning around again.

Someone is holding my hand. The hand with the bell.

The bell slips away from under my thumb.

'Who didn't believe you, Cass?'

Nobody believed me, not after Mum's performance, not right away. But then he was gone, vanished out of our lives, and they began to believe that what I wished I hadn't seen, what I wished I hadn't told, was true after all. A lingering kiss, not a familial embrace. He had smoothened down my bed, as a last little fatherly gesture, a sign of forgiveness, I always liked to think. But then he had hung his clerical collar on the swan-neck steering tiller, a sign of all the things I tried not to think about.

'Can you hear me, Cassandra? It's taking a little longer for you to come back from the sedative. You shouldn't be this sleepy any more. Are you sure you haven't taken any other medication today?'

'Tell her, Cass. You must tell her if you did.'

Later, as the full moon shines onto the still calm water, mirroring the boat perfectly, the collar on the swan neck seems even more tantalizing in reflection. I whip it off and throw it like a Frisbee down the canal. It lands, breaking the moonlight into ripples on the surface, floating for a moment before sinking below.

Silly girl.

'Who's a silly girl?'

Cassandra.

The beach girl.

'She's not making any sense, shouldn't she be awake by now?'

Shouldn't I be?

But this is really lovely.

My eyelids are too heavy to open to see who is holding my hand. Every part of me is leaden. I'm woozy and drowsy and light-headed too.

What was it she gave me? An opiate? Am I goofing off?

'That was only a medium sedative we gave her, we didn't want to go IV just for claustrophobia, but I'd expect her to be talking back to me by now. We'll have to do a blood test, see if there's anything else in her system.'

'Could you understand anything of what she was saying?'

The voice is light and airy, or is it the fan making it seem like that? Blowing it distortedly at me.

It's all a bit distorted in here. What the hell was I saying?

'I'm sure you'd understand it a lot better than me. Even with the sedative she certainly seems to have a lot on her mind at the moment.'

'Will she have any memory of this, being in the machine, her fears about it?'

Of course I bloody well will.

'It's hard to tell, really. I didn't expect her to sleep so much, and usually, if the patient sleeps through it, they remember very little.'

'Ah, good.'

A tight squeeze of my hand.

'Yes, she is very claustrophobic, so this will be best forgotten, poor thing.'

Ah, good. Poor thing.

Like my father used to say. It sounds a bit like him, muffled as it is to the whirr of the fan.

'Cassandra? Can you hear me, Cassandra? The scan is finished. You did very well. I'm turning the machine off now so you'll be able to hear us properly. It's time for you to open your eyes.'

Even now, as all around me descends into a quiet lull, there's a ringing in my ears.

It morphs from the sound of the fan, to the crashing of waves, to the groan she was making, to her caterwaul, a high-pitched call, but why? Why did she do that and who was she calling to?

Was it me?

Was she calling out for me to save her?

'Okay, Cassandra, it's time now. Open your eyes.'

I don't want to.

My head feels heavy now, as if I've been out on the tear. I want to keep my eyes closed and just lie here until it all goes away.

FEBRUARY

NINA

Nina arrives for her Friday-night shift in the family chip shop a little earlier than usual. The place could do with a little sprucing up. So much outdated plastic and steel. Faded posters with local classes and events, phone numbers ripped off a strip at the bottom. The circus that has already been and gone. Tatty. Grimy, even if hand-sanitizer dispensers dot the place. It needs something else. Customers need something beautiful to look at while they wait, instead of staring at the shiny plastic pictures of cheeseburgers and Coke on the price list or salivating over the uncooked battered sausages in the display unit. She likes the customers, in the main, especially her older regulars. Friday is still fish day for many of them and they drip in from teatime onwards, with an ease about them, keen to hear how Nina is getting on. She bats off questions about herself in favour of hearing about their week. It's a welcome break.

She twists her long, heavy hair up into a net and ties a red apron around her waist. The business is thriving and Friday is the busiest day of the week which suits Nina. There's nothing quite as bad as a slow Wednesday on the chip-shop floor. She sets about her work, tearing down the circus poster that has been annoying her since Christmastime and replacing it with one of her many posters of Fellini's *La Strada*, humming Nino Rota's soundtrack as she goes. The clown-like Gelsomina, elevated and clinging onto a thick, solid wooden pole, arms and legs wrapped around it, smiles out at Nina, encouraging her on. She rips off old sheets advertising Pilates and T'ai chi classes, leaving the yoga one up, as none of the phone numbers have been torn off the bottom yet. It's good to give a person a chance.

She removes the freshly laminated photographs from her backpack and sticks them up. Sand. Shells. Sea. Why didn't she think of doing this years ago? A fish-and-chip shop with a seaside feel. Perfectly simple. Perfectly natural. Maybe this is what her mother was thinking when she stuck up a reproduction of *The Birth of Venus* which had another effect altogether before it was ripped off the wall by one of the customers. A drunk. *I'll take this home for myself now, I didn't know it was a porn chippy you had here, Mr Ruzza*. Nina's eldest uncle called the police. *You shouldn't let her show all her bits like that*, the drunk had shouted, bloodshot eyes on Nina as he was escorted out of the shop.

Nina prepares to open up. She restocks the display unit with battered cod, sausages, and onion rings, and lines up buckets of potatoes, chopped into chunks, ready to toss into the oil. She's wiping the steel surface, again, when her uncle Stephano walks in.

'Little Nina.' He bends down to embrace her in a bear hug, lifting her slightly without meaning to. Her mother's youngest sibling, Stephano has always felt more like a big brother to Nina than an uncle.

'Hey. So your fiancée has released you for the night?'

He runs his forefinger under the rim of her net cap, releasing one long corkscrew curl which bounces off her nose. 'Just for tonight. Good of you to tear yourself away from those film studies.'

'The customers could do with the treat of someone nice serving them on a Friday night, I like to think.' She blows her hair off her nose and tucks it back in.

'Could they now?' he says laughing.

She slaps him on his bare arm.

'They could. Someone who can chat about something other than football and going to the gym.'

Stephano's skin is clear and tanned, his body trim and taut. He looks misplaced here. There's a hint of rose about his cheeks from the ride in.

'Looking good though, it has to be said.'

'Thanks. You look tiny. I hope you're managing to eat something other than pomegranate all day. Now promise me, no philosophizing tonight and no quizzing me. It's been a long week.'

'That's because you missed me last week. That fiancée of yours is upsetting our flow. My little titbits help to set you up for your week. They lessen the drudgery. She'd thank me if she knew.'

'So I'm a project you're working on. I don't think that's even legal. If I don't know that you're trying to improve me and you do it in a sneaky way, I'm pretty sure I can sue you.'

They both laugh then. They've always had an ease together, a closeness and a rapport which lately has benefitted from a weekly dose of mutual slagging. With eight years between them they are just like siblings. Siblings without the rivalry.

The oil makes an occasional chugging noise, asking for something to be tossed into it. But they wait. They do not cook in advance like in some of the bigger shops. Each customer is greeted and treated as if they're the only person they will see all evening.

'Right. Bets on,' Stephano says.

They play a betting game when they work a shift together. How many customers will come in tonight? How many will be drunk. And miscellaneous — some random thing that will happen. Nina likes betting on this the most. She gets out her notepad to write the bets down and rips out a page for Stephano.

'No cheating,' she says, jotting her guesses down. For miscellaneous she scribbles that someone will hit on Stephano. Male or female. She's seen it before, after all.

'What's the prize for the winner tonight?' she asks.

'We'll see,' he says, grinning, as the door pushes towards them and a regular, a woman in her late sixties, comes in.

'Ah, Mary, how are you today?' Nina asks as Stephano

lifts his face up from his list and nods, a signal asking Mary if it's her usual order.

'One and one,' Mary says, with a seriousness, as if it's something different she's saying tonight. Nina wonders about her when she sees her each week. A widow these past few years. What is that like for her? She carries her grief as a fresh thing, as if time doesn't diminish it at all. Ordering just for herself on a Friday seems to sting her a little, to scrape at the wound. Nina is quick to divert her.

'How was the bingo on Monday, Mary, any luck at all?'

'There's all these young ones coming in to play now, Nina. Not as young as yourself, mind, but like himself there.' She tips her head in Stephano's direction.

'Maybe he should try his hand with you, what do you say, Stephano?'

'I say Mary's luck would worsen drastically if I went along.'

'Ah, don't be saying that. I'd be a star anyway bringing a handsome lad like you in. It would be the same as winning.'

'Is that a date then, Mary? Stephano here is off on Monday nights, isn't that right?'

Nina lets out a gentle laugh as she chucks some chopped potatoes from the bucket into the boiling oil, and they hiss and spit for a moment before quietening, settling down to their fate.

'Nina here is off every night except Friday, Mary. She'd be a great bingo partner. She says she's studying film, but you know what? I think she's making it all up. Sure how can anyone study film? You just watch a film and either you like it or you don't and that's the end of it. Isn't that so, Mary?'

'She'd be no use to me, Stephano. It's you I'd get the credit for bringing along. All the lonely old ladies, think of them. Sure I'd be doing them a great service. Just the sight of you.'

'Well, that's miscellaneous in the bag for me right there,' Nina mutters to Stephano.

'It's going to be a good night I think, Mary,' she says, winking.

'Can you do me a favour, Mary? Can you tell Nina to stop using her big college words in here, it puts the customers off their food.'

'I think she's wonderful, putting herself through all that, when she could be like you taking the easy way. Go for it, Nina, love. Use all the big words you want. You could end up in the films yourself – and when you're famous, I'll be telling everyone how you used to serve me fish and chips every Friday, always with a beautiful smile on your face.'

'The date is off, Mary,' Stephano says, mock-serious. 'If you can't even do one little thing for me, sure there's no reciprocity. That's a Nina word, I got it from her, do you see what I mean now, Mary? Could make a person lose their appetite.'

The three of them laugh together and it is as Nina shakes the vinegar onto Mary's chips that the door pushes gently open and there, standing in front of her, are Jeff Hogan and his son.

TUESDAY

CASSANDRA

It's all gone quiet. There's a fresh, citrusy smell close by. She's put something in here with me. Trying to wake me. But I don't want to wake up. Not yet. My eyelids feel as if pebbles have been sewn into them. I need to let her know about my pounding head. My tongue feels as if someone has come in and coated it with sand while I was out cold. I fumble for the bell she gave me. It's not in my hand. She's taken it away from me. Why would she do that? I'll tell her when I manage to open my eyes. First though, just another little sleep.

'I've been on to her GP and she says she's not on any prescribed benzodiazepines.'

Someone is talking in here, nobody is answering. I try to lift my eyelids. I'm seeing two of her, my child doctor with a mobile phone to her ear.

'And she's not waking when we talk to her, as we would expect her to at this stage. Do you think she could have had some alcohol today?'

Alcohol, during the day. No. No I'd never do that. No.

'No, Cassandra? Can you hear me? I think she's trying to say something here, which is good. She tells me she saw you today, when she dropped her son in to you. Did she seem under the influence of anything at all then?'

My poor mother. I told them not to ring her.

'Yes. Yes he was in here with her. He just left.'

Who? Who was in here with me?

My CPR friend? I wouldn't even be here at all if it wasn't for him. Why is he still hanging around? He's helped out far too much already. Although right now I wouldn't mind seeing him. Any bit of token familiarity would be a comfort.

'Her brother? Okay, sure, will do. If you just give me his number. Thanks. Yes. I'll let you know.'

Silence. Then different-toned beeps as she presses her keypad many times.

'Hello, I'm looking to speak to Henry Taylor, please. Oh, hi. Yes this is Dr Sanchez, senior house officer, calling from St Vincent's University hospital in Dublin.'

Tell him. Tell Henry quickly there's nothing at all to worry about.

'We have your twin sister here with us. No, nothing like that. We're just a little concerned about how she has been since we sedated her for an MRI. Yes, for claustrophobia. A moderate sedation. No.'

I'm herded onto the packed Ryan Air flight to London. The panic kicks in quickly, severely. It's too soon to be doing this. I'm still bleeding. Purple-black clots of residue fall out onto the nappy pads meant for after a birth. As if I need reminding of my failure every time I go to the loo. It was Jeff's idea. 'It would be good for you to go and spend a weekend with Henry. Take your mind off things. We'll be fine. Don't worry about us at all.' Then he went ahead and booked the flights. Friday afternoon to Monday morning. He's right. I know he's right. I need to get away from both of them and their disappointed hurt faces which I can't fix. But now that I'm stuck here in this tin can with a load of strangers, I can't find my breath. I'm sweating. My heart is pounding. I'm either going to throw up or faint. My usual tactics don't apply. Get up. Change location. Get a glass of water. Tell myself that it isn't dangerous and it will pass. I can't get up. We're taking off. It feels bloody dangerous to me. Henry?

'To be used at her discretion? How long ago was that? What dose, can you remember? Is there anything more recently that could have caused her to feel the need to use them again? Yes. Yes, I'll certainly ask him when he comes back.'

He's standing in the arrivals hall at Gatwick with a great big grin across his peach dimpled cheeks. He wasn't supposed to come. I told him not to. But here he is. Flamboyant and spruced up, as if we're going to hit the town. I'm in maternity jeans and a hoodie. He's impervious. He'd go ahead and hit the town with me looking like this, proud as punch. He doesn't know about it, not yet, but I feel better already for seeing him. I'll tell him it all, hold nothing back, and he'll do what he always does. What Henry does best. He throws his arms around me and then pushes my shoulders back to get a good look at me. 'Cassie, you're so pale, what have you been doing to yourself over there? Here, let me take that.' He grabs my hand luggage in his right hand and puts his left hand on my shoulder. We stroll towards the car park in companionable silence.

'Yes, she may have taken a Xanax at some point in the day. Did she seem anxious or panicked about anything at all to you?'

Did I take a Xanax? It's been ages since I've needed one. Why today?

'Her brother, when she visited him following her miscarriage in January.'

'You are always so brave Cassie.' We've queued for a seat at the Barbary in Covent Garden and are now sitting at an open horseshoe-shaped bar. The theatre of the chefs in front of us flame-grilling octopus is reassuringly distracting. 'So in control. You always know just what to do.' My appetite has been very poor since. This is perfect. Just small bits and pieces. Tasters. 'And you'll know what to do now. How to get over it. But give yourself a break, yeah?' That's what I intend to do, why I'm here. 'Yes, sir,' I say. 'Now when am I going to get to meet your new beau?'

The squeak of a door. Someone coming in or leaving.

'Her breathing is good. Yes. When she opens her eyes she looks very confused. Frightened even. Then she dozes off again.'

I don't feel confused or frightened.

I open my eyes and scan the room. My vision is blurred at first. It begins to settle.

That's when I see it. The stick. Hanging off the back of a chair.

He's here.

And I remember now.

FEBRUARY

NINA

She can see that Jeff doesn't recognize her, and as she looks at him his edges seem to shimmer and then blur, as if she is dehydrated. She turns abruptly so that her back is to him and she grabs a bottle of water from the cooler.

'Can you serve the next customer?' she mutters to Stephano. 'I'm not feeling that great.'

'Sure.' He hands Mary her food and works the till.

'Good luck with all that studying, Nina,' Mary calls out, and Nina turns just a fraction, but enough to see it dawn. Jeff Hogan now knows that it is her. She has no choice but to turn and face him.

'See you next week, Mary.' She unscrews the cap from her water bottle and takes a slug, with a teenager-style detached indifference, finding it hard to swallow as she stands there looking straight at him. A trickle of water seeps from the side of her mouth.

'What can I get you?' Stephano asks as Jeff stares at Nina quizzically. A stare that at any other time would have the pit of her stomach feel as though it is filling with melted dark chocolate. A stare that now makes her feel decidedly bilious.

'It's Nina, Dad,' Ted shouts out, high pitched with excitement.

'So it is. Well, well.'

Nina is now fully aware that Stephano has turned his head to look at her too. She is like a caged panther, everyone having a good gawk at her, this rare and dangerous specimen.

'Hello, Professor Hogan. Hi, Ted,' she says and she bends down to pick up the chopped potatoes. She hurls the whole lot into the oil, from higher up than she should and a spit jumps out catching her right hand, which she rubs off quickly with her left. She knows that it will kick in, the pain, in time, as it has done before. For now though the effect of the hurl is as she had hoped, a little reprieve as the loud sizzling helps to charge the atmosphere with a pragmatism.

'What can we get for you?'

Before Jeff has a chance to answer Ted is pulling on his sleeve.

'Look at the pictures, Dad. That's like the one you gave to Mum.'

'Just a minute,' Jeff says to Ted.

'The many lives of Nina Ruzza, eh?' he says, and he looks at her so intently that he seems not to blink.

'Ah, she has to tear herself away from those books occasionally,' Stephano says.

Nina knows that he feels her discomfort and that he's trying to do something about it. But the creeping tingle that has begun to map her neck and is making its way up her face seems unstoppable as she looks at Ted staring at her fresh array of photographs on the wall. She pinches the red hot patch on her right hand, hard. It will blister, she knows. But until then it serves a purpose. Lifting her for a moment, up and out of this place.

'A bit of the real world won't do her any harm,' Stephano continues.

'Dad, look, it's the same one that you gave to Mum,' Ted says a little louder now.

They all turn to look at where Ted is pointing. The picture of a fan shell is displayed alongside the picture of Jeff's footprints in the sand.

Nina slips into the backroom and waits.

TUESDAY

CASSANDRA

A light shines in my eyes.

'Cassandra, it's time for you to wake up and tell us how you're feeling now.'

I try to lift my hand up to my head, but I'm too weak.

The citrusy smell is stronger in here now.

It's him. His cologne.

I have to let her know. I begin to shake my head.

'She seems to be getting agitated again. That can happen when someone has too much in their system. Her focus isn't good either. I'll get the registrar to come take a look at her.'

'How serious can this get?' His voice comes from behind me. Soft with worry. Worry about what?

'It depends on what she's taken. Her bloods will be here soon, and we'll get a clearer picture then. Her skin tone is fine and her breathing is regular, not laboured, all good signs. We'll keep a close eye on her. I'm going to get the reg now.'

'No, don't go,' I call out to her.

'She's trying to say something; it's all slurred though,' he says.

'No,' I call out again, and begin to writhe about on the bed, thrashing my arms as much as I can.

'This can happen, agitation and sometimes aggression. It's a good sign. I'll just be a minute.'

The sound of the door swinging. She's gone.

I hear his bad foot slapping on the floor, getting closer to me.

A chair scraping along. Being pulled towards my bed.

My fight-or-flight adrenalin is not going to kick in, is it?

'It's all right, Cass. You're going to be just fine. Don't be afraid. Relax. Be calm. Sleep it off. I'm here now. There's nothing for you to worry about.'

He places his fingers on my left temple and rubs in a circular motion, slowly, methodically. The warmth of his fingers pressing on my skin sends a shudder through me. I feel as if I'm going to doze off again.

'There's something I need to tell you, Cass.'

I begin to shake my head from side to side. I don't want to hear it. But then he puts both of his hands either side of my head, holding it tightly. He begins.

'I don't know if you'll remember this later, but you need to listen to me now. I should've told you about it from the beginning. I know I should have. But you would not have approved.'

My eyes are firmly shut. I do not want to hear him.

'I didn't think that you had seen anything, which is why I didn't tell you. I didn't want you to worry unnecessarily. But then you behaved so oddly today. Not answering my calls. Leaving Ted with Eve. Disappearing for hours.'

I breathe in and out heavily, as if I'm having difficulty with it, to try to make him stop talking. He releases his hands from my head. He is hovering over me. He does not stop talking. My head is spinning, as if I have vertigo, but I'm lying down. I have to fight the drowsiness now.

I don't want to hear his excuses.

A little doze would guarantee that.

But if I doze, I don't know where he might put those hands next.

'. . . So I'm sorry Cass for what you'll have to go through now.' His voice fades back in. He takes hold of my hand. His hand feels clammy and wet on mine. He squeezes. Hard.

'I should've given you more credit. You'd have understood. You'd have known what to do.'

There's a snuffling sound. A warm drop of water splashes onto my arm. He's crying.

'And I knew it was wrong, in many ways. But it could've worked out well for us. For all of us.'

He sniffles some more.

I lie here, in a haze, wondering how much of a fool he actually thinks I am. We tell one another everything, or so I thought. But was he thinking I'd hold his hand while he picked up from where he left off with his pretty little women?

'And now, well now it's too late for me to tell you, and for it to be all right. Because now she's gone.'

The swoosh of a swing door.

I make my eyelids flicker and I can see the back of his head. He has turned to see who is coming in. No one.

He turns back to face me.

I feel him leaning in closer. He begins to talk again, in a whisper. There's a whiff of garlic from his breath. He has just carried on. Eating whatever he likes. Without remorse.

'But you already know that. She shouldn't have been there, Cass. Turning up at the beach like that as if it's all perfectly normal. As if I'd be expecting her. As if it's an everyday thing. She's done some strange things over the months. But this. This was just a bridge too far.'

Two voices getting closer. Thankfully.

'I'm Dr Boyle, registrar. My SHO here tells me your wife is having some difficulty coming out of the sedation for the MRI. Do you know if she was feeling panicky about anything earlier today that might have prompted her to take a sedative?'

'She dropped me off at work this morning and then went about her usual day, as far as I know. She's a psychotherapist and works from home – appointments with troubled teens and the like. She has natural ways to cope if she's feeling panicky. She does not take drugs for it.'

'Okay. Cassandra? Can you hear me?'

I try to nod my head. He pulls back my eyelids and shines a torch in.

'Good. Cassandra, it's taking a little longer for you to come out of the sedation than we expected. You might feel a bit confused and agitated. Try not to worry. Your husband is here with you.'

'How long will this take?' Jeff asks.

'Difficult to tell as we don't know why she is reacting this way. Is there somewhere else you need to be?'

'No. Not yet.'

'Good. We'll be in and out. Let us know if she wakes up. Or if there's any change at all.'

The voices fade out. Jeff begins to whisper again.

'It was frightening at first. I didn't know what to do, whether to put her off, let her go or let her in. I stalled for a while to work it out and could have lost her then. But she came back. Once I was able to embrace it, it was no longer frightening, but it was bewildering. A whirlpool of bewilderment. Her brightness and her beauty, spinning in front of me. Her grasp of my work and what I needed to do next, how to become unstuck. Her flightiness. Like a little robin sitting contentedly on a branch one minute, gone the next – and you just never knew what it was, what you said or did, that would cause her to go.'

'Stop,' I shout out and begin to writhe and to squirm on the bed to show my discomfort. I do not want to hear any more.

'Shush, Cass,' he whispers and he puts his arm across my chest to still me. 'This will pass, just stay calm.'

Tell them, why don't you tell them I'm waking up?

'Then she would flit back when you were least expecting it, often with something new, something that was enthralling her, and she'd share it. It was infectious, Cass. Elevating. Her enthusiasm, her zeal, her youth.'

'Any change?' a voice calls in.

He removes his arm from my chest. 'Not much. She's just thrashing about a bit. I'll keep talking to her. I hope it will help.'

'Yes, it should. Keep reassuring her that everything is okay. She'll be very confused for a while. Your voice is important here.'

I try to lift my hand up to wave to her, but it is too weak, and it flops back down with a thud.

'I'd been feeling stale for a long time. Stale and stale-mated. You knew that. The slew of rejections for *Joycean Influences*. I wanted that to be the book I'm most known for. The petty politics under Margaretta's gaze. Being stuck at assistant level for years. But it changed when she burst in. I changed. Something shifted in me. It seems ludicrous now, thinking back, that I stalled at all. It was perfectly simple. There, in front of me. I just needed to let her take the lead.'

He's holding my left hand now. Thumbing my ring finger, pressing deep into the groove.

'You must have noticed small things, Cass. I often wondered if you did. At first, how we were having more sex. Because that's what she did to me. She woke me back up. Made me want to experience every little bit of life to the full. We benefitted. You and me. Can you remember that?'

He stops.

Yes, I remember. Of course I do. That surge. *Supercharged*, I used to say to him.

There had been a frustrating dwindling in the months before. Talk of going to the GP for a blood test, even if just to be told it's a natural part of ageing. And then, out of the blue. Kicking off along with the new academic year. Early morning especially. A marathon of multi-orgasmic sex. The pregnancy.

'That was her gift to us.'

Gift?

'But then the loss. That grief was ours to share, but you seemed to want it all for yourself.'

He lets out a deep sigh. 'What are we going to do now, Cass? You, me and little Ted. It's all gone horribly wrong.'

I lift up my hand and swat the air.

FEBRUARY

NINA

Nina listens to the voices from the backroom and waits for them to die down. When she is sure that they have gone, left the chip shop, she re-emerges.

'That was a strange one,' Stephano says.

'What was?'

'Where to begin? Your professor guy saunters in here with his kid, pretends not to know you at first, but the kid knows you and then he acts like a prick.'

'How do you mean?'

'*Well, well. The many lives of Nina Ruzza,*' Stephano says, mimicking Jeff so well that Nina is impressed.

'That was a put down if ever I heard one. Cheeky bollox.'

'Why are you getting so cross? He didn't know I work in here, that's all.'

'Why the hell should he know? It's none of his business.'

'I think he was just taken by surprise.'

'Yeah? I think he knew,' Stephano says.

'Knew what?'

'Knew that you work in here on a Friday night. I think he came in on purpose.'

'Yeah, right,' Nina says, slapping Stephano hard on the chest, diverting his attention away from her smile. Could he have known? A frisson of delight pulses through her. A rush. As if she is at a water park, cascading down the winding slide and into the deep pool below. Could he have come in here especially to see her?

'What makes you think that?'

'It was plain for everyone to see, except you. So it seems. Sure ask Mary next week. I'll bet she noticed before she left. The way he was looking at you. He had it planned all right.'

'Did he say anything while I was gone?'

'Yes he did. He ordered the bloody chips and then discussed the pictures you put up with the kid.'

Nina had forgotten about that, how they were all staring at the photographs in silence as she slipped away. The throb of the burn announces itself now, as if it is linked to her embarrassment.

'Which I've been meaning to ask you about myself. Not sure the drab grey pock-marked sand is a thing of beauty Nina. I thought you had a good eye. You could do a bit better than that,' he says, leaning back on the counter behind him, surveying her.

'What did he say about them? Jeff, I mean, what did he say to the kid about them?'

'Oh, Jeff is it now? I don't know, something about scallop shells looking like fans and their bright, interesting colours.

The kid kept saying it was the same as some other one. He seemed pretty excited about that.'

'Who was excited?'

'The bloody kid, who else? Jesus, Nina, so many questions. Why did you disappear anyway?'

'I wasn't feeling great. Did he say anything about the sand one?'

'Okay. So this is the last question I'm answering. No, he didn't – but I did. The kid was pestering him saying, *What's this one, Dad*? So I said I wasn't sure what it was or why it was put on the wall, that it looked like a bit of a mistake – the kid laughed then – but that my niece probably had a reason for doing it.'

Nina stares at the picture, at the many ridges of sand, the lugworm casts spiralling here and there, and then at the magic of the centre.

This is no mistake.

'Now, my turn. Why are you asking so many questions? Is he going to test you when you next meet or something?'

'Very funny. Yes, at doctoral level it's all about the little personal tests.'

'I thought you were wasting your time in there but now I know for sure.'

'Cheers.'

'No problem. He asked me to tell you something, now what was it again?' Stephano says, strumming his fingers on the metal counter, taking his time.

'Oh yeah, he said to tell you they'll see you next week.'

'They?' It comes out louder than she would've liked. Tinged with disappointment. Tipping a smile across Stephano's face.

'That's what he said — *we'll see her next week.*'

She feels the blow fizzle in her, like a spray of water on a dying fire. Jeff is planning to bring Ted along again. She likes the kid well enough. He's sweet and funny, a great kid insofar as kids go. If she were his babysitter she could imagine having plenty of fun with him. Watching movies, crunching on warm popcorn, sipping Coke floats. Letting him play with her hair. He's an only, like she is. She knows this space, how to make it that little bit better. But for now, he just distracts her from everything. From the work. From Jeff. He's like a little buffer. Which she does not need on the rare occasions she actually gets to spend time with Jeff. She can tell that Jeff enjoys the rapport she has with Ted. He shoots her little bemused looks. Which is gratifying in a way. But not what she wants each time they meet.

'What's the suss with that dude anyway?' Stephano asks.

'What do you mean *the suss*?'

'Okay for starters, is that his grandkid? He seems pretty old to be the dad. He has a walking stick, for feck's sake. And what's he doing sneaking up on students while they work? As if he's ever eaten a chip in his life. It's completely unnatural that they would come in here. He wouldn't take salt or vinegar on the chips, even. You see? Completely unnatural. A ruse, dear Nina. He probably chucked them in the bin after he left.'

'Don't be an ass. He's actually pretty down to earth and funny at times.'

'Oh is he now?'

The door squeaks. It's being pushed open slowly. It's taking quite some effort. Then standing in front of her is little Ted again.

'Can I please have some ketchup, Nina? Dad and I are going to eat the chips down by the sea and he forgot to ask for ketchup.'

'Sure thing, little guy,' Nina says and hands him a styrofoam pot with ketchup in it. His dark brown eyes sparkle and then widen as he looks up at her.

'Can you come too?' he asks. Nina takes a long, deep breath.

'Afraid not, lots of very hungry people will come looking for food tonight. They'd be very cross with me if I disappeared leaving Stephano to do all the work. He's very slow at it, as you can see. He needs all the help he can get, isn't that right?' she says to Stephano, and she winks at Ted, his eyes large and ponderous now, almost sad, she thinks.

'Okay, see you next week. Thank you,' he says, and he pulls the door towards him, leaving the shop. She can see Jeff now, waiting for him at the corner, and then, as he takes him by the hand to cross the road safely together, Nina feels a light tug in her stomach, as if she's in a car that has just gone speedily over a little bump in the road. She unstrings her apron.

'I'm popping out for five,' she says to Stephano, and before he gets a chance to say anything she's gone.

There's no heartbeat. I'm sorry. You'll have to come in and have your labour induced. You're too far along for anything else. I'm sorry.

Are you sure? Can you check again?

Yes — look here on the screen, just here. If the heart was beating you'd see it but there's nothing.

See? How about hear? Can you turn up the volume, please?

Baby is measuring correct for dates. This has only just happened.

Is there anything you can do?

I'm sorry.

What could have happened?

It's unusual this late. It might be a virus.

But I haven't been sick.

Sometimes you, the mother, won't have any symptoms, but it can be deadly for the baby.

Like what?

Parvovirus.

Never heard of it.

There are many things. We'll do some tests. We should be able to get to the bottom of it. Come in on Saturday morning, to admissions, I'll be here.

What do I say?

Just tell them you're coming in to see me.

What do I bring?

The same sort of stuff you'd have in your labour bag, for yourself.

What do I do between now and then? What do I say to people, because we've told everyone, seeing as we were out of the danger zone? How do I untell? What about Ted? He knows. God, he's so excited.

'How's she doing?'

'She's muttering a lot, stuff I can't make out, I think she's asleep and dreaming.'

'Does she seem to be asking for anything? She will most likely be thirsty and she could have a headache. Let me know if you think she needs anything.'

'Thanks. I'll have to make tracks myself soon.'

'Yes, you go whenever you need to. We'll be shifting her from here anyway. She'll be admitted for sure now.'

Admissions. Proud fathers walk past me swinging empty car seats, ready to carry their alive babies home in. I'm wearing my favourite maternity top, white with little black leaves laced around it. I didn't know what to wear. But the bump is still here, and I can't fit into my other clothes. Strangers look at me and smile. You too. We're all in the same club. For now it all looks the same. I carry my labour bag, this curious thing packed as if full of potential. At first, when I see him, I ask for another scan. To be sure to be sure. Maybe the scanner in his room was dodgy that day. He does it. The black and white stillness on the screen is numbing. I stare but I understand now. That our baby is dead at seventeen weeks. So I say to him that I think I see a little flutter of something, a joke to lighten it somehow, to let him know that it's okay now, that I understand, but he says he's sorry again and that he'll get to the bottom of it. You're not with me for any of this. You're with Ted. You'll come in later when the induction takes hold and we can birth our dead baby together. I think about how I don't want you to come in.

'We're going to admit you, Cassandra.' My eyelids are pulled back again and something is shoved into my ear which beeps immediately. Now someone is pressing into my wrist. Fingertips. Blunt nails digging in.

'Okay so her body temperature is a little high. We're still not quite sure what happened here. She was given a mild sedative just for her trepidation about the scan, as you know, and she's reacted in a way that is unusual, to say the least, but it can happen. Has she had any pain recently that she could have been taking something for?'

They ask if I need anything to manage the pain. The pain that I am not expecting, seeing as the baby would be so tiny. But the contractions are painful and even though they are not as painful as they were with Ted I opt for the relief. With Ted I said no to it all. We wanted it as natural as possible. But with Ted we were getting a baby at the end of it. The exhilaration of that carried me through. The prize waiting for me. Now I say yes please to the pain medicine and they inject pethidine into my thigh muscle. There's something comforting in the brutality of being stabbed with painkiller.

'She's only really complained of pain associated with constipation recently.'

'Okay. Some painkillers can cause that too. Has she been in hospital for any procedures in recent months?'

She flies out of me in a push as if I'm about to get the runs. Which is what I think is happening as I rush to the commode that they wheeled in. I wonder if I'm going to be able to look. I am, of course. She's there on the bottom in a gelatinous mass. Oh god, I say looking down at her. She's curled up in that blissful foetal position. Like a 4D picture in one of the pregnancy books. Oh god. Oh god oh god oh god oh god. There's a sense that this is happening to someone else. That I'm looking at a road-traffic accident as I drive on past saying, oh god help them. This isn't happening to us. The pethidine is doing a great job.

'No, well except for a miscarriage a little while ago. It wasn't a procedure as such, she gave birth to her without intervention.'

'Was she prescribed painkillers after that?'

'I don't know, it's all a bit of a blur. She was injected with something for pain during the labour which seemed to help.'

A blur. For you, maybe. Not for me. Crystal clear. She's handed to me in a little basket along with two instamatic photos of her. Perfect, my obstetrician says. She looks perfect. These words sting violently, as if I've been slapped all over with a wet towel. Perfect but dead, I say.

'She could have been prescribed codeine after the miscarriage for pain. But that was a while ago. Her bloods will be back soon. At a guess though, from what we've seen today – her dangerous reaction to the sedative, as well as the irregular heartbeat and you mentioning her constipation – I think your wife might be using an opiate-based painkiller.'

'Why would she do that? She doesn't have any pain. I'm the one living with chronic pain.'

There are different types of pain, Jeff, but I wouldn't expect you to understand that. You feel things differently. You can detach yourself at will. When they asked us for her name for burial in the angel's plot you didn't fall to pieces. You named her simply, pragmatically. Jo. Baby Jo. I couldn't do it. How do you pick a name for a dead baby? Is it a different name than the one we'd pick if she was alive? We always said we'd wait and see. Look at our babies first before naming them. So how did you pick Jo? Does she look like a Jo? What the hell does a Jo look like?

'Are you taking anything for your chronic pain?'

'No. I'm supposed to be, well, could be, you know, but I think it's best not to. I like to keep my head clear for work and things. The pain is just something I've learned to live with.'

'I'm going to check if the bloods are back. I shouldn't be long. Just keep talking to her.'

The swing door swooshes. I feel him getting closer.

He's making a tutting noise.

'Oh dear, Cass. Have you been going to the pharmacy and getting my prescriptions filled and then taking the drugs yourself?' He squeezes the palm of my hand so tight that I feel the bones rub off one another.

FEBRUARY

NINA

Nina grabs her biker's jacket and leaves the shop. She takes her beanie hat out of the pocket and pulls it on over her netted hair. She catches a glimpse of herself in a jewellery shop window, the image of a teenage boy reflects back at her. Perfect.

Trailing them, she leaves a gap of nine or ten metres. Just in case. Jeff is carrying the chips in his left hand and his stick in his right. Nina can see dark blobs leaking through the brown paper. Did Stephano forget to drain them? Jeff tells Ted to press the cross-now button and they wait. When the green man flashes and beeps at them they cross over the road and into the courtyard of the town's church. Nina hangs back until the red man appears and then crosses too. Ted has diverged off from Jeff. He's running in circles in the courtyard, laughing, while dozens of pigeons flee from him. They take off and fly a little bit and then land again in presumed safety, until Ted catches up with them, sending them scarpering into the air. The cause and effect never quite losing its appeal for him. Nina feels the pull. How she'd like to join him. Abandon herself for a few moments, run in circles, listen to the flap of the wings and the frightened little squawks. Like machine gunfire. If Jeff wasn't there, that is. If Jeff wasn't there, that's exactly what she would do.

'Let's go, Ted,' Jeff calls out. Nina has not heard him shout before now. In the lecture theatre he keeps his voice on an even keel, projecting lightly, as if there's nothing particularly exciting about what he's saying. Now little sprigs of pleasure are released in her. Hearing his voice like this, the wonderful timbre of it, raised, has a chemical effect on Nina. It is as if she has just been for a long run.

'The chips are getting cold.' He holds up his stick with the chip bag now dangling from the handle where he grasps it. Ted skips over to his dad and takes his free hand. They walk on together, down Marine Road towards the harbour. Nina waits for a moment, watching. What might it be like to slip her own hand into Jeff's? Just loosely. Just for a moment. The pigeons huddle together again, pecking at crusts that have been tossed their way.

'You're wasting your time on that one, love.'

Nina turns her head to the left where a middle-aged woman sits on the wall, pulling hard on an almost finished cigarette. She's looking directly at Nina. An alcoholic or drug addict. Nina turns her head again to watch Jeff and Ted saunter down the road.

'I'm telling you love, I can see it.' The woman's face is deeply lined and tanned, weathered beyond her years. A bright red scarf with a silver thread sits loosely on her shoulders.

'Are you talking to me?' Nina digs her hands deep into her jacket pockets.

'Yes, love.'

Probably from the methadone clinic up the road, Nina thinks. She usually sees them hanging around in groups though. 'I'm in a bit of a rush, sorry,' she says and begins to walk away.

'Don't go after him, love, it's not the way,' the woman calls out.

Nina stops. She likes how this woman is shouting her random thoughts, even if it's just because she's an addict. The woman stands up and stamps on her cigarette butt. Then she walks off towards the town centre, with a confident stride, no longer looking quite so much like a drunk or a druggie.

Nina glances down Marine Road. It is thronged with Friday-evening people ready to celebrate the end of the working week. She can no longer see Jeff and Ted. She breaks into a sprint, frightening a few of the pigeons into flight, and on down the road she goes until she glimpses them again. They are going in the direction of the pier. Nina runs across Queen's Road and down some steps into the car park below, sprinting another few feet and then walking through it at the same pace as Jeff and Ted on the footpath above her. She likes this feeling of Jeff being above her, matching her walk, as if they are all here together. She passes the Royal St George Yacht Club and loses sight of them as they walk past the monument, but she has the pace now and sticks with it. Coming to the end of a second car park, she passes the slipway for the boats where the lifeboat is stationed. Jeff and Ted are visible above her now, just as she knew they would be. She pulls her hat and netting off and loosens the clip so that her hair falls down on one side, bouncing off her right shoulder. Then she walks up the slope onto the pier, slowly, naturally, even as her heart thumps violently in her chest. They round the corner onto the pier and she converges beautifully with them.

'Nina?' The lilt of Jeff's voice as he says her name sends little spasms of heat right through her.

'Hi,' Nina says. She has every right to be here she tells herself, to try to save her face from reddening.

'Can you join us?' Jeff asks.

'I'm on a quick break before it gets really hectic at work, so maybe just for a bit.'

'I was surprised to see you there in the chip shop. You never told me you worked.'

There's a hint of something in what Jeff says that Nina likes. She can't quite put her finger on it. Quizzical with a frosty glaze. Annoyed almost. He's put out that she didn't mention it.

'No, well it's good to have a few secrets,' she says, and she smiles at Ted.

'So it would seem. How long have you been doing it?'

'Oh, you know, forever, really. It's the family business.' Nina feels, for the first time, that she somehow has the upper hand. She's rattled some sort of nerve in him. Released a bat. If she had tried to do this, she would have failed. They walk on down the pier for a bit, without talking, watching as Ted straddles either side of the heavy black iron chain, designed to stop people from falling over the edge. They reach the bandstand.

'Let's sit, shall we?' Jeff says, motioning to a nearby bench.

'Yes, I'm starving,' Ted says.

They walk over to the light blue bench, turn to sit and without any orchestration on her part, Nina finds herself beside Jeff, with Ted on her other side. This is the closest Nina has ever been to Jeff. It is electrifying. She has never known a feeling like it. Every inch of her skin is tingling with alertness. If she pulled up her sleeve now, even the soft, downy hair on her arm would be standing erect.

'So tell me about your family,' Jeff says and his eyes seem to singe hers. She does not think that she can speak.

'Can we eat the chips now?' Ted says and Nina breathes out heavily, relieved by the distraction.

'I'd forgotten all about the chips,' Jeff says, smiling as he hands the bag across Nina to Ted. For a brief moment, Jeff's outstretched arm glances off Nina, the sleeve of his maroon jacket brushes her chest, and it is suspended there, taunting her until Ted reaches up and grabs the bag, breaking the spell. Jeff withdraws his arm and puts it across his lap. He rubs the tip of his thumb across the tips of his four fingers, in a circular motion, over and over, as if he has something pliable that he is trying to make into a ball. The hypnotic pleasure that Nina feels as she follows his beautiful, long fingers in motion is intoxicating. She crosses her legs. Jeff looks out across the moored boats towards something in the distance. As the wind tickles the sailboat masts and a concert of chiming and tinkling rings around them, Nina thinks that this must be the most perfect moment. She would like it to go on and on.

Ted holds up a ketchup-laden chip and offers it to Nina, wrenching her out of it.

'No thanks. I have rules,' she says.

'Rules like in school?' Ted asks.

'I guess. Except they are all to do with food. I'm never allowed to eat from my own shop. And I'm never, ever allowed to put ketchup on otherwise perfectly delicious chips.'

'Why not?'

'So many questions little man,' Jeff says and he reaches out to grab the chip from Ted. Nina watches as Jeff tilts his head back slightly and sucks the chip into his mouth.

'But rules are made to be broken,' she says and she delves her hand into the bag, pulls out a chip, dips it into the tub of ketchup and pops it into her mouth. Ted's light laughter rings about them as Jeff shifts on the bench, angling his legs slightly more towards her. Nina is euphoric. Her perfect moment just got better. She holds the chip in her mouth, salivating on the salty sweetness that Jeff has just experienced too.

TUESDAY

CASSANDRA

I open my eyes to the sting of a fluorescent light blinking at me. I turn my head, left and right, again and again. Where the hell am I? There's a probe on my finger and a monitor flashing my pulse back at me. I'm going to throw up. I hear the sound of someone's rasping breathing nearby.

'Hello?' I call out. Nothing. A television mumbling on low. The pains. In my calf muscles, as if I've just run a marathon. In my stomach, twisting, stabbing. On the top of my head, pressing, like a slab of concrete. I'm sweating.

'Hello?' I call out, louder this time and I pull the sheet up over my face to shield me. Something is very wrong. Meningitis. I peer at my arms for signs of blotches the way I do for Ted when he's poorly. They are clear. There's a tag on my wrist. *Cassandra Hogan 2/3/'79.* That's it.

'Help,' I call out and then I hear a beeping noise. I pull back my sheet to see what the monitor is doing. Is this it? Am I going to die now? A woman's voice. Croaky. Hoarse.

'The person in that bed is very agitated.'

The beeping stops and the curtain whips open to the sight

of a small, round-faced nurse. Black gleaming shoulder-length hair. Filipino.

'You're awake now. Good, good. How are you feeling?'

'Why am I here? What's wrong with me?' Hot, fast tears sting my cheeks as I ready myself for bad news. I've always known this day would come. Alone in a hospital with the end in sight.

'You had a bad reaction to the medicine for your scan. Do you remember the scan? You had a fall?'

'Yes, the fall, but I was fine. Now though. Now I feel like I'm going to die. Is there a bleed?'

'A bleed?'

'Yes, a bleed on the brain, because the pressure in my head, I've never felt anything like it and I'm nauseous. Am I concussed?'

'No, no, nothing like that. The scan was clear for your head. Good news. Very good news. The doctor looking after you will come soon to talk about what has been happening. Your husband had to go, he'll be sad he missed you waking up. He was waiting a long time,' she says and she smiles at me.

Jeff's been here.

'When did he leave?'

'An hour ago, maybe a little more.'

'Did he say anything to you?'

She nods.

'He asked me to tell you it will all be fine. He'll be back in when he can with a bag for you. Such a nice man,' she says with a twinkle in her eyes. Jeff working his charm on a young woman again. Even now.

'You're lucky, he takes good care of you. He worries about you.' She smiles at me. A wistful smile. What the hell has he said to her?

'Can you give me something for the pain?' I can't think straight. Not with the twisting in my gut and the pressure in my head, as if someone has placed a paving stone directly on my crown and decided to stand on it for good measure.

'No, not until the doctor sees you. It's okay to sip at the water there beside you, it will help. I'll get a bowl for you now.' She flits off, leaving the curtain open.

Directly across from me a woman, mid-thirties, is shouting into her phone with slightly slurred words. She hangs up and looks straight at me. 'Here, you can have this if you like.' She holds up a paper cup. 'It's my tea, I don't even like tea, I put two sugars in it, so you can have it if you want. Go on. You look like you could do with it.'

I shake my head, which is a bad idea. If I just close my eyes maybe this will all go away.

She puts the tea on her table, picks up a remote control instead, and points it at the television. The mumbling now becomes distinct words.

The Gardaí are appealing for anyone who might have seen anything to contact them at Blackrock station . . .

'Ah, god, the poor thing, raped and killed. She must've fought. That's when they get killed. I'd just lie there letting on I liked it. That'd scare him off and I'd come out of it alive, for the kids you know?'

Jesus.

'Did they say she was sexually assaulted?'

'Nah, but *partially clothed*, so that's rape for sure. Killiney beach, right near where I live. Hard to believe something like that could happen there. The kids love it, they do. It won't be the same now. Knowing someone's been raped and killed there.'

She wasn't raped I want to shout out.

'It won't be long before they get him. All those trains going past high above the beach. A bird's eye view of the whole bay. Someone will have seen something. He must've raped and killed her somewhere hidden, up in the grass near the tunnel, I'd say, and then dragged her down to the water. To make it look like a drowning. The bastard.'

She takes a swig of her tea and turns her gaze away from the television to face me. I thought she said she didn't like tea.

'So what has you here in the respiratory ward? Asthma like me?'

If only.

'I shouldn't be here at all,' I tell her and she laughs, wheezing like a walrus.

'I'm always in here, it's like a second home only without everyone at me, demanding things morning, noon and night. People giving me dinner instead of the other way around. It's a great little break, to be honest, when I'm not too sick with it.'

Can you please, please just stop talking I want to say.

'I'm not feeling great, do you mind just pulling my curtain across, I'll try to sleep it off.'

'Sure, hun, and you just call out if you need anything, I'll get the nurse for you.' She jumps off her bed and pulls my curtain. A snake tattoo curls from her left ear lobe down her neck.

I sit up and pour water from a jug into the plastic cup left out for me. I take a sip. Tepid. Metallic. I gulp the rest down, hoping it will help to clear my head. I need to remember it all but at the moment I'm in a haze. My mouth is dry, sandpaper dry, despite the water. It's as if I'm having a fight with someone and I have no saliva to help me spit out the words.

I glance around my curtained-off section. Sparse. A faux leather dusky blue chair, with an indentation where Jeff must've been sitting. An empty bedside locker. I have nothing. I need something to jot it all down on. This morning. Before. After. The scan. The fear of being trapped, and then something else. Some worse fear.

'Hi there,' I call out. I hear her feet hit the floor and then she slides across in her slippers, pulling the curtain and smiling.

'Need the nurse?'

'No, thanks. I just wonder if you have something I could borrow to write with?'

'You want to write when you're sick as a dog. What are you, a journo?' she asks, laughing.

'No, a counsellor for kids, and before I was brought in

here I had some notes from a session I was supposed to write up. If I don't do it today, I'll forget, you know, what happened, what I've asked her to do for next time.'

'I had a counsellor once. Very good he was. I don't think he was too fussed about writing anything down though. Here, I have this drawing pad and colouring pencils for the kids when they come in. You can have them for your notes. The kids never bother with them anyway.'

She pulls a plastic shopping bag out of her locker and hands it to me. 'Work away,' she says and pulls the curtain again.

I tip the contents of the bag onto my bed. Unopened, unused pencils and a blank sketch pad. I shift myself into a more upright position, and as I do so, I feel the stickiness beneath me. I'm glued with sweat to the sheet. I must begin, however rotten I'm feeling. I must begin to write what I know. I choose the colours with care. Red for before. All the little warning signs that I failed to see. Black for after. A mourning colour. All the loss that will now come our way. I begin to scribble.

There's a click of shoes approaching my bed.

I stash the pad and colours under the covers. A swift, deft flick of the curtain reveals a tall, slim, golden-haired man holding out his hand to me.

'Hello, Cassandra, I'm Dr Carroll. You gave us a bit of a fright earlier.' He pushes his glasses up his nose and stares at his clipboard. 'How are you feeling now?'

'Worst headache I've ever had, nauseous, sweating, dry

mouth. Not great, all in all. But I don't understand why. The nurse assures me there's no bleed after the fall, the scan is clear, so what's going on with me?'

'You'll need to help us with that, Cassandra. Your bloods came back with surprising levels of an opiate derivative. You ticked the "Not on any other medication" box on the form before your scan, before being considered for sedation. We've checked this with your GP and she confirmed that you are not. That you were for a week after a late miscarriage, but not since then.'

'It's just codeine occasionally. Well, most days, I suppose. Every day, really.'

'Why didn't you mention this?'

'It's not a tranquillizer. I didn't think there was any point.'

'The combination of the codeine in your system and the sedative for the scan was dangerous. You were in respiratory depression and you were very confused and agitated. It took much longer for you to wake up completely. You were drifting in and out of consciousness. Something like this could leave you with brain impairment. We'll monitor you over the next twenty-four hours.'

'What for? I'm fine now, apart from the pains and sweats.'

'You're going through withdrawal, Cassandra. You'll have missed your usual doses and your body is looking for it. You've become dependent on the opiate. It happens easily enough.'

Withdrawal. I help teenagers with this. Shit.

'The thing is, your heart arrhythmia, the dizziness, the

fall – it's possible they were caused by the ongoing use of codeine. It can also cause confusion. Have you noticed being confused about anything recently?'

Very, but nothing I'm about to tell you.

'Not at all. In fact I feel sharper on it. After the miscarriage it worked well for pain, like the worst period pain ever. But when I stopped taking it the mental pain and grief over the loss seemed much more acute. I couldn't get on with things, get through the day, see my clients. So I thought I'd take it for another little while. It's prescribed for my husband but he doesn't bother with it. It works though.'

He checks the monitor.

'Your breathing and heart rate are getting back to normal. I'll get the nurse to give you paracetamol for the pains and make sure you drink plenty of water for the sweating. You're at the worst of it now. Just try to rest and don't worry about anything. It'll be over soon enough.'

Just give me some bloody codeine and I'll be out of here in no time, I want to say to him as he waltzes off, leaving the curtain open. My snake tattoo friend is sitting up on her bed flicking far too quickly through a magazine. Pretending she hasn't just heard everything. She's smiling though. She knows the cut of me, clearly.

I pull my pad and colours out from under the covers and get back to work. My red list. All the warning signs. Was I missing a whole load of them because of the codeine?

The sudden night-time meetings.

Why didn't I quiz him instead of just letting him go?

Reeking of whiskey when he got back and he's not supposed to touch a drop of that, since it nearly wrecked him completely before. I smelled it and said nothing. Sat opposite him and watched as he dozed off in the chair.

What did he do all that time I was in London? Do I even want to know? Why was he in such a good mood when we'd just suffered a horrible loss? When he's not even happy at work? I thought he was just doing it for me, trying to lift my spirits, to jog me along the bereavement road. Blind, I think now, with my red pencil poised ready to scratch this evidence across the page.

'Ah, there he is now.'

I look over at my new acquaintance who is no longer pretending to read. Her head is tilted up and she's greeting someone.

'She's awake, in there – writing up her notes, would you believe?' she says, and she laughs. The tap of his stick sends a shiver through me. Then he appears around the curtain at the foot of my bed, as if this is exactly where he should be.

'I'll head out for a smoke, leave the two of you to catch up in peace. Don't tell the doctor where I am.' She directs this at Jeff. Smiles at him, a sweet coy smile. Then she pulls her grey and white polka-dot fluffy dressing gown on.

Don't go, I try to tell her with my eyes widening. She's still not looking at me.

'She's very brave, you should be proud of her,' she says to Jeff, and she's gone.

FEBRUARY

NINA

Nina gets up from the blue bench and breaks into a sprint without looking back. If she had stayed a moment longer, she would have acted. Some little thing said or done that couldn't be unsaid or undone.

Sitting there beside Jeff, tasting what he was tasting, hearing what he was hearing, seeing what he was seeing, Nina Ruzza felt utterly defenceless. Unsafe from herself. As if she had been sliced open for all the world to see. The kid was a buffer for her and she was glad of it now. Without him there she is quite sure she would have blown it. She could sit there and fight it, or she could take flight, like the endangered pigeons she had seen earlier. Which is exactly what she has chosen to do.

Back in her flat Nina pulls the heavy red velvet curtains around the sitting room bay window. She hasn't bothered to do this for a long time but she's not going to risk a passer-by looking in. She lights her white jasmine scented candle on the hearth. Then she unzips her jacket and lies down on the couch, picturing him. His eyes sparkle as he smiles at her.

His thumb rubbing the tips of his fingers, circling them. She begins to do the same thing with her own fingers, summoning him into the room with her. Putting her hand up inside her T-shirt, she makes her way to her left breast and she circles her areola with her thumb, but it is his thumb that she feels now on her, soft and strong, circling. Her inverted nipple responds, pops out and glances off the barbell piercing. She licks the middle finger of her left hand and slides it down inside her jeans imagining, not for the first time, that it is Jeff Hogan that she will lose her virginity to. She counts as she pulses and contracts onto her finger. More this time than ever, as she knew there would be. She lies like this, glowing in her own wet warmth, until she feels the tug of a peaceful sleep envelop her. Just five minutes she promises herself, pulling the lilac throw from the back of the couch over her.

She startles to the sound of the intercom crackling. Someone is at her door. Could he have followed her? She leaps off the couch, zips herself up and runs to answer it.

'Nina?'

She buzzes him in.

'What the hell, Nina?' Stephano stands in front of her, jacketless, goosebumps on his bare arms.

'First you tell me you're not well. You looked awful. Then you disappear and don't come back. I was worried about you.'

'I'm fine now, thanks. What about the shop?'

'I had to close. Tell me what's going on, Nina. Your

professor dude with the kid came back. Handed me this. Said you left it behind.'

Nina stares at the purple beanie hat that Stephano is waving at her. 'Aww, how kind of him,' Nina says, smiling now.

'Kind? Nina, he says he was calling after you but you went off so quickly, running, he says you were running. What were you even doing there in the first place?'

Stephano's quizzing was beginning to diminish her high.

'Chill, Stephano. I bumped into them on my break, sat down for a bit, began to feel a little sick again, came home to sort it. Okay?'

Stephano takes in the room. The drawn curtains blocking out the light. The scented candle flickering in the hearth.

'Were you expecting company?' Stephano says, like a proprietorial older brother. 'Or do you have someone stashed in here hiding from me? You look a lot better than earlier anyhow. A good flush to your cheeks. However you sorted it, it seems to have worked a treat.'

'Let's go,' Nina says, blowing out the candle, and then inhaling the puff of white jasmine smoke deep into her lungs.

'I was ringing you at first,' Stephano says as they stroll through the main street. 'And there it was, your phone vibrating away by the till. Interesting image on your home screen.'

Nina pictures it, shuddering away on the counter. The screen grab of a street view. Grey double-backed roofs. Parked cars in a line. The red circle with a little arrow marking the spot.

'What's that about?'

Nina ignores the question. 'You're an awful worrier lately, Stephano. Worse than Mamma. That fiancée of yours is having a bad effect. Or maybe she likes you fretting about her?'

'She does.' He punches her lightly on the arm.

'The more you worry, the deeper the love?'

'For sure. It's as simple as that. You'll see someday, little Nina.'

'I think I'll have to work on a different formula for myself. That one just doesn't appeal somehow.' She looks in the window of McDonald's as they pass.

'All our customers have migrated,' she says about the long queue inside. 'We'd better up the pace.'

'They'll come back. They always do,' Stephano says, in no hurry at all. 'I went out to see Maria on Sunday, by the way. Thought you'd like to know,' he says.

Nina pictures her mother the last time she saw her, in full flow, loud, rapid speech, arguing with her at dinner on New Year's Day, telling her that she's wasting time, that she should forget about UCD, the cheek of them not accepting her straight away, that she should go back to Trinity for her PhD. Their loss, she had said, dropping her fork from a height onto her half-full plate, then walking around the table and hugging Nina tightly from behind, planting a kiss on the top of her head.

'How is she?'

'Ah, you know, not taking care of herself, worrying as

always. A mother's job but she looks wrecked on it. Puffing away, more than her usual. Not great to see my big sis like that. She says you're very hard to get hold of these days. She needs to see more of you.'

The guilt springs from Stephano's words and infuses her, muddying her thoughts. It has been far too long, she knows. But it's so hard to be there, as the sole recipient of this colossal, passionate care, being championed when she doesn't need it, when she'd just like to be left alone to work it out for herself. Nina thinks that she will do it now though. She'll make the effort to get out to see her mother next week. She won't cancel again. But she won't say it out loud to Stephano either, just in case.

'I told her you're grand, insofar as I can tell from what I see of you Friday nights anyway. Now I'm not so sure what I'd say to her.'

'Cheers.'

'Hey,' he says, stopping at the doorway of Dunnes Stores. 'Promise me you'll be careful.'

They walk on in silence, past the closed shoe shops and the charity shop with a silk sage-green dress draped on a mannequin in the window. Nina stops to stare for a moment. She thinks how Stephano knows full well that she doesn't make promises, and careful is a word that she would never choose to use nor apply to any aspect of her life. She could get into this with him but decides to let it go. She's tired now even if the euphoria of the last hour fizzes in her a little still. The signs she has been waiting for, confirming that Jeff

Hogan cares about her and wishes to be with her, were there for all to see tonight. She could throw her arms around Stephano now and thank him for bearing witness to this truth. Which would probably alarm him all the more. They reach the corner around which their own shop lies.

'I guess all bets are off for tonight seeing as I've skewed the numbers by absconding,' Nina says.

'New bets are on now, little niece,' he says, putting the key in the door. 'And I've got the best one for miscellaneous.'

The pain from the burn on Nina's hand begins to kick in again as they step back into the shop. She wonders how she hasn't felt it until now.

TUESDAY

CASSANDRA

He stands there with his little-boy-lost look that I usually find so endearing. His hair is freshly combed through with the cologne that I love to sniff at, but that now seems to be making me even more nauseous. The collar of his shirt is jutting out over the lapel of his maroon jacket, that little bit of haphazardness that pulls on the maternal strings in me, would have me jumping up, tucking in, patting down and then kissing. But not now.

Now at the foot of my bed stands my husband, the stranger. Someone I have poured every little bit of myself into. The primal urge that I had this morning to protect him and our family, no matter what, has vanished. Maybe the codeine was clouding things all along. He knows that I know. He knows that I saw. He knows that I'll do now what I should've done this morning, as soon as I can.

I pick up the wire dangling beside my bed and press the bell. The beeping begins behind my head as Jeff stares at me, his eyebrows meeting quizzically. The nurse arrives much more promptly than I'd have thought possible. She greets Jeff with a big, wide smile.

'The doctor said that I can have paracetamol, which I really need. I'm feeling too sick for visitors tonight, so my husband is leaving now and can you make sure no one else comes near me?'

'Too sick? The doctor says you're sitting up writing and feeling much better now, he's happy about that,' she says, more to Jeff than to me. He smiles at her, his eyes sparkling with it, as if they're in cahoots. His gorgeous, dazzling, dangerous smile.

'He says to hold off on any pain relief unless you really need it,' she says, slowly.

Jeff swings his hand up and plonks a black Tesco bag down on my bed. The red pencil rolls off onto the floor. I close the sketch pad and look directly at the nurse.

'I really need it,' I say.

Jeff turns around and begins to walk away. Click, tap, slap, click, tap, slap.

The nurse follows him.

'She'll be much better tomorrow, if you come back and see her then,' she says, and Jeff speaks in a whisper as the sounds of his footsteps fade away down the corridor.

I'm more than a little surprised that he goes off like that. Without a word. Without a fight. It holds us somehow still in the before. Not speaking it out loud. The way I wanted it at first, but not now.

I think about how easy it was for him to stand there asphyxiating her, his half-naked young lover, and how seamlessly he returned to the car and carried on. I pick up the black pencil, open the pad and flick over the page to begin to scratch out the after. All my actions to unearth the truth about who she is and what Jeff was up to seem hideously naïve now. Waiting to hear if she was dead or alive. What if she was alive? Was I just going to push it to the back of my mind, take a few codeine and let it wash away? I don't know. I'll never know, because she's dead and my gross inaction, the fact that I didn't go straight to the police after walking Ted to school will haunt me for ever.

'He's gone already?' the woman opposite says, sliding back towards her bed. 'That was quick. What did he bring in for you, anything nice in that bag?'

'Sorry, my head is pounding, can you pull the curtain again please?'

'Sure, hun.'

As soon as she does it, I tip the contents of the bag onto the bed and search.

FEBRUARY

NINA

'Hi Professor Hogan,' Nina types in an email on her phone. He has told her to call him Jeff, more than once, and she does in her head, of course. But she cannot type it. Not yet.

> It was lovely to bump into you and Ted on the pier. Sorry I had to rush off, I had to get back to my flat for something. Thanks for returning my hat to the shop, very kind of you.

She pauses to read over it. There is no hint of what she would actually like to say to him. She will save that for their meeting, now that she knows.

> I'm afraid I won't be able to meet you in Starbucks on Thursday afternoon. I have an appointment. I am free to meet any evening after 8, except Friday, if that suits. The Royal Marine Hotel has an open lobby where people often meet to discuss work and it's handy for both of us.

Has he actually ever told her where he lives? She knows. Of course she does. But she got the address from looking up his wife, a child psychotherapist who sees clients in their home. She deletes 'for both of us' and changes it to 'for me, not sure about you, just let me know.'

She reads over the whole thing now. It's not enough. It will need something more enticing to make it worth his while.

> I'm so excited about what I'm working on at the moment –
> I think you will be too.
> Best,
> Nina

She reads it one more time. The goal that she wants to achieve is there. Before she presses send, she thinks about the email she would really like to write.

> Hi Jeff,
> It was so special to spend time with you on the pier.
> Sorry I had to rush off. I was so turned on that I had to
> get back to my flat for privacy, to, well, you know how it
> is. Thanks for returning my hat to the shop – another
> little sign that you care. I don't want to meet you in Star-
> bucks this Thursday because I don't want Ted to be at
> our meeting. Perhaps some evening when he's bound to
> be in bed? Let's meet in the hotel that's close to both our

homes. I'm so excited about seeing you – I hope you will
be too.
Love,
Nina

Nina presses send on the actual mail. Cancelling the
Thursday meeting is not something she would have done a
week ago. It's a risk. Maybe he won't see her at all. But a
new confidence sings in her now, since last night. It is as if
she's just been told that her exam results are excellent and
she knows she'll most likely get the scholarship. It is this
delicious in-between time that she likes the best. The waiting time. Will she, or won't she? It doesn't really matter. She
will dance in this no-man's land, knowing, as she does, that
she has done her best.

She checks her sent mail box, to make sure that it did actually go, and there it is. It's Saturday morning, a little too early
for most people to be awake, but Nina hasn't managed to
sleep at all yet. How could she with the chip-shop shift ending at two-thirty, riding pillion home with Stephano
shouting from the front of his Honda about the great form
she had been in for the rest of the night and then buzzing
away, leaving her to run it all over in her mind. She hears her
stomach growling now but hasn't the energy to search for
food. She switches off her phone, and curls her legs under
herself on the couch. In a little while, she thinks, after a small
doze, she will do all of the things that she is supposed to do.

TUESDAY

CASSANDRA

He has done well, but not well enough.

I think of him rooting around in a panic for what to bring in for me.

Necessities. My toothbrush. Hairbrush. Moisturizer. Shampoo. Conditioner. How long does he hope I'll be in here for?

Underwear. The good stuff for special occasions. Why? Black leggings and vest tops, because I don't do pyjamas or nightdresses.

Mascara and nude lip gloss. He knows how much I love mascara, springing my tired eyes back to life.

He's put some thought into this. What to choose and what to leave out. The book that's been on my bedside locker, underneath the lamp for months. Jonathan Franzen's *Freedom*, a parking-ticket stub sticking out of it, acting as a bookmark. A third of the way through. I'll never finish it. Not now. Is he telling me, by the contents of this bag to just carry on as normal? To act as if nothing of any significance has happened. To spruce myself up and wear the things that

I love. Then to just sit up in bed and read until this all blows over?

My Chloé perfume. I take the heavy glass lid off it and sniff. A burst of reassurance. My everyday smell. Clever of him. Very clever.

The nurse slips back through the curtain holding out a tiny translucent cup with two white pills in it.

'You'll feel better soon.' She glances at the mess of my stuff spread all over the bed.

'A lot of things,' she says, smiling. 'You let me know if you want to shower and change. I'll take you, to make sure you don't fall.'

She leaves again, like a ghost, barely moving the curtain. He has thought of every little thing. How long did it take him? Did he make a list and move around the cottage ticking things off like I would, or did he rummage in a panic and just get lucky? I try to picture him, there alone, filling the bag with all the little placatory bits. I cannot see him at all. He has put my little black pumps in. Better than my runners, but not essential. I pick them up to put beside the locker when something slides out, hits the floor and rolls. I unclip the monitor from my finger, jump out of the bed and get down on my hands and knees, searching. Nothing. The coolness of the floor is enticingly soothing. I stretch out and lie face down. Even my throbbing head feels better down here. I can see under my bed and the other beds on the ward. Slippers and bags. Chair legs. Then across from me. Right beside the wheels of her table I see it. The little green bottle.

Then a hand. Her hand. Reaching. Whipping it up. Why would he pack them? Why the hell would he do that? She slides her feet into her slippers and shimmies across. I can't get off the ground quick enough.

'Looking for these?' She holds the curtain back with one hand and shakes the bottle with the other. 'Only it says Jeffrey Hogan on them, so maybe they came from somewhere else.' She tilts her head backwards, as if she really thinks someone else on the ward owns them. She knows full well. She's been listening in.

'Thanks,' I say, getting up off the floor and crawling back onto the bed.

'I used to be hooked too,' she says. The sheet is soaking wet beneath me. It's some sort of underworld I'm in now. I'm a sinner, not quite in hell, not quite out of it, but being pursued, chased down by the likes of this hornet.

She'll want to sting me soon.

'Very hard on everyone. You're going through the sickness. I know all about it.' She's enjoying herself now. The trace of a smile. A glimmer of something verging on smug. 'Thing is I don't think I should give you these. You'd just take them to stop the sickness, but at the end of the day, you're better off without them.'

There it is. The first little sting. Not too bad. I've no intention of taking them. I pull the covers up around me as a hint for her to leave.

'I suppose it makes you a better counsellor if you've been through the shit yourself,' she says, and she lets go of the curtain. I hear her sliding back across to her bed for a moment and then further. Off out of the ward for a smoke. Or maybe to swallow some of my pills. I think of how I only said one word to her and how she revealed so much to me which reminds me of why I really enjoy my job. Did really enjoy it before, at least.

I shake the black Tesco bag one more time and, as I suspected, it's not there. I feel through all the other bits spread across the bed, just in case it got stuck in something, but no. It definitely isn't among my things. I think of how carefully he selected everything except the thing that he knows I need the most.

This is not an oversight.

Just as he thought about putting the painkillers in, he thought about leaving the phone out. He wants me drugged, dangerously so, and unable to make that call.

The main lights are turned off now. I sort through my things, doing just what he wants, lining up my toiletries on the bedside locker, leaving the book within easy reach, as if I might just grab it and have a read. I fold the clothes that I will wear tomorrow and put them back in the bag and inside the locker. I remove the lid from my perfume, and this time I spray a little onto my wrists and dab them along my neck. Then I sit bolt upright in my bed with the bell in my hand. Even though I feel like crawling under the covers, pulling them over my head and not coming back out, I know that I can't. I know that I must be hyper alert to the sounds on the ward. To the sounds of what might be coming my way.

FEBRUARY

NINA

Nina,
Tuesday evening, say 8.00 in the lobby? Send on a copy of
your latest work in advance for a fruitful discussion.
Jeff

Nina stares at the phone in her hand. Then she widens the
blurred words on the screen with two fingers and reads
them slowly again. Clipped, terse, as if he's in a rush. Or is
it that he's now a lot less formal, since the pier. He's dropped
the *Dear* and the *Best*. He's using the short form of his name.
She likes it. He's coming to meet her at night, in a hotel,
without the boy. At her request.

She takes her time standing up, but there's a rush to her
head. Black dots spin in front of her, as if she's got up too
quickly. She blinks them away and runs the cold tap at the
kitchen sink, filling a pint glass with water. She gulps it back
and fills it again. Her body is all dried out, as if she has just
completed a marathon. She slips a couple of slices of soda
bread into the toaster and waits. Tuesday. Which means

she'll have to get the piece to him by Monday. The piece she has not even begun to work on. She smears Marmite onto the toast and eats, standing, while wondering how she's going to do it. She has promised him something great. Would he even be meeting her without this promise?

She could rustle up a good enough piece on The Sea in *La Strada*. The fertile daytime opening of the film with a young woman and lots of small children running along the beach, laughing and chattering, accompanied by waves crashing, the sea a symbol of procreation, of movement, of life, compared with the barren night-time ending with a lone male, felled on the shore, sobbing, the sea a symbol of loss and regret. Does the sea throw up these gifts and these monsters, both in equal measure? Is the sea a companion in life, as well as in death? This she could do easily enough, but she would like to offer Jeff a little more to chew on.

Nina can feel herself un-wilting now, her cells sucking hard on the tardy infusion of sustenance. If she's going to be able to write well, to throw up oblique angles for discussion, she will need to take better care of herself. She takes a vial out of the fridge and rolls it between her hands for a few seconds. The cloudiness disappears. Then she washes her hands, lathering back and front, and plucking any residue from under her nails. As she does this, she sings the happy birthday song, just as her mother used to.

Tanti auguri a te

But it's not my birthday, Mamma.

> *Tanti auguri a te*
> *Tanti auguri a Nina*
> *Tanti auguri a te!*

Every single time.
Brava Nina, brava.

Nina goes to the freezer and grabs the tray of ice. She squeezes a cube out, takes her T-shirt off, and presses the ice onto her stomach between her navel and her pubic bone. When the cube has melted and the spot is nice and numb, she continues with the ritual.

She waits until it kicks in before flicking open her phone to email Jeff back.

Tuesday evening it is. Expect a copy to hit your mail by Monday afternoon.

She presses send, pleased that she has taken Jeff's dropped salutations a step further. No names are necessary now. Step by little step, they are letting one another know.

WEDNESDAY

CASSANDRA

I listen for him in the early hours. I know that he will be back. It's easier than I had imagined to keep wide awake. Insomnia must be one of the things that accompany withdrawal. A good thing now because when he comes back in to say whatever it is that he thinks will make this all better, I'll be prepared. No more whispering to me as I lie semiconscious, as I know he was doing, even if I couldn't grasp what he was saying.

The hiss of someone's oxygen into their mask is worrying me. I might not hear him at all. I didn't notice it earlier among all the other noises but now it is startling in the silence. A rhythmic whoosh. Someone fighting to stay alive. Did she fight to stay alive? She made that sound. A singing wail. Is that a fight? There's a mumbling coming from another bed. An old person talking to herself or talking in her sleep.

Did I see everything or miss something crucial in the shock of the moment?

Was I shocked enough or was the codeine doing a good job of dumbing me down?

If I wasn't taking it daily, would I have reacted differently or would I still have thought I was doing the right thing? Keeping silent. Protecting the family. A little codeine, as prescribed for him, just to take the edge off the pain. It worked. Allowed me to get on with seeing clients. Helping other families to muddle through and navigate their tricky worlds with troubled teenagers. I didn't feel dumbed down on it, I felt like myself before the miscarriage. It just helped to put that pain on hold. Enough that I could take sneak peeks at the photos on my phone and smile, proud of her for trying to get here, for almost making it, instead of weeping uselessly for failing her. I could look at her and marvel at how her eyes were shaped just like Ted's but her nose was different, button to his long one, and so she would've been a good mix of Jeff and me, the best bits of each of us for our perfect little girl. Ted's little sister Jo. Ted and Jo. My children. Our children. Children. How much better it sounds than child. Now, without the protective layer of codeine, these thoughts gnaw at me, flailing my skin red raw. Ted will not have a sibling. I will not have children.

I am woken by loud clanking. I sit bolt upright, annoyed with myself. How could I let myself fall asleep? I scour around for signs of him, traces that he has been here. The curtain opens.

'Tea with your breakfast, love?'

'Yes, please. What time is it?'

'Twenty past seven.' She puts down a tray with cornflakes,

milk, slices of brown bread, butter and marmalade, before adding the tea pot, and rattling the cup and saucer down. A proper cup for this time of the day.

'See you later, love.' She leaves the curtain wide open.

Across from me, the woman with my pills sleeps on, thankfully, a light snoring coming from behind her curtain. She's accustomed to the noises of the ward, no doubt.

If he's been in, he didn't try to wake me. I would've woken easily enough. I was certain he'd be back, when it was all quiet, when I couldn't protest. I was certain he'd come in to tell me what he has done or to ask me what he should do. He knows that I saw. He knows that I don't want to know, not really. Or that I do want to know about it all up until the beach. He'd know that about me. I'd want to understand every little bit of it. I don't want to know what happened in that moment, how he was able to do what he did. Not yet.

I pour the tea and drink it, black, without thinking. It scalds the roof of my mouth, and I don't care. I deserve this, for being so naïve, so unseeing. There must've been so many signs, while I went about my crusade of numbing the pain of loss and marching forwards with our life. Or am I a bit more like Mum than I'd care to admit? Did I know, underneath it all and turn a blind eye? Could I have stopped him from doing what he did on the beach by noticing weeks, months before, and confronting him? I take another slurp of tea. There's a little peeling just behind my front teeth. It feels good.

The curtain opposite opens, and she stands there, wiping her eyes.

'He scared the life out of me,' she says, looking straight at me, black eyeliner smudged onto her cheeks.

'Who did?' I say, but I already know. He's been in.

'Your fella, what's his name? Jeff. There should be rules about it. Shouldn't be allowed to just wander in like that in the middle of the night. Mind you, he wasn't exactly wandering, poor man, with his stick an' all. Must take a lot out of him.'

'Did he try to wake me up?'

'Ah, no, he didn't want to do that. I asked him what the hell he was up to sneaking in like that. He laughed and said he just had to leave something in for you. Said he wouldn't be able to get in again for some time. I bet he travels, does he? He looks like the type who travels a lot.'

'Where?'

'Where what?'

'Where did he leave it?'

'No idea, I was on my way to the loo and when I got back he was gone.'

'Thanks.' I push my table aside and get out of bed to close the curtain.

'No worries. I'm going to put the television on if that's okay with you, if you're not trying to sleep again or anything.'

'Fire away,' I say smiling at her, before welcoming the relief I feel from closing the curtain and shutting her leering face out.

I begin my search.

Nina chooses the table in the hotel lobby with great care. It's in a corner behind the door to the bar at a good distance from all the other tables. She pulls two chairs side by side and then disperses the remaining ones as if they're for random passers-by. There will be no doubt when Jeff Hogan walks in as to where he is to place himself. She flips open her laptop and clicks on the piece she has written for today. The piece she sent to Jeff just last night and to which he did not reply. She begins to read it, again, while she waits.

Representations of the male body in Fellini's *La Strada* – From Eroticism to Asexuality

Much has been made of the physicality and diminutive stature of Fellini's lead female character, Gelsomina, in *La Strada*. The fact that she is played by his wife, Giulietta Masina, has also attracted much debate as well as speculation about the internal dynamics of such a relationship.

The words on the page begin to blur, bleeding into one another, until Nina seems to be looking into a soup. Which is how she feels about the writing now too. It is not as sharp as she would like it to be. Words swim up to her and drop away. *Sexuality. Redemption. Childlike. Religiosity. Desire.*

She stops trying to read. It has taken her too long to get to the heart of what she is analysing, the character she is most fascinated with. She should have begun with The Fool, Il Matto, and worked back to the leads. The unique contribution she will be making to the field, centres around Il Matto, after all. She glances around the lobby. No sign of him. He's five minutes late. A barboy approaches her table, pristine white shirt tucked neatly into black trousers complete with central crease.

'Can I get you anything?'

She had wanted to wait to see what Jeff would order, to take her cue from him, but with disappointment beginning to fizz in her, the niggling feeling that perhaps he won't turn up at all, she decides to go ahead.

'Yes, a pint of Bulmer's please.'

'Do you have any ID on you?' he asks. Whippersnapper. Will she ever stop being asked this? She's twenty-two years old, but everyone guesses about sixteen. She looks up at him, at the glimmer of fear dancing in his eyes. Maybe he hates asking as much as she hates being asked. She pulls her old student card out of her bag and waves it at him. Her fourth-year student card. No date of birth on it but he can work it out.

'Oh, okay, thanks. So you've finished college?' One eye is slightly more closed than the other when he smiles. 'Sorry for asking, I got it wrong before, nearly cost me the job.' He doesn't seem to be in any hurry at all, now that he has the information he needs, to actually get her the drink that she really does need. 'What are you up to now, then?' he asks.

'Still a student, well, kind of,' she says. She can hear Jeff before she sees him. The click of his stick on the marble floor. This is perfect.

'Working on it at least,' she says, flashing her eyes at the soupy words on the laptop and then back up at him, clearly outlined, simple. She smiles at the contrast. 'How about you?'

He places his circular empty metal tray on her table. He's on for a chat.

'Oh, you know, just killing time before deciding the next move. It's between a one-year master's, travel or looking for a real job. Which I probably wouldn't get without the master's. A vicious circle, isn't it?'

The clicks are getting louder. He must be wearing his soft-soled Clarks shoes. She can't hear the slap.

'Sounds like you've solved it already to me. Travel. When will you get that chance again? If it was me, that's what I'd do.' She holds his gaze, smiling right into him. He places his hand on the back of Jeff's chair and tugs it a little towards himself, as if he might just sit down.

'That's what everyone says to me, but when it comes down to it, not what they do themselves. Fear of being left behind or something. All the other millions of graduates gaining an advantage while you loll about on your personal odyssey, getting to know yourself better, deepening yourself . . .'

'Steady now,' Nina says, laughing, trying to get it back to light-hearted banter. She's obviously hit a nerve.

'Even you said it just there, you're trying to get onto a course, while recommending that I travel.' The clicks have stopped. To the right of this irked peer stands Jeff, looking vaguely amused, his hair damp, the silver waves more clearly defined. Nina pinches the burnt skin on her hand. The pain is less acute now, but it helps to divert her from being too conscious of the thudding in her chest.

'Old friends?' Jeff asks, smiling down at Nina.

The barboy snaps his head to the right.

'Professor Hogan? Whoa, long time no see. What's up with the leg?'

The edges of the people standing in front of Nina begin to blur now too. She closes her eyes, shakes her head for a moment and opens them again to the sight of Jeff patting the barboy's shoulders.

'Jack Conroy, well, well. Good to see you. The leg, a terrible bore, really – nerve damage, they think. Still, it gets me a bit of sympathy all round. I just have to swim every morning and it should improve. How about you – you haven't come looking for that reference yet, I take it you're still undecided?'

Nina's dizziness worsens.

She closes her eyes again and this time keeps them closed. She half listens, letting Jeff's voice swim about in her head.

'Isn't that so, Nina?'

The skin on her arms tingles in her jacket sleeves.

'I'll be back in a minute,' she says, getting out of her chair and snapping down the lid of her laptop.

'Looking forward to that Bulmer's, Jack,' she says and turns her back on both of them, making her way across the lobby, past reception and out into the crisp night air.

WEDNESDAY

CASSANDRA

It's all just as I left it before I went to sleep. My toiletries are lined up on the bedside locker, along with the book. Inside the locker is the bag with my spare clothes. I pull it out and shake them onto the bed. Nothing new. I pick up the book and fan through the pages, expecting something to fall out.

What were you doing in here?

What have you done?

I pick up my black pumps and shake them. Nothing. You were lying to her. You didn't bring anything in, did you? You came, as I thought you would, to tell me what I already know. To see if I can help you, again.

A hand on the curtain.

'How are you feeling this morning?'

My nurse.

'Much better, thanks. A bit of a headache, slight nausea, less sweats now, nothing like last night though.'

'Okay, that's good. You let me know if you need anything before I finish my shift. Someone else will look after you today.'

Her face is smiling and open, as if she's seen it all and could weather any storm.

I could just tell her. Splurge it all out to this neutral safe face and ask her what I should do next.

'My husband came in during the night,' I say instead.

'Yes, he asked me if he could leave something you need. I said he could leave it with me but he said he'd be quick.'

'I can't find it, whatever it is.' I can hear the crackle in my voice as clearly as she can.

'It's okay, don't worry, I'll help you.'

She pulls the curtain closed and it's just the two of us. She looks right into me, and as I feel the full force of her kind stare, the first of the tears springs unbidden, stinging my cheek. Her eyes widen, and it is as if I am attached to her, as if her little movements prompt mine, an invisible string between us, because now the tears are flowing freely, cascading down, and I don't even care.

I feel safe with her.

I slump down on the bed.

'It's okay, this can happen in withdrawal, you get a bit low. It will pass.' She puts her arm across my shoulder and pulls me close to her. I breathe her in. She smells like the vanilla perfume oil from the Body Shop I used to wear as a student.

'I don't think it's withdrawal, it's just I have a lot on my mind, a lot to work out, you know?' I say, and my nose begins to run to match the tears. She pulls a blue hand towel from the dispenser over my sink and gives it to me.

'Yes and things can seem much bigger than they are because your body's crashing, looking for the drug. When withdrawal is over you'll know how to work it out, what to do. For now all you need to do is rest.'

'I wish,' I say, like a petulant teenager. She takes her arm away.

'I need to do your blood pressure in a minute, when you feel a little better. Would you like me to help you find what you're looking for?'

'No, that's okay, thanks. He didn't leave anything, I've been through it all.'

'Maybe he'll bring it today. When he comes back.'

'He's not coming back.' I need to stop myself. I know this. Too vulnerable, too much to be said, regret. There's a term for it, something I'm careful about with my clients.

'Yes, he said, "See you tomorrow". I tried to say I'm not here during the day today, but he had his back to me and didn't hear. Don't worry, he'll be in soon. You can talk to him about what's on your mind then. I'll take your blood pressure now, and after that you can have a shower. You'll feel much better.'

She wheels her machine in, unfurls the Velcro and wraps it around my left arm. She sticks a peg onto my right index finger. As she pumps and the Velcro tightens on my arm I think of the girl, the tightening across her face, every little bit of her screaming for release, but not fighting, not really, not enough. A little flailing, that's all. Maybe she's like my neighbour here, thought she'd come out of it better if she didn't fight. The nurse releases the pump and I picture the girl falling to her knees, hitting the stones hard, then the sideways fall, as her torso keels.

Slumped like a ragdoll.

'It's a little high. Maybe because you're worried. Finish your breakfast and we can check it again.'

'Thank you.'

'My next shift is tonight. I'll see you then if you're not discharged today.'

Discharged.

Back to face it all head on.

I don't think so, not today. I don't think I can do it today.

I do as she says now. I smear marmalade across the bread and eat, ravenous all of a sudden. I eat both pieces and then tip two sachets of white sugar onto the cornflakes and cover them in milk. I eat rapidly, glad of the curtain hiding this spectacle. Then I throw my shampoo and conditioner into the clothes bag, slip on my pumps and make my way out of the ward and along the corridor to the shower room.

It's too early for other patients to be in the showers, it seems. I strip off and dump my dirty clothes on an orange plastic chair along with the bag. In the shower I tilt my head backwards so that the spray pummels down on my face, ridding me of the residue of my tears. I shampoo quickly, using the leftover froth to cleanse my body. I condition, for the smell more than anything, sweet coconut, not unlike our sun cream, which always makes me smile, remembering.

But now you've taken those future sunny days away from us. Relaxing, on holidays. Playing happy families. Although I didn't know we were playing. Only you did.

I get out, and realize you've forgotten to put a towel in for me. It's not a bloody hotel I'm in now, Jeff. I dry myself with my worn clothes and then slip into the good occasion lingerie you've selected. Lacy purple. Once again, as if you're thinking it's a hotel I'm in and we're going to have some fun. You and me. Or do you think we'll have some fun as soon as I'm discharged and home with you? That I'll ask you what it was you liked doing with her, so we can replicate it?

I feel the welling of tears again, but I push them back. I slip the leggings and vest top on, along with my pumps. I look as if I'm heading off to a ballet class. Then I dump my dirty stuff into the bag and leave.

Back in my cubicle, I moisturize my face and neck. Using the mirror that's attached to the brush you've thoughtfully packed, I apply some mascara and nude lip gloss. I brush through my hair, too easily — too much conditioner now that it seems to be thinning. I spray my perfume onto my wrists and then dab it on my neck. Then I pick up the pillows so that I can sit upright on the bed.

I see it.

My phone.

You've placed my phone under the pillows.

I key in the code quickly, our wedding anniversary, and I see them all, all of the missed calls from you, from my mum.

Then a text message from you. Just one. Sent at three minutes past two this morning.

After you left?

My fingers are trembling.

Do I read this or not?

What the hell do I do?

FEBRUARY

NINA

Outside, Nina is shaking. It is as if she's standing on the shore, naked, after a long swim in the icy sea. She sits down on the ground, unzips a pocket on her biker's jacket and pulls out a strawberry-flavoured Chupa Chups lollipop. She wrestles with the wrapper, her fingers shaking too much for her to be able to get a firm grip. She puts the lollipop in between her teeth and bites the plastic away, spitting little bits out as she goes. Then she sucks it hard between her tongue and the roof of her mouth, before swapping it between her cheeks, the extra saliva helping to dissolve it all the more quickly.

How clearly has she been thinking, she wonders now. Inviting conversation with the idiot barboy instead of concentrating on her submission and how to excite Jeff about it. A man in a suit, late thirties, wheels a travel bag past her, cutting it close to her toes. Nina pulls her legs in, and then narrows her eyes at him.

'Taking a break?' he calls out, beaming down at her. German. If she wasn't feeling so off, she'd take him on. Stand up. Tell him how very rude it is to almost shave her toes with his bag. Ask him why he has a wheelie bag anyway, horrible, noisy, attention-seeking things that they are. Why the hell doesn't he just use a holdall and slip into the hotel with some manners. Instead, she turns her head away from him and sucks all the harder.

Then she waits.

Nina crosses the lobby slowly. Jeff has his reading glasses on, his head bent down, a copy of her paper before him. Beside him a pint of copper fizz shimmers. In his hand, a tumbler with some golden liquid. Good, she thinks.

'Sorry about that,' she says. He peeps at her over his silver rims.

'I'm celebrating your piece with a decent Scotch. Cheers.' He holds his glass up to her, his eyes twinkling.

She takes a seat opposite him and reaches for something to say. It is all just as she hoped it would be. Except for the cloudiness. The urgency and the bite have gone from her. She can't think of a single thing to say. She picks up her pint and drinks without stopping until it's drained. She doesn't know what else to do. It is as if she is sleepwalking and can't wake up. It will pass. She just needs to wait it out.

She tucks her head into her shoulders and curls her legs up underneath her.

'You're very pale, Nina. Are you okay?'

She smiles and nods. She would like to raise her hand, put

up her index finger and let him know that she needs just a minute, but she does not.

'This is the beginning of a very special piece of work, Nina. We need to discuss the direction it could go in.' Jeff takes a slug from his glass, swirls it about in his mouth for a moment, puffs his cheeks out with it, holding it there as if it's mouthwash, and then swallows. Nina watches the movement of his Adam's apple. The sharp point of it, moving up and down. She places her forefinger on her own neck and swallows.

'If we work on it together over the next few weeks, we could submit it to one of the journals for publication. I'm thinking *Camera Obscura*, *Film Criticism* or *Film Philosophy*.' He puts the tumbler to his mouth and gulps back the remaining Scotch as if he's in a rush. Then he twists the empty glass, around and around. The light from above catches on the crystal, refracting diamonds onto his hand. 'It will be great to get you a publication, get your name out there and known, get you started on the peer reviews.'

Jeff looks across the lobby as he speaks, as if something interesting is taking place on the far wall. Nina feels herself beginning to sharpen a little again, even if she is a bit woolly about what he is saying. It's not making sense to her. She stands. Elevation might just help to clear her head.

'I don't get it. How can I put a paper forward for publication when I'm not even registered for a PhD?'

'Don't worry about that. We'll do a joint paper. My name will carry the weight for the publication. You're right, of course – on your own it would be next to impossible to get into a peer-reviewed journal.'

He looks down at her paper, as if he is reading from it. Nina stares at his eyebrows, thick and black and unruly. A perfect contrast to the silver waves on his head. One stray long hair juts out from his right brow.

'Isn't it a little early to be thinking about publications? I'm at the start of developing the concept of male hysteria in Fellini's work. If I jump the gun with a publication introducing this, what would be the unique contribution of the doctorate? Wouldn't someone else just pick it up and run with it?'

Jeff shuffles backwards in his seat and then looks up at Nina. 'We could leave the concept out for now. The piece is strong enough without it. I think we should tweak the title. *From Eroticism to Asexuality – an analysis of the male body in Fellini's* La Strada would work. It hasn't been done, Nina, and it's a great forerunner for your analysis of male hysteria when it comes to the PhD.'

Nina thinks about how she should be feeling ecstatic. Her name on a publication, twinned with Professor Jeffrey Hogan's. Shouldn't she have to kill for that? But there's a dull ache about her head and an unfamiliar reticence flooding through her. She ought to be chomping at the bit. Instead, she feels a vague, fuzzy sense of disappointment, which she wishes would either just announce itself fully or go away. It is as if she is veiled, her face covered with mesh, and how she is actually seeing things will not be revealed until the veil is removed. She is, she thinks, probably in the process of messing things up, but she doesn't seem to care. The barboy flits past and Jeff raises his hand.

'Same again please, Jack,' he says motioning to the two empty glasses. Then he looks directly at Nina. 'There's a ball at your feet, Nina Ruzza. It's up to you what you do with it.'

'Right now I'm not sure what to do about anything.'

Jeff removes his glasses and his eyes widen. Expecting more.

She takes her time, mulling over her options. Say nothing, don't risk it. Say something, test him out. There's a deliciousness to savour in this pause. Something she knows she'll return to when she's alone. His eyes shimmering with expectation. His hands clasped together, long fingers intertwined, resting on her words on the table in front of him. He presses his lips together as if he's trying not to say something. He wants to hear more. Wants to enter her addled mind and help to iron it out. She gives him something.

'There was a suspected leak at my flat today. A carbon-monoxide alarm went off in a flat above but they're pretty sure it's coming from mine.' As she says the words, slow and deliberate, she sees it. Just a slight flush on his cheeks. Coral.

'Dangerous stuff. Are you all right? Yes, now that you say it, you haven't seemed yourself this evening. You mustn't go back there, not until it's safe.'

'No, I won't.'

'Good, good,' Jeff says, slowly, looking directly at Nina,

singeing her skin with his stare. She feels the veil rising. Her camera lens coming in to focus.

'So I'm going to take a rest now,' she says, standing up. 'I'll think about what you've said. It will be clearer in the morning. I'd like to discuss the content of the piece with you before making a decision. Can you meet me again here some other evening this week?'

'Absolutely. I'll double check with Cass, but I think tomorrow night would work.'

Cass. Nina has never heard Jeff speak her name and didn't know that he shortened it. It sounds so natural, so friendly. Jeff and Cass, Cass and Jeff. Jeff, Cass and Ted. Why didn't he just call her Cassandra, like she did? She could feel the mapping start in her neck.

'Let me know,' she says and turns away, just as Jack approaches the table with the drinks.

Back in her room, Nina showers, allowing the hot fall to drench her before removing the shower head and twisting it to the central massage mode. She holds the nozzle and aims, first at her right breast for a moment, then at her left, circling the areola with the strong jet until her nipple stands proud, tingling. She thinks about Jeff, here in the same building as her, just two floors below as she moves the pulsating jet down her stomach and along her pubic area, onto where she is swollen. She comes almost instantly, unable to slow it, shuddering to the warm jet which is him, some part of him, any part at all, touching her there.

She slips into the white fluffy hotel robe without drying herself first and perches on her bed. The orgasm is helping to clear her head, the oxytocin flooding her, shaking off the uncertainty she had been feeling down in the lobby. She goes over it all again. Jeff Hogan has read her stuff, loves it, wants to get it published. He has come here tonight, and will again tomorrow night, at her request. There was something different about him, certainly different from Friday night sitting on the pier. It's as if he's allowing himself to step right into it. Without Ted he can embrace it. Just as she'd thought he would. She was different herself tonight; she knows this and maybe he was reacting to her. Or maybe something is going on at home that has him unsettled. That frisson, the warm electrical little pulses that she feels when she's close to him were not there this evening, but no matter. There's plenty of time, especially if she decides to go ahead with his suggestion – then they will be working closely on a publication together. She gets off the bed to flick the kettle on and hears a gentle tapping on the door. She stands in the middle of the room wondering what to do. Then she hears his voice.

'Nina? It's Jeff.'

The rest she does not hear. He is still talking but the words are muffled now, as if she's trying to make them out from under water. She walks, in a trance, and swings her door wide open.

WEDNESDAY

CASSANDRA

Cassandra, my love, try to remember who we are together and be the strong person that I know you are. Don't let this destroy us. I could see it in your eyes, your protective detachment, full glow, but I'm asking you to cast your old fears aside now and use your wonderful brain. I'm sorry that I didn't know you were suffering so much with our loss and that you were self-medicating. I think you will see things much more clearly once the codeine fuzz has lifted and you can be your excellent rational self. I will be there for you.

I read over the text three times and at first, I must admit, you get to me. I am right there remembering who we are and how I don't want us to be destroyed, how I don't want Ted to be destroyed. So if I just switch off my emotions and turn on rational mode it will make this all okay, will it? I won't mind that you were off screwing a beautiful young student and then killing her when she started to make a fuss. Now as I read it over I see all your clever little ways. Not

235

mentioning what you've done. Complimenting me, and then putting me down. You'd fit the classic controlling-husband criteria. Coercive control. Knowing how to get exactly what you want from me. Why did you bring the phone in? Do you think your message will be enough to stop me from doing what I know I must do?

'I knew they'd get him quick.'

I open my curtain and I read it before I hear it. TV3 news with the headlines flying across the bottom of the screen. *A man is being questioned by police in connection with the death of a young woman on Killiney beach yesterday morning.* Everything in the room begins to spin. My knees buckle and I fall to the floor. Bells go off all around me from other patients. My neighbour screams for a nurse and then bends down and takes my hand.

'Your blood pressure is probably after dropping there. You'll be grand, we'll just get you up slowly, come on.'

But I don't want to get up.

What would I be getting up for?

It's all over.

We are in the after zone, our safe little world, the one I wanted to protect and you asked me to, gone.

'Come on, love.'

I close my eyes and lie here. Mute and unmoving.

The bells keep ringing. I can't hear the news readers, and I'm glad.

I know all I need to know.

Someone tugs at me. Scoops me up. I don't care who it is or what they want to do with me.

I am placed back on my bed. My wrist is squeezed. The Velcro noise again, the pump.

'Ah, yeah, she just came out and collapsed on the floor there.'

'I'm okay.'

All these good people wasting their time trying to figure this out.

'Good. You ate today?' A male nurse this time. They must call the male ones to lift and drag.

'I ate. I showered. I'm grand. Just a dizzy spell.'

'Yes, and that's what you were admitted with too, wasn't it, a fall, blacking out?'

'That was different.'

'How so?'

'I hadn't eaten and I was running. This is just part of the withdrawals I guess.'

'Not that I've seen before. Still, you're in the right place. Your blood pressure is fine now. I'll ask the reg if we should send you for another ECG just to check.'

I'm going around in silly little circles in here while you're out there turning our lives irreparably inside out. There must've been another witness. Someone else has dobbed you in. How did it happen? Did you leave here, and make your way home to police waiting on our doorstep?

She comes across to me, this neighbouring patient without boundaries.

'They got him,' she says. 'Poor girl.'

'Handed himself in an' all. Now that's a new one on me.'

You handed yourself in?

'Can you turn the volume up?'

'Yeah, he must've known he was a goner. All the trains with commuters from Bray going into town passing overhead.'

The man, who is in his late forties, went to Blackrock police station in the early hours of this morning. The young woman has been named as Nina Ruzza, a twenty-two-year-old Dublin student.

Ruzza. Italian. Of course.

'Late forties? A paedo uncle and she was going to rat him out. The bastard.'

You didn't want me to do it, after all, did you? You've saved me from having to make that call. Something from our past gushes up in me. A memory of the game of scruples we used to play.

Is that what you're doing now, reminding me?

What would the question be this time, Jeff?

You kill your lover in a tussle on the beach and your wife sees you do it. Do you hand yourself in to the police or wait to see if your wife will?

Is that what you're doing, claiming the moral high ground now?

Is it known at this time whether the man has been arrested in connection with the death?

A crime reporter stands outside the station where you are, on Sweetman's Avenue. Do you know that's what it's called? If that wasn't you inside and we were watching this together, you'd make a joke about it. Highlight the irony. Dissect it and we'd laugh.

The reporter's face is pursed with seriousness, a little flushed, and he nods as he listens to the all-important question, as if the answer is yes, yes of course you've been arrested. There's a slight delay. The wind whips at his lilac tie. He opens his mouth to speak and I close my eyes.

That information isn't available to us at the moment. What we can tell you is that this man presented voluntarily and so he is free to leave at any time. If the police have reasonable grounds to suspect that he has committed a serious offence, then he will be placed under arrest.

Have you not told them yet?

The body, which was found partially clothed, was examined last night at the scene by the Assistant State Pathologist. It has now been removed for a post-mortem examination.

Assistant State Pathologist.

You'll like that.

The person examining your crime hasn't made the grade to the full title. I wonder if they're hankering after it like you are.

Thanks Paul. Can you tell us what we know about the young woman?

Yes, Susan. We know that Nina Ruzza was from a well-known Irish–Italian chip-shop-owning family. She is a former student of Trinity College. A relative has told us that she was taking a year out and was due to enrol for further postgraduate study later this year.

On the screen now her photograph shines out.

A purple wool hat is pulled tightly over her head,

compressing the curls around her face, but they dance on her shoulders, dark with bits of copper shimmering.

Those curls that our son, Ted, tells me he has put his little fingers in.

She's not looking directly at the camera but off to her left, as if at something in the distance. Her eyes, that I was sure would be brown, are a light turquoise, almost unnatural, as if she has coloured lenses in. Her bottom lip is pierced in the centre, drawing the eye to it, to its beauty, plump, a fresh cherry red. She is otherwise pale and thin, like a child who still has some growing left to do. She is thinking about something, unaware the picture is being taken. The person who is taking it loves her.

It would be easy to love her.

That was Paul Shorthall reporting from outside Blackrock police station in South County Dublin where a man in his late forties is being questioned in relation to the death of twenty-two-year-old Nina Ruzza, whose body was found yesterday morning on Killiney beach.

'That's too sad, seeing her picture. Beautiful she was.'

I look at my neighbour as she wipes the tears from her cheeks onto the grubby grey sleeve of her dressing gown.

'Her whole life ahead of her. Bastard. There should be something worse than prison for the likes of him.' She pulls up the hood on her gown and walks away, her slippers clacking loudly as she goes. Off out for an indignant smoke.

A little sample of what we're in for when everyone knows it's you in there.

FEBRUARY

NINA

He stands before her, his edges shimmering like a mirage. Nina is ready for this. A little too ready. For six years now she has preserved herself, waiting for the right person. The right moment. The boyfriends in her past were never going to get close. The one who pressed himself against her, begging, and then told her she must be a nun or a lesbian. Silly little boy. The boyfriends that she enjoyed, the ones that seemed to really care about her and didn't put her under pressure. The one that told her, instead, that he thought it was beautiful she was still a virgin.

Conor. She loves Conor, but she's not in love with him. She kissed him once, in the back seat of the top deck of a bus on the way home from the cinema. All the way home, in fact, the bus bumping along, jerking their heads together and separating them as they laughed. Or maybe it was just Nina who had laughed. It was not ideal for a first kiss, she had thought at the time, not then knowing that it would happen only the once. Kissing a best friend was different. She was free to be just herself and she was having fun with it. She had seen Conor through his first love, a stunning Swiss girl, who was not a virgin and persuaded him to leave that status behind also. He had deliberated. Discussed it with Nina first of all. Then he broke up with the girlfriend without mentioning it to Nina. Until that night. Nina luxuriated in the kiss. His lips were surprisingly warm and he moved his tongue around the outside of her mouth, slowly first of all, as if happy just to taste her. Then she did the same to him, licking his popcorn saltiness before their tongues met and it began. Sucking and bumping and laughing along. She was there, in the moment, savouring it, feeling herself swelling and tingling unexpectedly, a little alarmingly, then stopping to look at him.

'I wish I had waited for you instead,' he whispered to her. Which changed everything. She shunted a little bit along the seat, away from him.

'Sorry,' she whispered back.

It was never spoken of again.

Jeff Hogan is the person that Nina has waited for. She knows it just as intuitively as she knew with all the others that it would be wrong. He is swaying slightly, despite leaning on his stick. Then she sees why. In his left hand he is holding her laptop. Holding it out to her, unsteadily.

'You left this behind, and we don't want anybody running off with it now, do we?' he says, smiling down at Nina.

'I guess,' Nina says, reaching for it. 'How did you know I was here?'

'I didn't. Not at first. I thought you might come back for

it, so I waited. Had another couple of whiskeys, maybe not the best idea.' He puts his free hand against the door frame. 'Then I told Jack that you had left it behind and I didn't know what to do with it. He said he thought you were staying at the hotel, saw you taking the stairs, apparently. He checked it out for me at reception. Then he offered to bring it to your room. I think he likes you.' Jeff smiles for a moment before casting his gaze beyond Nina. Down to the back of the room.

'But you brought it instead.' Nina keeps the door open with her right foot and holds onto the belt of her gown, slipping her thumbs through it, her fingers splayed and pointing down.

'Yes, well, just to be sure you got it.' He removes his hand from the door frame and takes an unsteady step backwards.

'You look like you could do with a coffee. Come in, if you like.' Nina is surprised at how steady her voice sounds. Tinged with pragmatism.

'I won't, thanks. Cassandra phoned. Ted is running a fever. Looking for me, apparently.'

Cassandra. Now that's better.

'If I could just pop in to use your toilet, that'd be great. I probably shouldn't have polished off your cider,' he says and he laughs.

'Sure, just in there.' Nina gestures to the bathroom and removes her foot from the door, leaving it to slide closed gently behind them. For a moment they stand together in the darkened entrance before she reaches to the bathroom light switch and flicks it on for him. Back at the window she decides to boil the kettle again. Maybe when he comes out the sound of it bubbling will entice him to stay. She sets two cups on saucers at the little round table and sits down to wait. It's a pity, in a way, that it's night-time. The view that she enjoyed earlier out across the bay would be lovely to share with Jeff. Now lights on the ferries out at sea twinkle a different sort of charm into the room.

She hears the toilet flushing and with it the start of the heat in her face, an unfortunate blushing. Quickly she makes her way to the corner and clicks the lamp off so that now the room is lit solely by the blue glow of the television screen, a channel as yet to be selected. He seems to be taking his time though. She takes her iPhone out of her robe pocket and checks. 21.57. She flicks to her voice memo, presses new recording, and slips her phone back in her pocket. Nina pictures him washing his long fingers with care, maybe even cleaning under his smooth nails with their perfect half-moons. An indicator of good thyroid health, she discovered when she googled it. She looks briefly at her own moonless nails, bitten down, although less so than when she was a child. A little tag of skin stands proud from her right index finger. She wonders if he has noticed this about her.

Even with very thorough hand washing Nina decides that he is taking far too long. The kettle is well boiled and there's no sound coming from the bathroom. She walks across the room and listens against the door. Nothing. Then she inhales deeply and knocks.

'Jeff?'

No reply. She turns the round black handle and, holding her breath, she pushes the door open. Jeff is sitting slumped against the bath, his eyes closed, the zip on his cream chinos half down, a splash of wetness in darkened spots on the material. He is holding a towel in his right hand. For a brief moment Nina wonders if there has been an event, but then she sees his chest moving peacefully, in and out. He is sitting on the damp mat Nina used for her shower. She feels the heat going out of her cheeks now.

'There's a ball at my feet,' she says, smiling into the mirror at his words. She will take her time to decide what to do with it.

WEDNESDAY
CASSANDRA

My phone rings and I jump, letting out a little yelp of fright. I look down at it, at Mum on the screen. She'll be frantic. I answer.

'Cassandra, darling, at last. How are you feeling now? Jeff told me what happened.'

What did you say to her?

'Don't worry, Mum. Is Ted okay? Did you get him off to school?'

'Oh no, darling, he's too upset for school today, with you in hospital. He's not himself, not talking much. Not to me anyway. It's all a bit unsettling for him.'

He knows.

'Put him on to me.'

She calls him, I hear her walking, slowly, to the living room, opening the door, the television blasting, the same morning station we have on in here.

'Ted?'

Then I hear her leave, closing the door behind her.

'He's crying, Cassandra.'

Jesus.

'Mum, tell him not to worry at all, everything is going to be okay. Turn off the television and later on only let him watch CBeebies. No news channels, Mum, he's too little. Ask him if he'd like to go with you to the house to feed Tuppence this morning, then bring her back with you. That will comfort him.'

'Okay, darling, yes. I have my keys. How long do they think you'll be in for? I'll ask Jeff to bring Ted in to see you this evening. They can take a taxi. Ted would like that.'

'No, you keep Ted with you and don't come in. I have everything I need and I should be out in no time. Heart arrhythmia, apparently. Wouldn't even know about it if I hadn't gone out for that run.'

'Your father had that.'

'God, you should've told me that years ago. They've been asking if there's any heart stuff in the family and digging around for other causes.'

She doesn't respond. I shouldn't be guilt tripping her, not with all she's about to be hurled into. Another public humiliation. A lifetime of public humiliation.

'It's okay, Mum, just mind Ted for me and if he wants to talk to me send a text and I'll ring him. I have to go now. The doctor is coming.'

The footsteps are loud, purposeful.

'Cassandra Hogan?'

I look up and stare directly into the face of a policeman. Familiar somehow. His arms are folded across his chest and his eyes, slightly shadowed by his cap, are tinged with alarm.

'I'm Detective Inspector Ian Kennedy.'

Ian Kennedy, Sheena's dad. I smile at him in recognition. He takes a step towards me but stops, unsure of himself.

'Apologies, Dr Hogan, I didn't realize it was you I was coming to see. I'd have sent someone else.' He pulls my curtain across and lowers his voice.

'Your doctor has said it's okay for me to ask you a few questions. If you don't feel well enough to respond at the moment, or if you'd prefer that I send someone else, that's no problem.'

I nod my head and he sits down on the chair, placing a recording device on my bedside locker. He presses a button.

'Time, nine twenty-five am, Wednesday, April twenty-second. Witness Dr Cassandra Hogan.'

Then he looks up at me. I'm higher than he is now that he's sitting and I'm on the bed.

'Are you aware that your husband has presented himself for questioning at our station this morning, in connection with the death of a young woman on Killiney beach?'

His face flushes. He is even more uncomfortable than I am. Am I well enough to be questioned? Would I ever feel well enough to be questioned about this?

'No.'

'No?'

'I'm not aware.'

'He says that you might be able to help us with our inquiries.'

How, Jeff? How do you want me to help?

'Did you drive your husband, Jeffrey Hogan, for a swim at Killiney Bay in the early hours of yesterday morning?' He whispers. I wonder if his device will pick it up.

'I did.'

'And did you leave him there as he says you sometimes do, coming back to collect him when he's finished, or did you stay in the car park above the beach?'

How I wish I'd left.

'I stayed.'

'And did you see any interaction between your husband, Jeffrey Hogan, and anyone else on the beach yesterday morning?'

Did I?

'Jeff went in for his swim, as usual. It's too early in the morning for other people to be around. I watched him swim for a bit, and then I checked my emails. Ted was lying down in the back.'

'Ted?'

'Yes, our seven-year-old son.'

'Your husband didn't mention that he was there.'

You didn't mention him. Trying to protect him. Too late.

'Did you see anything at all that might be able to assist us with our inquiries?'

I think of her photo now.

I see her eyes and her lips, shining.

I see her running up the beach to greet you. Running towards her death.

'I think I did, yes,' I whisper, and I see the colour drain out of Ian Kennedy's face.

FEBRUARY

NINA

Nina opens a sachet of Nescafé Gold and tinkles the granules into the small white cup. She pours the boiled kettle water over them and stirs. Then she puts the cup back on its saucer, along with two fingers of shortbread in a maroon tartan wrapper, and she returns to the bathroom. Jeff is still in the same position, but now his mouth is drooping slightly. She tries to remember the signs of a stroke. F.A.S.T. She calls out these letters and thinks she remembers that the F is for face drooping. Is Jeff's face drooping? She kneels down beside him, placing the cup and saucer on his far side. Peering at his face, she takes note of the details that have escaped her so far. A small, dark mole at his left temple. A bump on the ridge of his nose. Bottom teeth slightly overcrowded. Plenty of asymmetry, but not drooping. She remains in this position, allowing his whiskey-sweetened breaths to blow at her and she adjusts her own breathing to match his. She could stay like this, just breathing along with the man she loves, for a very, very long time. The other letters for signs of a stroke should be checked out too. For that she will need to rouse him. But something else first of all. She reaches across to his crotch, pulls the trouser material straight and zips him the rest of the way up.

Jeff lets out a loud snort, juddering him awake. He is staring straight into Nina's face, and as it seems to dawn on him, where he is, what must've happened, the look of fright that dances in his eyes indicates to her that this is not a person experiencing a stroke. She waits. She will take her cue from him.

'God, Nina, I'm sorry. I had a bit of an accident going to the toilet there and I just sat down to dry off for a minute. I must've dozed. This *is* embarrassing.'

S. Slurred speech. Maybe just a little.

'Can you move your arms?'

'What? Of course I can. It's just my leg that's dodgy, thankfully.'

'Show me.'

Jeff raises both arms together and then lets them flop back down into his lap.

'Okay. Good. Any weakness while you were doing that?'

'Are you secretly training to be a medic, Nina Ruzza?' he says, smiling. His mesmerizing asymmetrical smile. His lip curling up just that little bit more on the right side.

'Now that's an idea,' Nina says, feeling a little silly – all this concern over nothing. Like an anxious wife or mother. Something that Jeff may well be trying to get away from.

'Just the speech that's a bit off. How many whiskeys did you have?'

'Four, I think. Then your pint. Thing is I don't really drink any more. The odd glass of wine or two, maybe, but not this stuff. I'm not sure what got into me this evening. I should know better.'

'Don't worry about it. We're allowed to let ourselves go every once in a while. Now that I've decided you're not having a stroke, how about you get up? I've made you some coffee there if you'd like to have it first. Then we can see how you're set.' Clipped and terse. A mixture of a let-down wife and an efficient nurse. How is this happening, she wonders. Jeff Hogan is here, alone in her room with her, and all she wants to do is fix him.

'I'm not sure I can,' Jeff says.

'Not sure you can what?'

'Get up. I'm sorry, Nina. Just to add to the embarrassment, there's no way I can get up from this position without some help.'

Nina bends over him and offers her hands. He reaches out, and as his hands touch hers, she stops. She does not pull him up. She stands there holding his hands, palm to palm, hers tiny in his, and she closes her eyes, allowing him to flood her entire body. It is as if every little part of her life so far has been leading to this one great moment. She is aware that she is naked underneath her robe. That as she bends over him, he may or may not be able to see this. It doesn't matter. She doesn't want to entice him any further. This is just perfect. When she opens her eyes again and looks at him he is staring directly at her mouth.

'Is that sore?'

Nina runs her tongue on the inside of her lip, needling the back of her piercing, and the tiny turquoise stone stud placed in the centre of her bottom lip juts out, catching the light.

'Not this one,' she says and she watches it register. That there are more, hidden.

He closes his eyes for a moment, imagining where perhaps, but he does not ask. 'A symbol of virility and courage in ancient Roman times. Nipple piercing,' he says, then, and she feels his right hand tighten slightly on her left for a moment. Some sort of reflex action. As if he knows it's just that one side.

'I tell a story about it in one of my lectures,' he says, his voice trailing off as he begins to move, bending his good leg in preparation.

'I know,' Nina whispers. She tugs his hands to help him to stand and as he tugs back, she gets pulled down towards him so that her hair brushes off his, her long strands dancing on top of the wave of his.

'God, I feel suddenly very old,' Jeff says, and he smiles up at Nina with sad eyes. 'And you're too slight to be able to pull a heavy old man like me off the ground.'

Slight. Nina bristles at this. Even as she understands what he means, it feels abrasive, insulting somehow. As if there's an insignificance to her. That she's lacking substance. She lets go of his hands.

'Thanks. I'll get your stick and maybe if you throw your arm behind you, you can lean on the bath for support.'

She is glad now though. That little annoyance has clicked her back into helpful nurse mode. Pulled her away from the precipice. From the verge of telling him how she slips into his large first-year lectures on occasion, just to hear his voice. How his lecture on symbols of virility through cinematic time, peppered with his own story of youthful symbolic misadventure and the scar that has been left as a forever reminder, had her book an appointment for herself. How her left side had always felt slightly deformed, but not any longer. How this is one of the many gifts from him to her.

Back from the precipice, Nina is fully sure that while this is the man she is in love with and will lose her virginity to, it will not be like this. He will not be inebriated. He will not be wistful. It will be much more beautiful. There is no rush. As she hands him the stick, she pats the top of his head, a little maternally, and leaves him to it.

He emerges unsteadily, somehow carrying the cup and saucer, clanking along, and makes his way to the little table where Nina sits looking out at the twinkling lights on Howth Head. He places the cup and saucer on the table and pulls the second chair out a little before sitting down. He takes a sip of the coffee and winces, baring his top front teeth. Perfectly straight top front teeth, concealing the imperfect bottom ones.

'I'm sorry about this, Nina.'

'No worries.'

'I think it's just that I'm so excited by it all. Your writing.

The angles you're coming up with. It's so fresh and you're incredibly young. It's puzzling in a way.'

Again. That fizzle of disappointment. Just that little bit insulting.

'So drinking helps you to work the puzzle out?'

'God, no, not at all. But it does bring me back to the early days. I was a bit like you, you know?'

Nina cannot imagine what he means. She shakes her head.

'You know, idealistic, passionate about my subject. English and the classics more than film back then. Plenty of exciting ideas. Nowhere to put them.'

'How do you mean?'

'I didn't find the right mentor, someone to match my passion, to recognize it, even.'

'So what did you do?'

'I drank it away mainly. Slowed myself down. Became less excited, less productive. Did enough to get through and to establish an academic life, no more.'

Jeff's tone is becoming unappealing. Melancholic. Nina is not a person who indulges self-pity in others. It is most likely the alcohol, the depressant after-effects, as she has never seen him like this, but it's beginning to irk her. 'A good life,' she offers, to get him back on track.

'Oh, yes, yes. But if I had continued with that passion, much as I'm sure you will, I would've ended up somewhere different.'

'Where's that?'

'Another university. Maybe in another country. Perhaps a

full professorship. Who knows. But I just stayed where I was, ticking along, ending up in film studies instead of English. I took the easy way.'

'That's not what it looks like to me. You've published so many papers. You wrote the seminal text on film theory. Not edited – wrote. Your *Mythologies of Masculinity in Modern Italian Film* is widely sourced and quoted. You're very much admired.'

'Thanks. But when I tell people I'm Assistant Professor of Film Studies I feel a sort of gnawing emptiness. A visceral thing, you know? I can't explain it. I just don't feel that I'm taken seriously.'

'Then why are you taking my work seriously?'

'Yours is completely different, Nina. It's singing with freshness and potential. The depth of the grasp you have on Fellini is astonishing. I can see where I might be going wrong with my latest book draft now, how I can improve it, so it makes me believe that there's still a contribution to make. Maybe an excellent one. Even at this stage. It makes me think that this is exactly the right place for me to be, after all. I know it may seem silly to you, but it's given me a lot of hope back.'

'Well, let's hope you don't drink that away,' she says, surprising herself with her tone. Parental almost. Out of kilter with this string of compliments. She needs to pull it back, somehow. She digs her thumb nail into the burnt skin on her right hand. A pleasing pain pulses through her.

'Yes, sir,' Jeff says, saluting now. 'Aren't you a bit too wise for a, what's this you are, twenty-five-year-old?'

'Twenty-two.'

'Twenty-two,' Jeff repeats and looks out the window, as if this is a number which is worth some deep thought.

'What were you up to at my age?'

'Oh god. Up to my neck in Joyce, I suppose.'

'What about the drinking?'

'Later. Yes, that came a good bit later,' he says, his gaze drifting off again towards the sea. 'I'd like you to do something for me, Nina.'

Nina feels the sudden ferocious thud of her heart, a hammering that he might just be able to hear. She will, she thinks now. She'll do whatever it is.

'Read the Molly Bloom soliloquy in *Ulysses*.' He places his cup back on the saucer and, leaning on his stick, he gets up from his chair.

'Why?' Nina says, irked that this random, out-of-left-field thought is all he seems to want to say.

'It will inform our work together,' he says, and he walks towards the door. Sombre and serious, as if heading off to battle, his loyalty – or is it his lack of disloyalty? – stinging her with his every step away. He places his hand on the golden handle and, pulling the door towards him, he leaves the room without looking back.

It is as if Nina is treading on a half-inflated bouncy castle, swampy and uncertain. She did not wish for anything to happen tonight, not while he was drunk. Yet here he was, with her, alone in this room and he didn't even try. She wonders if perhaps he is even more like her than he alluded to earlier. Maybe he has the same values and wishes to wait until he is sober. Which could be as soon as tomorrow night. She feels herself begin to steady, to calm back down. So much progress has been made tonight. He came to her room, entered it, saw her in her bathrobe, displayed a drunken vulnerability and allowed her to help him. She had held his hands, his long fingers wrapping around hers, craving her support. He could have tried anything on and claimed misjudgement due to the alcohol, but he did not. There's a comforting decency to that, Nina tells herself now. This is as important to him as it is to her.

She returns to the little round table, picks up his cup, and drinks the dregs of his coffee from it, placing her lips exactly where his would've been, tasting him as she looks out across the bay. For tonight this is enough. She begins to feel the tiredness envelop her. She listens to her body. Does what it tells her to do now. She climbs up onto her bed, loosens the belt on her robe and takes her iPhone out of her pocket, checking the time. 23.01. She pins in her code, the room number on his door in college. Then she sees the blue line racing across the screen, the little white lines following it, bouncing on the black screen like a heart monitor. Still recording. She had forgotten she had done this while she waited for him. She presses done. Then she slips between the tight starched sheets and presses play. Closing her eyes, she listens to the sound of his voice, the timbre of it. Melodic and soothing. She listens to the moods. Apologetic and embarrassed at first, humorous for a little bit, wistful at the end.

Each one causing a different feeling to thrum in her, a heady mix. A whole hour of a recording of his beautiful resonance that she can play whenever she likes, as if he's with her, here in her room, still. She can pause and replay over her favourite middle bits, when Jeff is teasing her for her medical vigilance, when he is at ease with her and lets her know. This she will play many times. Jeff has given her homework to do for tomorrow night and she will do it, she has plenty of time. First though, she must sleep. Just after midnight she presses play again and slips further down in the bed. She succumbs to the drag of sleep just after Jeff says, *I'd like you to do something for me, Nina.*

WEDNESDAY

CASSANDRA

I whisper it out to Ian Kennedy, as if in a trance, not looking at him, but picking a spot on the wall, a brown fleck that I deliver it to, and I don't think I even stop to draw breath, because what is the point, it was all so quick, too quick to know what was taking place and he needs to understand that too. I can slow it right down in my own mind, of course, slo-mo the whole thing, every step, every movement of hers and yours, even the waves crashing behind, the glint of early sun on the water, her shirt being carried off on a slow gust, her breasts against your bare chest, her mouth moving ceaselessly, her head tilting back and her long hair swinging as she seems to laugh up to the sky, you putting her down, shaking your head, her scream.

That's how I most often see it, in slow motion, and freezing it in certain places too. When I do, it's not intense jealousy or rage that I feel. It's something even more unnerving. So I press fast forward now and tell it rapidly, staring at the brown fleck on the cream wall. Then I turn to Ian Kennedy.

'Yes so that's what I saw, or what I think I saw, because as

I'm sure you already know I am withdrawing from codeine and how reliable I am as a witness or otherwise is debatable,' I say, to my surprise, and then the gush of tears, out of nowhere. The relief of having now told, having spoken it out loud.

'What did you do next?' he asks, pushing through, ignoring the emotion.

'I drove him into UCD and took Ted to school after breakfast. Came home again. Put on a wash.'

'And did you wash your husband's items from his swim?'

He knows the answer. I can tell. I nod.

'You nodded your head there. Does that mean that you did wash the items from your husband's swim?'

He wants it recorded.

'I did. Yes.'

'And did your husband ask you to do this?'

'No. It's just something I do every day.'

He switches the recording device off and he smiles, shaking his head.

'My god.' He stands up, towering over me and drops his voice to a low rumble. 'You witnessed your husband killing that poor girl on the beach and then you went home and continued on, having breakfast, throwing on a wash, seeing my daughter and me in the guise of a helper. You were completely calm. Popped a few pills, had you? You make me sick.'

He slashes through the curtain, talking still. 'He's denying it, by the way, so your statement will be most helpful to our investigation. Might bring you in too. Question you about concealing evidence, perverting the course of justice, that sort of thing.'

I listen to him leave and then I jump off the bed and look around to see if anyone on the ward has seen him come and go. My ribs sink down in relief when I see the empty bed across from me.

It's like sticking my finger in the wall of the dam.

I know it's coming, the terrible flood.

It's here already, waiting to be let loose.

But if I can just keep it back until I get out it will help.

This last little bit of control.

The old lady across and to the left is wheezing into an oxygen mask, eyes closed.

I'm safe for now.

You told the police I was there so you wanted me to be a witness, or is it that you expected me to lie? To say I was there and saw nothing whatsoever? You'll know I had read your text by the time they were coming my way to question me. You'll think I've taken your cue from it, taken your flattery well, cast doubt on myself because of the codeine. You'll be assured that my rational self will re-emerge triumphant and sort it all out for you. Well, when it comes down to it, bare-faced lying is not something I can do. I can put telling things off until I'm ready, but as you know I'll always seek to speak the truth. So your flattery and gaslighting didn't work. Not on me.

I open the text up again, and glance at the words. *Don't let this destroy us.*

There's a clacking sound getting close to me.

'Got this for you down at the shop,' my neighbour says, thrusting a can of Coke at me. The coldness of it in my hand is soothing.

'It's good for the headaches and you'll be craving the sugar like I was.'

I'm not quite the opiate addict you were, or are, I want to say.

'Thanks.'

'I was nearly knocked flat by a policeman when I was coming out of the shop. Furious he was. Didn't even say sorry, the cheek of him,' she says, and she flicks the television back on.

'Ah, look.' She turns up the volume, and the headlines dance across the screen.

It's done.

A man in his late forties has been arrested in connection with the death of twenty-two-year-old Nina Ruzza, whose body was found early yesterday morning by a dog walker on Killiney beach in South County Dublin.

'Now they just have to charge him,' she says, and she smiles and shakes her head at the same time, just like Ian Kennedy did minutes ago. That's what you do to people. What you've always done. Make a contradiction out of them.

'I got this in the shop too. I'm finished with it, here.' She hands me a copy of the *Daily Mirror*. A different picture of Nina takes up most of the front page. She's looking directly into the camera, her head tilted up slightly, as if it's a selfie. The shot picks out the copper highlights that pepper her otherwise dark ringlets. Her mouth is slightly open, unsmiling, but her eyes are sparkling, as if she is pleased about something. Her skin is smooth and pale, relieved by the contrast of the colour in her eyes and lips.

'I know. Stunning,' she says.

FEBRUARY

NINA

Nina sits at the little table by the window in her hotel room, a freshly made coffee in the cup that Jeff used last night, and she googles Molly Bloom's soliloquy. She reads it through, quickly at first, searching. Then she reads it slowly, out loud, wondering when she should take a breath, how she takes a breath, without punctuation. What does Jeff mean, this will inform their work together? Google offers her the option of listening to it, to an actress performing it. It is now, as she listens to Angeline Ball, that she begins to get it. What he's asking of her.

She flicks to her email and presses to create a new message.

I've read it. Didn't get it until I listened to it. Now I do.

She sends it. Then she goes to her recordings and plays Jeff talking to her, as she looks out at the harbour and across the navy-blue sea to Howth Head. To where Molly got

Leopold Bloom to propose to her. Nina would like to be able to block her own voice from the recording, sounding, as she hears it now, like a bossy older sister, an unmistakable air of irritation and impatience, as if with a wayward little brother. Jeff should've got up and left much sooner, which is what Nina herself would have done if the tables were turned. Instead, he had opened up, let her in. Then he had left her with instructions on how to move on from here. Rattling within every line of the soliloquy were clues for her. Now all she had to do was wait to hear from him again. Then she would let him know exactly how well she understood.

Yes I said yes I will Yes, Nina says out loud, sitting on the toilet in the bathroom, and as she wipes herself, and sees that it has now begun, the bright red stain luminous on the sheet of toilet paper, she laughs. Another little sign that he is perfectly in tune with her.

Nina puts her phone in her jacket pocket, zips it up and leaves the hotel. The hours of checking for his response, repeatedly, ever more frequently, has had a physical effect on her. Each time her iPhone screen tells her that her mail has been updated two minutes ago, she feels a little surge of hope. He could easily have responded in the last two minutes. She rubs the screen down, until it tells her it is checking for mail, trying to find his words. Then the plunge, in the pit of her stomach, a downward raw force, as the screen tells her that it has updated just now. The only thing for it is to get out and walk them away, the thoughts that are spinning in her, spiralling her downwards.

The cold bite of the early-evening February air, crisp and clear, is immediately soothing. She should not have stayed in the stiflingly hot hotel room all day, allowing her thoughts to marinate into a sticky gelatinous mess. Already, as she cuts down past Teddy's ice-cream shop and crosses the road to walk along the promenade, she can feel her thoughts loosening, dispersing. She breathes in the seaweed-infused air rhythmically, holding it inside and counting to five each time before releasing it, all along the walkway. As she does so, she untangles the blame. He is not responding for a reason unrelated to how she was or how she seemed to him last night. She may have come across a little bit judgemental, a small bit preachy, but he was drunk and unlikely to have noticed. If he hadn't been drunk, their time would've been very different.

A small dog, a Cavalier King Charles spaniel, runs over to Nina, offering himself to be stroked. She puts her hand on his soft head and he looks up at her, large, dark eyes expressing gratitude, before he darts away to walk alongside his owner. Nina can feel something change in her, some pleasure hormone flooding her, endorphins or dopamine, perhaps, from this physical contact with the dog. She picks up her pace a little as the night lights spring on above her, shining down on the walkway. As she gets to the end, beside the little exercise park, she cuts off the path and steps up onto a walker machine. She pumps on it for a minute, looking out across the darkening sea, and it is during this time that she decides.

She will continue on out to Dalkey to see if there's any sign of him. His day at college will be over and he should be home soon.

WEDNESDAY

CASSANDRA

I wake from the depths of sleep to the sound of the lunch trolley coming my way. For a brief moment I am serene. It does not hit me immediately. I am my old self, in our world, safe. It is as he clanks the plate down on my tray and removes the tin cover, revealing a grey mass of meat that it comes to me like the backlash of a whip.

'Tea?'

'Yes please.'

Roast beef and Yorkshire pudding. How I used to love this as a child. The Sunday roast. Dad would have finished his work for the day, and we'd sit, the four of us, and devour it. I'd tell him how I had helped to make the pudding, always keen to shine near him.

Well now, that has got to be the very best Yorkshire pudding in the land, he would say, each time, pulsing a warmth through me.

Yeah, and I slaughtered the cow, Henry would throw in sometimes, making him laugh. Something I was never able to do.

'I'm a vegetarian,' I tell the orderly. He clanks the metal

tin lid back on the plate, removes it and then replaces it with another one. He takes the tin lid off this plate, and before I have a chance to say a word, he's gone. A salmon darne sits amid a congealed mass of white sauce flecked with dill. Two scoops of mashed potato. Some deflated-looking peas. He didn't want to know whether I eat fish or not. Tough shit if you don't, he seemed to be saying. What will it be like for you, I wonder. Prison food. Queueing up with your tray with the other inmates. Not quite the university restaurant. I think of all the times we met for lunch in there, among the busy buzz of the students, and how exhilarating I used to find it, seeing you at ease in your zone. Students and colleagues, nodding or saying hello to you, sometimes without you noticing, as you would be so focused on me, on our conversation, as if it was the only thing in the world worth your time. That is something you could always do back then. You could always look me in the eye and make me feel that my words were of the utmost importance to you, pivotal to the rest of your day. Even just telling you how Ted was going off to school, what he did or said, and then some little domestic details, smoke curling out of the tumble dryer, Tuppence peeing by the fireplace, some little drama. You'd listen and you'd make me feel as if it wasn't humdrum at all. That it was just as special as your day, the lectures that you love giving, the irritating daily politics. You'd let me speak much more than you would, as if it was more stimulating than anything you'd have to say yourself, and I'd go off, back out to the suburbs for my next appointment, feeling valued, excited even, about the rest of the day. We both know that I'd be working differently if it wasn't for Ted. That while he is little I've chosen to be a glorified stay-at-home mum. One who can pepper her day with appointments, working from home, tailoring it to suit Ted's needs. We'd discussed how when he's older I could go for a full-time post, get back out there and drink up the conviviality, the validation. You'd often finish off with something along the lines of it not being all it's cracked up to be, all the conviviality being twinned with equal amounts of depressing reality about human nature, competitiveness, back-biting, almost cancelling any benefits out. I'd drive away feeling so very lucky, with you and Ted and my world that I am designing away from the pitfalls of the workplace. I'd leave feeling very special, to you, to Ted and even to myself.

Now I wonder about it all.

Was that just a way you had of controlling me?

FEBRUARY

NINA

She sings the address over in her head, remembered from when she googled Cassandra Hogan, and there it was, offered right up to her. *Dr Cassandra Hogan, Child and Adolescent Psychotherapist, 'Hestia', Tubbermore Road, Dalkey, Co. Dublin*. It had unnerved her at the time, a little pang of something hitting her physically, drying her mouth. The Dr bit, maybe, or the fact that she had taken his name, Nina had not been expecting that. The address itself, even. Not only could she picture that this would be a lovely place to live, but the name that they had given it, or inherited from previous owners. Their home had a name. At the time this had made Nina feel nauseous. Not now though. Now as she says the name, rolls it around in her mind and then says it out loud twice, it is not jealousy she feels, but something else. A little frisson.

She begins to jog, down by Bullock Harbour, past two seals, their dark heads bobbing in the waves as fish ends are tossed into them by a small group of teenagers, laughing and chattering above. She drops the jogging to a fast walk pace, down Convent Road, and then slower again, as she sees the junction of the road on which he lives. As she sets foot on his road, a high-pitched whining noise rings in Nina's ears. It has happened before, coming and going without rhyme or reason, something she has discussed with her GP and manages well enough when it occurs. But it is not until now that she recognizes the probable cause. It happens just when she needs to have all her senses finely tuned, to be on high alert, to find him. It is far from ideal. She keeps going though, on up the road, until she is standing outside his house.

The name is not on the gate post but she knows that this one is his. She's zoomed into it from above countless times on Google street view. Deceptively small from face on now, she thinks, knowing as she does about the double roof stretching it back. The skylight indicating that the cottage space is well used. Now she stands at the narrow path that divides the garden in two and leads from the gate up to the front door, a burnt sienna red. A palm tree stands close to the cottage, casting a shadow enhanced by the street light, directly onto the magnolia-painted front. The walls either side of the walk-in gate are taller than Nina and a leylandii hedge just in front of the wall is taller again, overlapping the wall and secluding the cottage further. There are no lights on inside. They are not home. Home. She lets her eyes search for the name now, and when she sees it, just to the left of the door, chiselled into granite stone, she feels the same sensation as she had when she read it for the first time. *Hestia*. Virgin goddess of the hearth and the home. A tightening in her chest, as if someone has a fist in there and is squeezing, hard. She begins her deep breathing again.

A dog barks, which could be coming from the cottage or from somewhere close by, it's difficult to make it out with the ringing in her ears. She steps onto the little pathway, between the garden walls, and steadies herself by holding onto the open gate for a moment. The bay windows either side of the door are without blinds, and if they have curtains, they are drawn so far back as to be invisible to Nina. Inviting, she thinks, as she steps onto the grass and makes her way up to the living-room window. She cups her hands over her eyes and peers inside. Wooden floors, a white rug at the hearth. Sparse, really, from what she can see. Nina is about to try the other window when she hears a car pulling up outside. The slamming of doors. Voices. She runs down to the bottom corner of the garden and squishes herself into the dark leylandii.

'Tuppence is going mad,' she hears, and it's Ted speaking, close to her, and then she sees him on the little path, walking quickly up to the front door.

'She must've heard the car.' A woman's voice, English accent, northern. She sees her walk behind Ted, tall, so much taller than she had imagined, with silky white-blonde hair tied in a ponytail. She is holding a key out towards the door and then Nina watches as Jeff walks up his garden path, briefcase in right hand and stick in left. Cassandra stands a full head above him. The door is flung open and the alarm beeps, waiting to be turned off, which Cassandra does with an easy efficiency, turning the lights on too, and the barking gets louder and louder as Ted opens a door inside and makes a fuss of the dog in the hallway. She sounds indignant and shrill until Jeff closes the front door and she calms down.

Nina can feel the thud of her heart in her neck. The dog could've run out of the cottage and exposed her or any one of them could've turned around and spotted some part of her, something sticking out, but they did not. The lights flick on in the living room, revealing black wooden beams in the ceiling, a crowded bookshelf beside the fireplace to the left, an antique mirror above it, a collage of family photographs framed all together to the right.

Cassandra walks in. Graceful. Her coat is shed now and she's dressed simply, a white grandfather shirt hanging over black leggings. She kneels at the hearth, doing something that Nina can't quite see, a couch concealing her, but then Cassandra stands up and steps backwards and Nina can see the orange flames of a freshly lit fire licking up the chimney breast. Cassandra is still, staring at her creation, until Ted and the dog join her, the dog jumping up at her, jumping high off the floor with excitement and Cassandra scoops her up into her arms and kisses her on the head. She's smiling at the dog, a cute tricolour Sheltie, talking to her, and Nina can see Cassandra's face reflected in the mirror, a subtle prettiness shining out, a kindness about her eyes. If the circumstances were different, Nina imagines that this is a person she wouldn't mind getting to know somehow. She needs to push this thought back down. It would be better if she hadn't come, better if she could still picture Jeff's wife as a blank, bland person who somehow got lucky. She cannot un-see what she has just seen, but she will do everything she can to shove it away.

Lights in the other front window flick on and it is Jeff now walking into that room as Nina's heart pounds, thumping violently in her chest. He stands for a moment, holding on to the mahogany post at the end of the bed. Their bed. Perfectly unmade. A crumpled cream duvet is strewn halfway across it. Pillows dimpled to the shape of their heads. They left in a rush. He sits on the red-sheeted mattress, and bends over to reach his shoes, untying his laces. All of his movements seem laboured, as if Nina is watching him in slow motion. He is never like this when she meets him. Even with his limp and stick, he's swift somehow. Vibrant. He sits back up straight, shoes removed now. He is still wearing his shirt from yesterday. Faded lilac. A perfect complement to his olive skin. Nina thinks of how she noticed that the cuffs come down just that little bit long on his hands, as if the shirt has been passed on to him by someone larger, expecting him to just grow into it. She smiles, remembering. Those beautiful hands in his lap on the bathroom floor, gripped around her towel. The darting dance of his dark eyes as he woke and worked out what was taking place.

Now, as he fiddles at the waist of his chinos for a moment, Nina lets out a sound, a soft mewling sound that she has never heard herself make before. He tilts onto his side and lifts his legs up onto the bed, and lies there in a foetal position before shifting onto his back, his hands folded across his chest. It's too early, way too early for bed, but then Nina thinks of how tired he must be, drunk last night, a full day at work today, and all that must be playing on his mind. All that she has given him to think about. No wonder he didn't answer her email, poor thing. She watches his chest rise and fall, rise and fall, and the rhythm of it is making her feel tired herself. How she'd love to join him, lie down there beside him, put her hand in his and doze off to his breaths.

The cold air is beginning to bite at her, now that she's not moving. It's time to go. She crawls out of the bush and stays down on her hands and knees, inching towards the little gate. She hears the dog kick off again, louder and louder, and she glances back to Jeff's room, his head now turned, his eyes looking out the window, looking directly down at her. He sits up as she makes it to the gate. Then she stands up and she runs as she hears a window opening, Jeff's voice ringing out, 'Hey'. She runs as fast as she can, down his road to the junction and then left up to Finnegan's pub.

WEDNESDAY

CASSANDRA

I keep the newspaper on the pillow beside me. She's looking into me, her beautiful, happy eyes glinting, telling me something. The nurse comes and goes, checking my blood pressure and my pulse, saying nothing, not that I'd want to know anyway. I lie back down. When they work out that the withdrawals have eased and it is no longer necessary for me to be clogging up the system, blocking a bed, they will release me, let me go home.

Home. Whatever that is now. I'll leave the country. That's all I can think. I'll take Ted and Mum back to Sheffield. Stay with Henry at first in London. Rent out the cottage to tenants here, Mum's house too, unless she wants to sell. Start over. My reputation is ruined here, Ian Kennedy let me know that. I'm sure that's what you'd want for us. Not that I'll be consulting you. You can get on with the new life you've created for yourself. When I'm called to give evidence at your trial, I will travel back for it and I will tell the truth about what I saw, be humiliated by my own actions or the lack of them, maybe even more than by yours. The codeine dependency will come out, be all over the newspapers, along with photographs, and England won't be far enough away from it. I'll have to move again after that.

'Would you look at that,' says my neighbour, pressing the remote at the television, shaking it, as if that will help. I get off the bed to pull my curtain back across again. I'm in no humour to talk to her, but then she says it.

'They're after letting him go.'

I run out to her, grab the remote and point it, pressing until the volume goes up beyond what is reasonable, and the newsreader bellows the words out.

A man in his late forties has been released without charge in relation to the death of twenty-two-year-old Nina Ruzza whose body was found in the early hours of yesterday morning on Killiney beach. Paul O'Connell is reporting from Blackrock police station where this man presented himself for questioning some hours ago. Paul, what can you tell us?

'They haven't enough to charge him, not yet,' she says, and she lets out a little mocking snort.

I sit on the end of my bed and put my head between my knees, to stop the feeling that I'm going to faint coming fully on.

'Shut up, will you?' I blurt out at her, and I listen.

Yes, Cliona, all I can tell you is that this man, who cannot be named, was arrested in connection with the young woman's death at ten o'clock this morning, having presented himself at the station six hours earlier. He has now been released without charge.

Is it known why he was released, Paul?

We have not been given that information yet, Cliona, this is an ongoing investigation, but I do know that the police were waiting for the results of the post-mortem carried out last night, with initial results from the examination by the Assistant State Pathologist at the scene proving inconclusive.

Thank you, Paul. We'll return to this later in the programme should any further developments take place.

I climb back into the bed and I wait.

I hear my phone beep with a text message and I ignore it.

I pull the dangling cord with the bell into the bed beside me, thumb on red button.

You weren't named.

I know you're on your way.

FEBRUARY

NINA

Nina ducks inside the pub, out of breath now but relieved to be among strangers. Up at the bar she orders a hot whiskey and the barman smiles at her, a kind smile as if to say she looks like she could do with it. He doesn't ask her for ID but tells her instead that he'll drop it down to her. She chooses the alcove by the fireplace, the fire as yet unlit. The hot whiskey arrives, steaming, a red napkin wrapped around the glass, cloves sticking into a slice of lemon. She rubs her hands together, her fingertips numb and tingling slightly. Then she wraps her fingers around the glass and waits for a minute before taking her first sip. It's good and sweet, just what she needs, and the taste of cloves makes her think about Christmastime for a moment. Christmas in Hestia rather than her own home.

She unzips her pocket and takes out her phone. On the screen she can see a text message from Stephano. 'Call me.' He needs her to go into the shop, most likely. She takes some more soothing sips. Maybe a stint in the shop would be a good distraction, take her mind off Jeff and all that has happened in the last twenty-four hours. She checks her emails first of all. He hasn't responded. Then she checks her sent box, just to be sure. It's there, so he should've got it. It doesn't demand a response as such, and as she reads it back she can feel herself getting annoyed. It's a little too cryptic. If Jeff has seen it, which he must have, he may not know what she's on about. *I've read it. Didn't get it until I listened to it. Now I do.* Why she didn't finish it off with, *Let me know which night suits best to meet and discuss,* she doesn't know. Seeing him just now in his own home has shifted something in her, created a little chasm, confused her somehow. She should not have gone along. She drinks down the rest of the whiskey, sucking hard on the glass to drain the dregs.

'That good, eh?' the barman says, smiling at her. She's beginning to warm back up.

'Same again, please.' She notices a couple in the alcove across from her, huddled together, glancing her way before continuing with their chat. A few years older than her, making their plans.

'I'll just light this first, nippy out there tonight,' the barman says. It's a gas fire, a good imitation and instant gratification. She thinks of Cassandra lighting her real fire, the earthiness of it catching Nina again now. Earthy and competent. Not what she was expecting. Nina removes the cloves from the slice of lemon in her glass and places them on the table before popping the lemon into her mouth and sucking down. The remnants of the whiskey and sugar go first and she is left with a pleasing bitterness. The door swings open and closed again as people come and go, a blast of biting cold air each time, along with a little residual hope. If Jeff saw that it was her crawling out of the garden, he might just come looking for her. What he called out, a soft, questioning 'Hey', could have been for her or just because he saw something and the dog was barking. At the time, in that moment, Nina had hoped that he did not see her, and convinced herself that he couldn't have, with the lights on inside the cottage and the deep darkness of outside. Now though, with a little distance and the whiskey warming her, she would quite like it if he did know. She spits out the lemon, and pops it back into the empty glass just as the barman arrives with her second one.

'Will I take those?' He picks up the glass and motions to the five little cloves on the table.

'No thanks. How much do I owe you?' She hands him a twenty-euro note.

'Back with your change in a minute,' he says, disappearing off.

She fiddles with the cloves, breaking the tops off for eyes and working them into different emojis.

The door swings again.

Nina looks up to see Cassandra standing before her, holding the door wide open.

WEDNESDAY

CASSANDRA

The phone beeps again and I pick it up this time. It's not you. A message from Mum. *Ted needs to speak to you.* I ring her immediately. Ted answers.

'I told her not to go away, Mum.' His voice is muffled.

'Who, darling?'

'Nina.'

'Nina?'

'Yes. She came to school at going-home time, and she said she had to go away to Italy and I asked her not to go because I really like her and now she's dead, and I think it's my fault because she didn't go and when I told Dad he was very cross that she spoke to me at school.'

I get up from my bed, walk down the ward and out onto the corridor so that I can't be overheard.

'No, sweetheart, it's not your fault. I'm very sorry that you're so sad. I know how much you liked her. Tell me, when did she talk to you?'

'On Monday. I was waiting to get the special bus with my friends to after-school club and she was there, laughing and

285

giving me big hugs and being funny and her eyes were sparkly and her face was wet and she was talking a lot, Mum, and I had to get on the bus then, so I said don't go to her, I said please don't, Mum, I remembered my manners and she didn't go so it is my fault.'

'Did she say why she was going?'

'She said she was going home.'

'What did Dad say when you told him?'

'He said it wasn't appo, approp—'

'Appropriate?'

'Yes. He said he was going to tell her never to do that again, the same as when she came to our house one night. He told her not to do it again, that it wasn't appropriate. He was very cross when she collected me from school one day too.'

I can hear his muffled sobs.

'And now she won't be able to, and we can't invite her in for a cup of tea when she's a student, like he said, and you would have invited her in, I know you would, but Dad says you wouldn't.'

'Did Dad ask you not to tell me any of this, Ted?'

'No, not really. He said it was against the rules and no one knew about it except me and that you had enough on your plate.'

'What rules?'

'His work rules. They'd be cross if they knew he was helping her, and you'd be cross about it too because you like rules, but Nina says rules are made to be broken.'

I've made it all the way to the café. I need to get the hell out of this place, get back to Ted, reassure him, somehow.

'You know what, Ted, I'll be home very soon, I'm feeling much better. We can have a proper chat about it all then. Just look after Tuppence and Gran for me and try not to worry. It's not your fault.'

'I wish I'd told you about Nina before, Mum. You'd really like her too.'

'I know, angel, but you did what you thought your dad wanted you to do. You were being a good little boy, doing your best. I'm proud of you.'

'That's what Nina said, too. Then she gave me something to put in my school bag, in the front pocket, and she said to wait until Friday when she'd be happy in Italy and we could open it, you, me and Dad, in Hestia, in front of the fire. That's what she said, Mum.'

What the hell did she give him?

His voice is no longer crackling at least, comforted by the words that Nina and I seem to have shared with him. I pull a chair out and sit at a table, sugar granules crunching under the weight of my elbow as I hold the phone to my ear still, wondering what I can possibly say next.

'Mum?'

'Yes, that's okay, Ted. It's only Wednesday, so let's do as she asked and wait until Friday. Good boy.'

I say goodbye to Ted and switch my phone off. I let my

arms flop across the table, soaking up slopped drops of coffee from earlier visitors or patients.

I know what I need to do now, it's just how to get to do it.

I feel my calf muscles cramping, as if I'm out on a long, cold swim.

FEBRUARY

NINA

Her neck begins to map and she hangs her head down, staring into her glass, before thumbing her phone, busying herself. Lots of voices, all women, and they file in through the door. Nina can feel them scanning for a seating area. Mercifully, her section is too small and she sees, peripherally, the group gravitate to the right, to a large section on the other side of the door. She allows herself to look up fleetingly as Cassandra passes, her sleek hair down now, resting on her shoulders, her clothes changed, thick black tights with blue suede ankle boots, a plum skirt just above the knee, a swing jacket tied at the waist.

'Ladies,' the barman greets them as they begin to undo their coats and settle themselves.

'It's book-club night again already?'

Laughter and chit-chat fill the air.

'A good one this time?' he asks

'I didn't get to finish it, but don't tell this lot. By the time they've had a couple of glasses they'll never know the difference.' Cassandra's voice, unmistakable now to Nina, rings out and the others laugh.

'I'll take your orders in just a moment.' He walks over to Nina, and even as she stares hard at the fire, she can sense it. Cassandra's gaze following him, landing on her. She holds her breath.

'Thanks, love.' He puts her change down on the table and she doesn't acknowledge it, doesn't say a word. When he leaves her table to return to the ladies she lets her breath go and allows herself a fleeting glance. Cassandra's jacket is off now, her straight hair resting on the shoulders of a black shirt. She's looking down at something, her phone perhaps, and a line creases down the centre of her forehead.

'We'll have to fire you,' one of the ladies booms out with a deep, husky voice.

'How many times is that now?'

'I know. Seriously lax at the moment, girls, sorry,' Cassandra says.

'Ah, no, I'm only messing with you. It's just that you admit it. I bet if we ask everyone to put their hands on their hearts and tell the truth you wouldn't be alone.'

'Right, what can I get you ladies?' the barman says, standing in front of Cassandra, blocking Nina's view. She listens to the women, all white-wine orders, Pinot Grigio, mostly, and then to Cassandra.

'A pint of Guinness, please.' Nina hears herself say *wow*, it slips out. Everything about Cassandra is different from what she had imagined. The barman leaves with the orders. The women have formed a circle around the table and they're taking their books out, waiting for their drinks to arrive. Cassandra is talking intently to the woman who teased her, head lowered, quiet words, while the others do table-tennis banter.

'Whose turn is it to chair the fun tonight?' one of them asks.

'I think it's mine, but if someone else could do it I'd be grateful, I haven't been feeling the best today,' Cassandra says, and the woman she's been talking to jumps in, offering, saying it's no problem at all. Nina sips her second hot whiskey, not that she really wants it now. She thinks back to seeing Cassandra in the living room and Jeff in the bedroom. To how she didn't see them together, interacting, talking. To how he hasn't sent her an email about meeting up. He must be in the doghouse. She knocks back the rest of her drink and gets up to leave, making sure not to look sideways as she passes the table of women. She pulls the door open, which then swings shut behind her, blasting the pub with a gust of cold night air.

Back at the cottage, the curtains are drawn across the two front windows now. Nina walks up the path and knocks on the front door, gently, in case Ted is asleep. The barking begins. The dog is at the door, sniffing for recognition. Barks are replaced by whines. Nina doesn't feel her mouth going dry, nor her heart pounding as it did earlier. She just needs to know that he is okay. It's her fault, after all, that he's in the doghouse. Even as she hears him approach and the door opens just a crack she feels steady and sure.

'Nina? Christ, what are you doing here?' He's bending slightly, holding the dog by the collar. He's in Nina's direct eye-line.

'Are you okay after last night?' she says, not perturbed by the irritation in his voice, the clouded gaze of his irises.

'Okay? Yes, yes, of course I am.'

'It's just that you didn't answer my email, and you had said that we could meet again tonight, remember?'

'Did I? Oh god, no, no, that wouldn't have been possible. Cass has something on. Look, Nina, I'm in the middle of reading Ted his bedtime story. I'm sorry if there's been some sort of confusion. I'll email you when I can to organize another meeting.'

'Okay. I wanted to let you know that I did as you asked, and I get it. And yes, I will work towards publishing that article with you.'

'Ah, good, good.' Jeff nods, but it is as if he's elsewhere, as if he's not quite seeing her.

'Dad?'

Ted stands behind his father and peeps out from his elbow. He's wearing light-blue-framed glasses.

'Cool,' Nina says and gives him a thumbs up.

'I'll be along in a minute to finish the story, Ted. Back to bed now,' Jeff says, pulling Nina's smile away from the child and back to him.

'Look, Nina I have to go,' he says in a loud whisper.

'Please don't come to our house again. I didn't know that you knew where I lived, but, you know, it's not really appropriate.'

Nina waits until she sees Ted reach the end of the hall.

'Appropriate? You didn't seem too concerned about that last night,' she says, turning her back on him and marching down the path, pulling the gate hard towards her and leaving it to clang.

She can feel her phone vibrating in her pocket and she whips it out, thinking that it is him, that somehow he's got her number and is calling her. Stephano's name flashes. She answers.

'You need to go home, Nina. It's Maria. I'll come and get you.'

WEDNESDAY

CASSANDRA

I stay at the café, on watch. If you're coming to see me, I'd rather we talk out here, in the open. The din of a central area in this busy hospital at visiting time will drown our words to those around us. You'll have to pass, and I won't miss you, not that you'd be out of place here among the crutches and the wheelchairs. You could slip on by, but it's not your stick or your slow, laboured slap of a walk that will alert me to you. It's how my body changes when I sense your proximity. I don't even have to see you or hear you. I just know. Even now, even after all of this, even before I can understand what it is that has taken place between you and that poor girl, I could close my eyes and feel my skin begin to tingle just with the smell of you wafting past. I'm not out of place either, in the clothes that you brought in for me. I must look more like a visitor than a patient, just trying to gather up the courage to go and see some loved one. When I catch sight of you, I will call you over here. I will get you to tell me every little bit of it. I will listen, squash the pound-ing in my chest, observe a neutral stance, as if in a session with a client. I will then let you know what Ted has told me, and you will crumble. He is your weakness. The thought of him being distraught about her will be enough. If you haven't told me the full truth, you will then.

'Do you mind if I join you?' I look up to see my ward neighbour, out of her dressing gown now, wearing a purple hoodie with black tracksuit bottoms, her hair pinned up into one of those giant topknots that sits precariously on her head.

'I'm just waiting for someone,' I say and I try to ignore the flash of surprise on her face.

'Well look-it, I just wanted to give you these.' She holds up the little green bottle with the codeine capsules rattling inside it.

'I'm getting discharged today,' she says, with a resigned look. As if it's a bad thing.

'I only took them so as you could go through your withdrawals, see how you feel after. You look much better, it's only right you have them back now.'

'Thanks, I won't need them any more,' I say and my eye catches onto a fast movement behind her. The brisk, brusque walk of Ian Kennedy, heading straight for my ward. A shiver runs through me.

'Feel free to join me for a bit until he gets here. It could take him a while,' I say and she doesn't need any further persuasion. I can tell, before she begins, that she's about to offload, a bit of counselling for free, and I don't mind at all. I'll sit here, slightly hunched, nodding, pretending to listen, interjecting with small redirections as she waffles on, and I'm shielded by her bulk. I'll do this until I see him leave again.

She slurps on her coffee, as she tells me how, in all honesty, it's a great break for her to get into the hospital every once in a while. How when she feels her asthma worsening it's a relief to her. How she stops taking her preventative inhaler and her reliever inhaler until she's in a right state and she gets herself to A & E, saying she's taken everything, so that they have to admit her. She's smiling about it.

'What do you find helpful about being in hospital?' I ask as I scan for you, hoping you don't come in and collide with Ian Kennedy. He could be looking for you, just as much as me.

'Gets me away from the kids, wreck my head they do, and him. He can't do anything for himself when I'm there, lazy git, but he can do it when I'm not. Makes them all miss me, you know? Then they behave for the first day or two when I get out, getting me this, that and the other, are you all right there, Mam? It's good for them to have to be more considerate, not think life is so easy, that they'll always have their mam doing everything for them, and him as well.'

I'm nodding away when I sense the gust of him approach, feel him slowing, even as I crouch further down.

'Dr Hogan,' he says. 'Can I speak to you for a minute?'

FEBRUARY

NINA

Nina hears the roar of his bike ripping through the village. He's going faster than he should, when there's no need for speed. It's too late for speed. She studies the clock opposite, above the supermarket. The black roman numerals on the white face tell her that at five minutes to nine on a dark Wednesday night in late February her uncle Stephano will screech up to tell her something that will change everything. The sharp, cold bite of this clear night is perfect, she can't help thinking. Numbing her in a protective way. Just as her mother would want it. When Stephano reaches her he leaves the engine running and says nothing at all. Instead, he nods and hands her a helmet. She straps it on and climbs behind him, straddling the bike, her hands on his shoulders rather than around his waist. His waist is for a fun ride and she'd like to keep it that way. He takes off with a deafening boom, back up Jeff's road. Nina looks over her shoulder into Hestia; the curtains in the living room are open again, he's making sure she's gone most likely. She makes out a silhouette by the fire. It must be him. Even now, with all she is about to face, she feels a fluttering of warmth pulse through her at the sight of him, or just the thought of him. She loosens her grasp on Stephano's shoulders and tilts back just a little bit, imagining herself floating in to join him.

'Hold tight,' Stephano shouts. 'We're taking the old road out.'

The bike climbs the steep Vico Road with ease. Nina is glad that he has chosen this route, the sheer drop to her left down into the sea is comforting to her now. She has never been up here at night. It would seem a little pointless when all the beauty is obscured by blackness, but not now. Now, the full moon lights up the sweep of the bay, the dark sea glistening. She can pick out Bray Head with the help of the moon too. Just below it the lights along the promenade twinkle. They will be there in twenty minutes, maybe less. The proximity will unsettle her in years to come she thinks now. How easy it would've been to get out to her. How she shouldn't have cancelled these last few times. Not yet though. The words have not yet been spoken. There's still the illusion playing in her mind. She's going home to see her Mamma, one last time.

Outside the house Stephano removes his helmet but Nina does not.

'Give me a minute,' she says, straddled on the bike still, unable to move.

WEDNESDAY

CASSANDRA

Her mouth hangs open as she looks at me and then at the uniformed Ian Kennedy.

'Jesus,' is all she says as she stands, picks up her coffee and backs away from the table. I'd very much like her to stay, to cushion whatever it is he is about to deliver to me. He sits himself down.

'I just wanted to come and tell you in person that your husband has been released without charge.' He whispers it out softly, but not soft enough. I look up at her, watch her eyes widen and her face blanch as she works it out. She no longer looks well enough to go home, even as she breaks into a run.

'In person? It's all over the news. So unless you've come to take me in also, which you threatened to do earlier, remember, I'd like you to leave now.'

'I'm sorry about that, Dr Hogan, I shouldn't have spoken to you like that.' He seems almost as vulnerable as he did in the cottage with his daughter. 'You can file a complaint if you like. I'm not here to stop you doing that. I just wanted to let you know that your statement was accurate, it corroborated your husband's statement factually and he was arrested on the strength of it.' His right hand rests on the table between us, his thumb twitching as if he is trying to tap with it.

'There was another witness who spoke to us today, which changed the picture for us. Gave us a different angle.'

What witness? I shift my bottom on the hard plastic chair, moving closer to Ian Kennedy, willing him to tell me every little thing.

'We let him go and we're now waiting for the post-mortem results. I just felt that I owed it to you to let you know where we're at. You've been so good to Sheena, you know so I just—'

'When will the post-mortem results be back?'

'I don't know. Here, take this and give me a call tomorrow morning, I'll let you know if there's anything new.' He hands me a card with the station details and his mobile number.

'Could he, you know, Jeff, could he be arrested again?'

'He could, yes. Witness statements are helpful but not always reliable. It will be the results later that will determine it.' He gets up to leave, a little bashful, and he glances back at me. His top lip is eclipsed just now by his bottom one and he smiles a semi-smile, as if he's only half pleased with himself for doing me this good turn.

I stay at the café, keeping watch, reworking it in my mind. Someone else saw too. What did they see? The numbers are dwindling all around me as visiting time comes to an end and there's no sign of you. You've gone home instead. I check my phone again for messages, emails, missed calls. Nothing new. The battery is going down, forty-three per cent. I switch it off. I need it to last through the night and into the morning. Right up until I'm discharged and on my way home.

MARCH

NINA

Conor stands in the living room of Nina's flat, looking around, shivering.

'Come and stay at ours, just until you begin to pick up a little, yeah?'

Nina knows that this is exactly what she should do, but isn't sure what to say. Everything takes such effort now. Like trying to wade through syrup and getting nowhere. She doesn't answer Conor and he doesn't press her further. He knows to give her the time to think about this.

She watches as he lights a stick of incense on the mantle before beginning the tidy up. He looks as though he's thinking he should've come sooner as he picks up a yogurt carton, half-full still with pomegranate beads which have hardened over the days. His face crumples a little as the odour hits him and he looks down at Nina as he might at a small child struck by a dose of flu. She had insisted that he stay away at first, but lately she's become worn down by all his messages. Now she wishes she had kept insisting.

She turns on her side, facing the back of the couch and she

listens to him making his way through it all, clinking the cutlery and scrunching up the detritus, every sound a little further insult that she feels as a tightening across her skin. The tap in the kitchen pulsing a solid stream, like a long thunder roll, makes her feel her thirst all of a sudden. It has been a couple of days now, more than likely, she thinks. She listens to the spray of cleaning fluids and then to the clunk of the hoover being dragged towards her and she'd like to shout at him to just stop. Give it a rest. Enough already. Yes, she'd like to scream that out but she hasn't got the reserves. As the hoover hums all around her she decides. She'll ask him to go and assure him that she will, most likely, stay at his for a while. In a couple of weeks. She has some important things to take care of first.

Fellini's *La Strada* is playing for an evening in the Irish Film Institute in Dublin city centre and Nina knows that she has no choice but to go. It will help her, one way or the other. She prepares herself, slowly and carefully. As she does so, she wonders if he knows about it too. A month ago she would've made sure he knew. Perhaps he would've made sure she knew. She dresses herself in black leggings, and a black long-sleeved vest with a tan tunic over it. Everything takes her much longer now. She laces her flat hiking boots and pulls her biker's jacket on. A glance in the mirror confirms what she already knows. The clothes are hanging off her like a scarecrow's. Earlier she had been watching a morning TV show about new mothers finding it hard to get anything done, to get out the door, to get anywhere at all and she thinks that this is what she is experiencing, only she doesn't have the baby to excuse herself from it. She's had a shock, a massive assault in a sense, and her reality has changed for ever now too. But she has nothing to show for it.

On the top deck of the bus she observes all of the normal people. A Polish man and his friend sit behind her, chatting in their native tongue, laughing. She listens to the sound of tin foil unwrapping and a sandwich is shared between them. A little bit of hunger fizzes in her now. The girl in front of her is a similar age to Nina but she is dressed for a night out. Long, shiny black nails click messages onto her phone and Nina can see the side of her face lift as she reads what comes in. A date night. Nina wipes a hole in the condensation on the window and looks as the bus pulls into the UCD stop. Her eyes are drawn up towards the car park where she fell asleep a few months back, waiting for him. He'll have been collected by now, or is it his day to have the car? She's lost track. She presses her head against the window and listens for the sound of his engine, just in case. Students pour onto the bus, off home or for a night out, and a lovely buzz, the hum of anticipation permeates around. Nina would like to get hold of this but it's a slippery thing, and not for her just now.

Getting off the bus at Trinity she is caught, not for the first time, with her what-if thoughts. What if she'd stayed where she was, in this college? It would've been the safe, logical thing to do. She could've had a safe, logical life. A life in which she'd never have known this. Never have found him. Not really. A shudder runs through her as she stands staring through Trinity's front arch. She turns around and walks away from it, up Dame Street and straight into the familiar embrace of the film house.

THURSDAY

CASSANDRA

An outpatient appointment for the cardiac unit will be posted out to me, I am told. Along with a rap on the knuckles. No more codeine. It might have caused the arrhythmia. I don't bother to tell them about Dad having it too. They might just decide to keep me in. A taxi is called for me and I wait at the main front doors, clutching the supermarket bag with my belongings.

Afternoon visiting time. A frightening number of people throng the place, bustling, pressing the red knob on the hand sanitizer. All these good, dutiful people, off to cheer their loved ones up. Dizzying. The surprise spring sun seems to be helping. Smiles are shot in my direction. A patient getting released on a nice day. There's a feelgood factor to that. If only they knew what I'm being released to. If only I knew myself. I squeeze the bag tighter and wish that the taxi would hurry the hell up.

I direct him the long way. Down to the coast road. He is respectful. Leaves me with my thoughts instead of bombarding me with hospital questions. My phone beeps in the bag.

A text message.

Took Ted to school. Hestia free for you. Rest.

Jeff. Carrying on as normal, as if nothing has taken place. A little terse and clipped. Ted shouldn't even be in school, not with all this and how upset and worried he is. What if it's out there? What if someone knows it was Jeff who was being questioned? It will spread like wildfire and Ted will be shunned.

It's high tide. We glide past Seapoint and I watch the heads bobbing in the water, people out of their depth, like seals, basking. The simplicity of it makes me want to cry. The brightness is distorting things, sunlight pinging off the pavement, rebounding. Everything seems so much whiter, so much more textured than before the hospital. Bigger, even. Two days and nights confined, cooking under the glare of artificial lights will do that to you. Or maybe it's the lack of codeine in my system. I slip my hand into the bag and root for it. I clasp the little green bottle. Run my thumb around the corrugated lid, remembering. Counselling. That's what the doctor suggested. Counselling for the psychological effects of dependency. *You were dependent on codeine, which is a nicer way of saying you were addicted. While you have managed to withdraw in here it's crucial that you don't go back to it. You'll be vulnerable over these next few days, so access any supports you can. I'd recommend you seek assistance from another professional counsellor.*

Vulnerable. A word I would never have used to describe myself. Until now. Nothing to do with the codeine though. I'm being released into the world to discover whether my husband will be arrested and charged this time. I am a witness. In the meantime he's knocking around somewhere acting as if we can just trudge onwards. Take Ted to school. Rest. It will all just seep away.

'Pull over for a minute, can you?'

I open the car door and get out. The driver puts his hazards on and they wink at me as I breathe the sea air in, deeply. Then I fumble in my bag for his card. I punch the unfamiliar number into my phone and wait. When he answers I exhale. His voice is softer than I remember. So I tell him. I'm on my way home and I am scared.

I do as Ian says and hold off. I ask the driver to pull into the Spar in Monkstown. Then I ask if I can borrow three quid. He can add it onto the bill. He doesn't flinch. Hands it over completely free from suspicion. I could just take it and run. Avoid the fare. Why does he trust me with this? There's a little Insomnia café in the Spar. Ordering a coffee should delay us enough. Hopefully we'll collide then. Pull up outside Hestia at the same time.

I pass the newspaper stand. The tabloids still have her picture on the front page, reduced now to a side column. *Man released without charge after being questioned in connection with the death of Nina Ruzza. Pages 2–4 inside.* I pick up a broadsheet. It's reported on the front page, minus the picture. I skim through what I know to what I want to know. There it is.

The post-mortem results determining the cause of death are expected to be known later today. Someone is hovering behind me and I realize I'm blocking access to the newspapers. I wonder if they've noticed what I'm concentrating on. I put the paper back and step aside, muttering sorry while not looking. I feel a hand on my arm.

'Cass?'

I turn. It's Susie. Dark circles hang beneath her eyes. She's not smiling. She knows. She takes a moment to figure out what it is that she will say.

'How are you?'

'Oh, you know, I've been better,' I say beaming at her as I feel the sting in my eyes. She nods.

'I got myself into a bit of difficulty when I went for a run, silly really, I hadn't eaten and passed out. Anyway I was kept in hospital for a couple of days there, which was pretty unnecessary. Bed blocking,' I say, and I laugh. I'm gabbling, I know. A single tear escapes from my left eye. I bat it away.

'Anything I can do, just let me know, won't you?'

'I will, thanks.'

'I can take Ted for you, any day. Just shout.'

'Did you see him today?' A sudden pang. I need to know. 'At drop off, you know, was he there? I fret a little when it's not me taking him in.'

'Yes, I saw him.'

'How did he seem?'

'Hard to tell, really. Maybe it's because he was in his uniform and it's a tracksuit day he seemed a bit glum walking up the slope. I said hello to him but he didn't hear me. In a world of his own.'

I try not to picture him in the wrong clothes, walking alone, with all that he's been through. Susie seems to be waiting for me to say something. To blurt it all out, perhaps.

'Poor thing, there's been a lot going on,' I say.

'Yes. Well look, I've to fly now, but do shout if you need me.'

I want to ask her. How does she know? Does everybody know? What does she think I should do? She picks up her newspaper and turns her back to me, queuing for a moment, before exiting without another word.

Other customers jostle past as I stand here, dazed. I go back out to the taxi and clamber in.

'No coffee?'

'Changed my mind. Here you go,' I say handing back the coins to him.

'You look like you could do with one though. Want me to pick it up for you?'

The kindness of strangers. Instead of making me smile it triggers something else, like it always does. If this begins now though it might never stop. I blink it back and he waits, patiently, for my response, looking at me in his mirror. I shake my head.

'No, thanks. It's time for me to go home.'

He drives on, slowly, taking the coast road down past the East Pier. Ted tried to tell me something about the pier a while back, eyes lit and shiny as if it was Christmas Eve, bursting with some taste of anticipated joy. But his story fell apart. He dithered. Stopped and started. Faltered. I remember having little interest in what he was saying. It was how he was saying it. I thought it might be the start of something else. A stammer. I observed without listening or probing, my face most likely blank, detached, as if he could be anyone's child except my own. I sat like this until he ran off into the garden with Tuppence. I followed, tiptoe quiet, with an odd old fear beginning to grip me. Henry. He was seven when it kicked in for him. I sat on the kitchen floor with the door open, just a crack, and listened to Ted tell Tuppence his story, free from any sign of hesitation. It flowed beautifully. Whatever this is, I remember thinking, it's not serious. The story itself went over my head. I do remember the final bit though. The punchline, so to speak. *But rules are made to be broken*, he said to Tuppence, and he laughed, a giddy little laugh, and I sighed in relief and flicked the kettle on. As I think about this now I wonder what else I missed. How many other things he might have been trying to tell me while I sat there analysing him instead.

MARCH

NINA

Nina orders an espresso in the film-house courtyard café, taking it to a little table along the back wall where she sits and waits. She's early for the showing, as she knew she would be. Facing down the narrow hallway that leads to the main door she begins to prepare herself. If he comes along too, she'll see him and hear him before he does her. She'll know then what to do.

The aroma of the espresso sparks thoughts of her Nonna. Thoughts she tries to push away. She sips and the bitter bite of it pleases her as it warms her through. Perhaps she should've eaten something, she thinks now. The line of glass singular floor tiles, lit from below, will pave his way towards her. Lights will shine on him from above as well, and as he enters the courtyard, she will get up and walk towards him, slowly. She will tell him that she knew he would come. They will watch the film together and she will hold off telling him what she knows she must tell him until afterwards.

She waits and she watches. This is a place where sitting all alone is usual. Going to see a film alone, as she has done so many times, is perfectly normal. As others straggle in, she wonders about them too. A middle-aged woman in a puffed red coat, black short hair, alone. A man in his thirties with a navy wool hat walks up to the ticket booth and then goes directly into Screen 1. Alone. Nina feels her stomach begin to cramp. It may be that the espresso is too strong for her as she hasn't eaten, or perhaps it is that she sees herself a little more clearly now, reflected in these people.

She waits until the film begins to be sure. He's not coming. Then she gets up and walks slowly to the door where *La Strada* is playing. She glances back one more time before she slips in, claiming an aisle seat along the back wall.

When the door opens, she knows. A chink of light shadows him in. The tap of his stick mere confirmation, not that she needs it. She sits bolt upright, readying herself, just as Gelsomina's mother sells her to the street performer. Nina puts her hand out and brushes the tail of Jeff's jacket as he walks past. He doesn't turn around. Instead, he gestures to a row of seats in the middle and Nina can see now that he is not alone. Cassandra follows behind him, her magnified silhouette moving across the screen. It is as if all the oxygen in Nina has been squeezed down into her fingertips where she cannot access it. She shakes her arms and then thrums her fingers on the empty chair in front of her as if playing the piano, trying to catch her breath.

Cassandra's head is in direct line with Nina's as she occupies an aisle seat also. Jeff has scooted further in, placing himself in the middle of the middle, the optimum viewing point, just as Nina knew he would. When he turns his head and sees that Cassandra is already seated, looking straight ahead at the screen, he gets up and moves to the seat beside her. Nina feels the tug of disappointment, a swirling sludge in the pit of her stomach, as if it is she herself making the compromise. Cassandra doesn't acknowledge the move, nor what Jeff says to her, her head in a fixed position staring straight at the screen. Her height, even when sitting, diminishes him. The protective surge that Nina had for him when she found him slumped on the hotel bathroom floor visits her again now, but it is different this time. She pictures herself clambering over the rows, down to the middle and claiming her place on the other side of him. Telling him, and telling Cassandra, and then clambering back over the rows and out of the cinema, leaving them to fight it out. But she does not do this. This is not how it will end. Instead, she watches him watching the film. She watches for any movements at all in him and she knows when they will come. The little gestures of assent and dissent that she mimics, the two of them in perfect unison, and it pulses through her, that electricity, those little static prods. Cassandra slips down in her seat, her head tilted away from Jeff, and Nina wonders if she's fallen asleep. Sometime later, when Cassandra stands up and walks out, Nina is seized by the opportunity before her but she pushes it back. She stays where she is, watching him watch and then watching him realize that Cassandra has gone. She watches him taking his time, looking at the screen as Gelsomina lies abandoning herself on the side of the road, his head moving slightly, tremulous. And then she watches him get up and leave the theatre to go to look for his wife. As he passes her, his eyes fixed in a glaze that she has not seen before, she breathes him in. There's a delicious fury bubbling in him, the tap of his stick a little more heavy than it needs to be.

THURSDAY

CASSANDRA

He indicates onto our road and I see the car parked outside, in a different spot than the one I left it in on Tuesday. He's been driving, despite what he was told at his last appointment.

'Anywhere here,' I say and the driver pulls up on the path behind our car. I feel my breathing change. Small, short breaths. My fight-or-flight system kicking in.

'I'll pop in and get your fare,' I say, even though I feel like just sitting here, not moving at all. I know the best thing is to push through this, to keep going. He'll be waiting here and Ian's on his way.

'Don't worry about it love,' he says. 'You were my last fare, but I forgot to put the meter on. I'm nearly home myself, knackered I am after a long shift. Go on in and get yourself sorted.'

I feel the stinging in my eyes once again. The kindness of this stranger.

'Thank you,' is all I'm able to safely say. I remove the house key from the Tesco bag and fumble to open the car door, pushing it then, as if it's a dead weight. As if we're under water. I can't work out if it's that I've no strength or I really just don't want to get out.

'Need a hand there?'

'No, I've got it, thanks,' and I'm out on the footpath, slamming the cab door a little too hard, as if I'm trying to prove something to myself or to him. I watch his left indicator twinkle and he's off. I set foot on our garden path and look at the house, our little home, tainted. It's then that I notice it. The front door ajar. The cracked pane beside it, a spider web of a pattern with a hole in the centre of it. I run up the path, shove the door with my shoulder and holler into our hallway for whoever is in there to get the hell out now.

The silence is deafening. No Tuppence pattering on the floorboards. I call her. Nothing. I step inside, pushing the sitting room door open. It is exactly as I left it on Tuesday. A heap of ash under the grate, waiting to be cleared. Wine glasses with ruby dregs on the mantelpiece. My tan tote bag on the coffee table, zipped up. I don't usually bother to zip it. Nothing has been disturbed. I go back into the hall and scour. A small stone lies on the floorboards. Everything else seems the same. I push the door into the kitchen and glance around. A Cheerios cereal box on the table along with a bowl and spoon. Clean and unused. It's as if they've been here and they haven't been here. Jeff and Ted. Then I hear them. Footsteps in the hall.

MARCH

NINA

Nina sets a timer on her phone for two minutes and when it beeps she presses stop, gets up from her seat and exits the screening too. She's given Jeff enough time to scour the immediate surroundings, to wait outside the toilet for Cassandra or to begin to go after her, wherever she is. As she emerges from the dark room into the bright foyer, Nina blinks to refocus her lens. She swings her head to the right where people are sipping their coffees. No sign. To the left then: more people dotting the place at tables, but not Jeff. Then down towards the exit. The single grid of underlit glass floor tiles picks him out. He is alone, reaching the last tile and about to step out onto the street. Nina follows, skipping every second tile as if she's a child playing a game. She needs to catch up to see the direction he will take.

He seems sure about where he is going, not looking around at all. He turns right into the cobbled lane and walks along before turning left onto Dame Street. He stops at a pedestrian crossing and then moves with the throngs across the road which will take him, most likely, up towards Grafton

Street. Nina waits for the next light and watches him cross. He is not the same now. She is not the same either. It has changed both of them, utterly. His emails, that she does not now respond to, show no trace of his knowing. His world continues on untouched, unfettered. He stops on the island in the centre of the road as a cyclist shaves past him, breaking the lights. This seems to have a knock-on effect. He begins to look around, first up towards Dublin Castle, then down towards Trinity. He stands there staring, as if in a trance, as the other people continue to cross. Then he turns his head further, back towards the crossing point where Nina stands, as if he knows. He rotates himself fully and is before her, smiling, mouthing something she cannot hear. It's only really now, the first time that she's seen his face since, that the full force of it hits her. The lights have changed and the traffic whizzes past again, drowning him out further and they stand, looking across at one another in this altered after space. He leans heavily on his stick, smiling still, waiting, sure of his next move, it seems. It is as the traffic begins to slow on either side of them, announcing the coming of the next crossing light, offering the opportunity for one of them to cross to the other that Nina decides. The green man flashes and Jeff takes a step towards her as she takes a step back, slipping away easily in the crowd, shielded and hidden. He calls after her, as she knew he would and his voice carries across the bustle, accompanying her as she ducks into the Foggy Dew pub.

THURSDAY

CASSANDRA

I fumble with the key in the back door and slip out onto the patio. I listen. Would Ian just saunter into the house without calling out? He'll have seen the broken glass. He knows I'm afraid. More afraid now than ever. My phone pings in the Tesco bag. I pull it out. *On my way. Wait outside*. It's not Ian inside. A yellow finch flutters past, landing for a moment on Ted's bird-feeding table before taking off again, as if startled. The beat of his wings mimics my heart as I crouch down and begin to crawl, hugging the perimeter of the cottage. I inch past a freshly deposited Tuppence poo. She's been out here today. I speed up, my hands and knees pressing painfully into the tiny stones we laid here last summer. Border stones to create definition. Jeff's idea. I didn't like it. Thought about how they'd get clogged in the lawnmower or spin out of the blades and fly up at one of us. Cause chaos. Wreak havoc. But he got his way. How many other things did I just give in to? I press on to the corner. Once I get around it I can get up and run. Let Ian deal with whoever is inside. I'm almost there when I hear the back-door handle pressing down, the slight creak of the door as it opens and then slams shut. I don't look behind. I get up and run.

It's like one of those dreams, the ones where you really have to run to get away and you manage a couple of steps before your legs turn to rubber and won't carry you. The side gate is padlocked and I approach it slowly as my mind races. He has staged this break-in. Taken Tuppence, so I'd come out here and look for her. He's been waiting for me to trap myself. I hear him crunching on the stones towards me. I scour for something to pick up to defend myself. Ted's wooden-handled spade is resting in the verge, dark specks of compost dotting the apple-green metallic end. Just a few short days ago we were out here, planting. A Saturday afternoon in the fresh spring sun. The three of us and the dog. Seeding peas, beans and radishes directly into the ground alongside a fresh mint plant. For our summer salads. I seize the spade now, raise it up and turn around to face him.

He stands there, this hooded person who is not Jeff. I open my mouth to scream.

He shakes his head and he's trying to say something.

He's not coming any closer.

He's muttering and seems to be shivering. His cheeks glisten.

'I just need to know,' he says.

'The police are on the way.' I say this in a low, calm voice, as if I'm in the office with a client.

His hands are deep in the pockets of his sky-blue hoodie and a wisp of damp auburn hair peeps out.

'Is that you?' I say as it begins to kick in.

He nods. Then he wipes his nose on his sleeve.

'What the hell. You broke in to my house?'

'Not exactly, no. The door was open. Look, I'm sorry. I just want to know. She said some stuff lately, told me things that didn't make sense but do now, kind of. I need to ask him.'

'Who told you things?'

'Nina.'

'You knew Nina?'

'Yes.' He takes a step in my direction.

I holler as he takes his hands out of his pockets. He winces at my noise, puts both hands out towards me, to show their emptiness, perhaps, but that is no solace.

Not when I know how easy it is.

I turn towards the gate and grab the rusty old padlock. It doesn't budge.

He's talking behind me, a jumble of incoherent words as if he's high.

Ted's orange go-kart is parked along the wall. I pull it towards the gate and step onto the seat.

There's a loud thud and I think about how I've somehow always known this. That there would be a small delay. A moment of realization that you've been hit before you fall.

I wait.

A voice chimes close behind me.

'You're all right, it's under control. You can get down.'

I turn to see Ian standing over the young man, felled as I

thought I would be. His eyes are closed and loud sobs come from him in convulsive waves as he wriggles about. I don't even think about it, I'm down on my knees beside him whispering reassurances, just as he was to me two days ago.

'Don't do that,' Ian says, pepper-spray can still in hand.

'I'm arresting you for breaking and entering and threatening the owner of this house,' he says, leaning down with handcuffs now.

'Let me wipe his eyes.' I get up to go inside and stop for a moment.

'I don't think he broke in and he didn't threaten me, not exactly. He knows Nina Ruzza.'

Ian's gaze drops to the heap on the ground, to the young man looking more like a little boy curled up in a foetal position, no longer writhing about. I've calmed him.

'Does he now?' Ian says, whipping a notepad out of his pocket.

Inside I rummage through the airing cupboard for a face cloth, my mind whirring. I seize on an old pink one, frayed at the edges. I run the kitchen tap, filling a mixing bowl with warm water and just a touch of soap.

Back outside, I kneel down beside him and dab at his face and around his eyes. Ian stands above us both, scribbling things down. The young man begins to blink and his tears stream. Good. Wash it all out. Then he opens his eyes and looks directly at me. Bloodshot. His mouth moves and he's mumbling something, but he's drowned out by Ian rattling off why he's under arrest, followed by a caution.

'Anything you do say may be . . .'

The young man goes quiet, looking at me still. Then he smiles.

'I'm coming with you,' I say.

As Ian leads him back through the kitchen I hear her nails patter on the floorboards. She runs past them and jumps up at me, her lead still attached, a high-pitched whimpering accompanying her frantic licks. I follow them into the hall. His stick hangs from the spiral staircase. He's in here somewhere. I don't want to know where.

I wait at the police station. Ian has asked me not to. So I tell him. This is the person who called an ambulance and did CPR. Got me to hospital. Possibly saved my life. I owe him one.

'On Tuesday evening, right?'

'Right.'

'Well, we'll need to find out what he was up to before that,' Ian says and he pushes through the swing door that a young female guard has just led the man through. 'We could be here a while,' he says, over his shoulder.

'I've nowhere to be,' I say back to him. I need this time now. I'm thinking what Ian is thinking, no doubt. That this is Nina Ruzza's boyfriend. That he found out about Jeff and Nina. That he was there at the beach on Tuesday morning too. I think back to my fall. To his irritating earnestness. To him willing me back to life. Did he already know me? Is he a student of Jeff's too?

The phone rings at the main desk. The guard who takes the call leaves the desk and pushes through to the interview room. A couple of minutes later Ian appears with the young man.

'You can go home now,' he says and then turns to me. 'Can you come with me for a minute?' My heart thuds in my neck. He's going to arrest me instead. I follow him into the interview room.

'Look,' he says. 'I shouldn't really be doing this, but I think you need to know. The post-mortem results are back.'

APRIL

NINA

Nina packs all she will need into a small red rucksack. It's a
chilly, crisp April morning but even so, she is dressed in
light clothes as if it is a warm summer's evening and she's
off to a barbecue. Underneath her white linen shirt and her
flowing turquoise skirt she is naked as a newborn. She
cycles, slowly at first, through Glasthule village and on
towards Dalkey. Her flip-flops and skirt aren't ideal for
cycling, slowing her more than she would like. It wasn't
the cycling part she was thinking about as she dressed and
prepared. She reaches Tubbermore Road and glances
around for the car in all the on-street parking spaces. When
she sees that it is not there, and then, when she glances into
Hestia, with the curtains already opened but no sign of
movement, it is then that a light panic begins to announce
itself. This is the day. It has to be. But they've left earlier
than usual.

She presses her feet hard on the pedals now, and they're
bending too much in the soft plastic. An image from her
childhood flashes before her. Wearing flip-flops, cycling on

her egg-yolk-yellow bike, she had wanted to turn the dynamo light on the wheel on. It was a July evening and not yet dark, with no hope of it actually getting dark, but she had wanted to show her light off to those around her, the boys and girls playing tip the can. As she cycled, she had put her right foot forward to flick the switch on with her toes. The flip-flop snagged, the spokes slicing through it, mangling it along with the sole of her foot. As the bike tilted over and she fell onto the tarmacadam all the children gathered around. Her foot was caught in the wheel now, blood trickling from it in rivulets up her leg, and all she felt was the imperative not to cry. Her best friend's mother appeared, calm, reassuring and she was glad that it was her and not her own mother. Hysterics would not have helped. Her friend's mother bent the spokes slightly, releasing the foot, and the throbbing pain of it, the slice of it right into muscle on the ball of her foot, was excruciating, but she wouldn't let on. Instead, she hopped, leaning on the friend's mother, into their house for bandaging. Someone else picked up the bike and the useless broken, blood-soaked flip-flop. *Don't tell Mamma*, she had whispered. She would think up another story to tell her mother. One in which she would not be accused of showing off or of doing something so obviously stupid and reckless as trying to turn the dynamo light on while cycling. She cannot remember now what it was that she had said, how her foot had come to be injured and her flip-flops were no more. But she does remember that whatever she said had worked because she was still allowed to play outside. Now she wishes she had been able to just tell her mother whatever the truth was instead of finding ways to soften blows for her. Her mother had always made Nina feel that she was a fragile creature, one who could succumb easily to the vagaries of life, one who needed to be protected from herself at times. She wasn't far wrong, Nina thinks now, as she presses ever harder, pedalling up the sharp incline of Vico Road, standing as she goes to get a little more purchase on each push.

At the top of the road Nina pauses to catch her breath and to take in the stunning panorama, the sweep of the bay glistening in this early-morning light, Bray Head and Dalkey Island hugging the sea, and she feels a drowsy peacefulness infuse her. She too would soon be embraced, at one with this natural beauty, basking in the element from where she feels she hails. On the way down she sits back in the saddle allowing the bike to take her, the wind rippling her shirt, her hair flying behind her, until she passes the high tunnel and car park where they would be and continues on down to the lower ones. She cycles through the stark, empty car park and into the small, dark tunnel which yields onto the beach. The shock of a sound like a light train clattering overhead stops her for a moment, almost throws her off. Then she sees them. Balls of hail bouncing on the tarmac beyond, rendering the landscape temporarily white. A blessing. Perfect.

She leans her bike against the tunnel wall and laces the coiled combination lock between the wheels, securing it. She removes her backpack. The insulin vials rattle in the bottom of the bag and she smiles. Three long-acting and two short-acting, more than enough to ensure success. She unbuttons her shirt and rummages in the bag for her syringe, the alcohol swabs, the small flask of ice. The ritual is to be the same today as every day, only more repetitive. She pulls her skirt down towards her pubic bone and begins to rub with the ice, numbing five spots in the shape of a star around her navel. She removes the vials and selects her first, a cloudy long-acting one, and she rolls it gently between her palms. She uses an alcohol wipe to swab her skin before inserting the syringe into the vial and drawing the liquid out. Then she taps the syringe to rid it of any bubbles – it's difficult to tell if there are any in the dark light of the tunnel. She begins the singing, her mother's voice in her head again now, chanting. *Tanti auguri a te.* She sings it slowly, as she empties vial after vial into her syringe and plunges it, over and over, into her body.

Tanti auguri a te.

But it's not my birthday, Mamma.

Tanti auguri a Nina
Tanti auguri a te!

As the needle pierces her skin and she plunges the syringe for the fifth and final time, she hears her mother's voice, raspy but clear. As if she is here with her.

Brava, Nina. Brava.

She gathers all of the used bits and puts them back into her bag and she moves quickly, hurling the bag into an open bin before jumping down onto the stony beach, shedding her flip-flops and beginning to run. Her research well done, she knows she has about thirty minutes before the process begins to takes hold. She looks out across the bay as she runs, hoping to see him swimming in the sea, and she will join him, let it begin there with him in the water as she tells him. This has been her plan. Swimming out to him, telling him, and then letting go. But he's not in the water. Something is different about today.

She looks up the beach now and spots him all alone, standing with his black towel around his shoulders, looking out at the sun glistening on the surface of the water. He's already been in. Nina picks up her pace, throwing her shirt off as she goes. She'll get him to go back into the water with her. He must be with her as it kicks in. She shouts out his name and his head turns quickly towards her, and in that moment she wonders if he already knows. It is as if he is expecting her. Not a trace of surprise, but something else. He's worked it out. Yet there's so much she needs to say to him, to explain it. If she can't get it all out, then at least Ted will be able to help. She sprints the last little bit and leaps up onto him, her arms around his neck and her legs wrapped around his waist, the towel falling down behind him onto the stones. Their skin touches properly for the first time, just as it should have over all the years. If it were to begin now like this, with him holding her like a little child, then she would be happy. She doesn't feel any sign of it yet though.

'What are you doing?' His voice. Soft and melodic. Calming. Not what she needs right now.

'Come swim with me. I've so much to tell you and very little time to do it.' She looks right into his face, searching for a sign that he knows now too.

'Come back into the water with me, everything will be fine, I promise, I just need you to be with me.'

She feels his fingers, cold and firm, touching hers, releasing her grasp from his neck. She unwraps her legs from around him and waits for him to assist her, and as he does, as his hands clasp her waist, and she feels him shaking slightly as he lifts her gently down, she feels her search ending and, for the briefest moment, a niggle of doubt. Maybe there was another way. She pushes it down.

'I love you and I understand why that is now and you need to understand too, you really do, and you will, I promise that you will, and take my work, make sure you do, it's all yours, fly with it, it's going to be great, you're going to be great.'

'Are you high, Nina?'

Nina can feel the trembling taking hold in her hands. It's beginning and he will be gone. She needs to keep him here just a little bit longer. Out of the pit of her stomach it comes, a guttural wail, which surprises her, the force of it, as if she is trying to rid herself of something. A birthing sound, perhaps. The stricken look in his eyes, like a wounded hound, as her wail builds towards a shrill, vibrating howl, is not what Nina would have hoped for, but then suddenly something changes. He seems to get it.

'Quiet now,' he says, and he places his right hand over her face and holds onto the back of her head with his left.

'*Stai tranquilla*,' he whispers, holding onto her still, but loosening his hands slightly. She is no longer trying to make any noise, no longer trying to do anything at all. His words. Special words for her.

'*Stai tranquilla, bambina.*'

He releases his hands.

Bambina.

This is the perfect moment to let go.

'*Grazie*,' she whispers, smiling at him before falling to her knees and then down onto her side. She listens to him dressing quickly, to his zip going up, to him stamping himself into his shoes, muttering something that she doesn't catch and then crunching back across the stones, stick slapping towards the steps and up to the car.

She lies perfectly still, waiting for it to strengthen, the cold sweats announcing themselves, her heart rate dropping, sure signs that it will be soon. She hears the engine start and the car drive away, stopping for a moment, which startles her a little. An intervention now is not what she needs. There is no better way than this for it to end. She hears the car move on and sitting back up she turns towards the car park and waves at the tail end of the car disappearing off up into the tunnel. Then she lies back down where he has left her and looks out across the bay, waiting serenely for death's grip to take her.

THURSDAY

CASSANDRA

He stands on the street corner, head bowed to the phone in his hand, texting. I tap his arm and he flinches. Afraid still. When he looks up and sees that it's me he smiles. His face is still an angry red from the spray, at odds with the open, quizzical look he gives me.

'I don't even remember your name but I could do with a drink if you'd like to join me. I've just been told something that I think you need to know too. Before you hear it on the news.' He puts out his hand for me to shake.

'I'm Conor.'

'Cass.' He has a strong grip, a solid handshake that you'd expect from an older person. Someone keen to hang on to life.

'I know,' he says. Of course he does.

We dip into the Three Tun Inn around the corner from the station.

'Another Wetherspoons, great,' he says. 'We go to the one in Dún Laoghaire, you know, the one called the Forty Foot? High up. Superb views out across the bay. She loves it.'

'Nina?'

'Yep.'

We order and pay at the bar and sit down at the back in a corner window seat, across from one another.

'Shoot,' he says, and he leans his head in his hand, his elbow resting on the table. He's nodding slightly, even as his eyes narrow in disbelief. I let him sit with it, although there's a thousand things I want to know. Was he her boyfriend? Who was she? What was she like? How long was she involved with Jeff for? Did he know or just suspect? What was he doing at our cottage?

The drinks arrive, interrupting my thoughts. His a pint of Bulmers. Mine a neat vodka. He gulps and I sip in silence.

'How?' he says but doesn't wait for an answer. Instead, the floodgates open and he pours. 'So that's why she left her stuff for the girls. She knew. How didn't I pick up on it? Her jewellery. All of it, just left in the bedroom. She stayed with us, you know? For the weekend. Came and stayed and played with the twins as usual. They adore her. We went out for a meal and a few drinks, the two of us, in Dalkey, just around the corner from you. She was in great form. On a high, even, I thought. She had been very down for a few weeks before that, you know, wasn't looking after herself properly, always a worry with her condition. But when she came to stay she was just her fun self, not preoccupied at all, didn't even mention the PhD for the first time in ages. Her mother, yes, she began to open up a bit about that, but not in a sad way. She'd accepted it, seemed to have anyway. She was more like her old self, before all of this, you know?' He stops for a moment to catch his breath as the million questions that I cannot ask hum in me. What condition? Before all of what?

'I really felt like I'd lost her when she began this thing back in October. She'd never been like this before. Always took her studies in her stride. Sailed through. But from the moment she embarked on the PhD something changed. She failed the interview, you know? The first time she'd ever failed anything and it was so important to her. It seemed to catapult her into an obsession about it all. She wanted it so badly, it took over. I lost her for those six months, more or less. She'd cancel at the last minute, or just not show up sometimes. Then last weekend she came back to me fully. I should've seen it, or wondered at least about what had changed for her, but I didn't even question it. It was just so great to have her back. She sent me a text late on Monday night, you know? *A swim tomorrow x*. I texted back, *Great, see you there*. I was so happy. It was another sign that she was back to herself. I went to Sandycove for high tide on Tuesday. That's where we always go and she loves to swim at high tide. I waited and waited, called her, texted her, swam in the end without her when the tide was dropping and everyone else had been and gone. That's when you showed up. And she was down at Killiney all that time.' He tips his pint to his mouth and swallows repeatedly, until there's just an inch left.

'Sounds like you were very close.'

He runs with this, tells me how they were childhood friends, in the same national school, before his family moved away from Bray and then they met again in Trinity. I'm only half-listening now. This is not getting me any closer to answering my own questions. A couple of men in high-vis jackets sit close by discussing the menu. It's curry-club Thursday. A page advertising the deal lies in front of me. I stare at the picture, at the small silver bowl of chicken tikka masala on a blue and white speckled plate with pilau rice, naan bread, poppadoms, a pot of mango chutney. A frothy pint sits confidently along-side it. How I'd love to have an appetite. For the greatest challenge of the day to be deciding which curry to go for.

'And so now I'll never know what was going through her head. She came in to me in the middle of the night, crawled in beside me. I cradled her, you know? Didn't ask her a sin-gle thing. Just held her there until the light broke through a chink in the curtains, sunrise on Sunday morning. She didn't want the twins to know, so she kissed me for a moment on the lips, smiled and slipped back into their room where she sleeps. I thought it was the beginning of something new. Instead, she was saying goodbye.'

He drains the last bit of his drink and I do the same.

'I don't get it,' he says. 'I'm going to head out there. Out to the bay.' He stands up and leaves without looking back.

I follow him. He walks down towards the train station. He crosses the road at the village chipper without care, putting his hand up to an approaching white van without turning to look at it. As if to say slow down if you like or just keep going, I don't mind either way. I pick up my pace a little, crossing behind him. He walks towards a small court area in front of the bank. A woman sits on one of the benches, throwing bread crusts to a flock of head-bobbing pigeons. As he passes she looks up and calls out to him. A beggar asking for change most likely. He stops and looks down at her, digging his hands into his pockets. She speaks again, looking at him and then at me. A face deeply lined and weathered, with the sparkling bright blue eyes of a much younger person.

'Let it lie,' she says, her voice smooth and soft. At odds with her face.

'What?' Conor says.

'Let it lie. Don't go digging around. It's not what she wants.'

She flicks her eyes between us, addressing us both. A mad woman rambling. The scarf on her shoulders glints at us in the low evening sun. Conor takes a step towards her, frightening the pigeons into flight. She doesn't flinch, doesn't even seem to blink as he gets down on his hunkers opposite her. She smiles at him instead.

'How do you know?' She doesn't answer him, just holds his gaze. He stands up and digs for change in his pockets. She shakes her head. The pigeons begin to gather again as she rubs crumbs between her fingers. Conor steps away and I follow him. He stops for a moment at a sculpted stone cross, staring at the face which bulges slightly from the middle of it. He's eye to eye with it, this ethereal image. He reaches out to touch it, before changing his mind and walking on. When we get to the corner to turn down to the train station I glance back. The woman has gone.

As the train emerges from the tunnel and the sweep of the bay comes into view, I can see it. The exact spot. Conor doesn't know that I was there and that I saw it all. He'll search for clues, just as I did, and he'll get nowhere. He's fast off the train, climbing the steps two apiece to walk the bridge above the track and cross over. He's not wondering if I'm coming too. This is a solo quest. He turns right out of the station, and crosses to the car park, walking briskly down towards the small tunnel that leads onto the beach. I take my time, wondering whether I should just walk home instead. Then I hear an echoing bellow and I run. In the tunnel I find Conor grasping the handlebars of a bike.

'It's Nina's,' he says.

'Look, she's even locked it. Why would she do that?' He leaves it back against the wall and exits the tunnel, turning right. The wrong way.

'She went left,' I call after him and he stops. When he turns around to look at me, I hang my head. I don't want to see his reaction to knowing now that I was here too. He says nothing as he walks back past me and I listen to his footsteps quicken, to him breaking into a sprint on the stones, just as she did.

★

He goes too far. I stand at the spot and wait. Dark grey clouds line the horizon and above them, closer to us, the sky is dusted with salmon pink. Night is falling. He turns and begins his walk back towards me. I sit. The stones and pebbles beneath me are cold, numbing. A good thing. I'm going to have to tell him and I don't want to feel too much of his pain. I dig my hands into the pebbles, picking up a purple one marbled with white in my right hand. An amber smooth one in my left. I sit, in lotus position, holding the stones looking out across the bay. I expect to feel a panic rise as he approaches, with what I am about to reveal. Instead, as he crunches towards me, I feel serene.

He doesn't flinch as I pour the words out. He looks to the right, as if he can see her running towards us now, shedding her shirt, her turquoise skirt with its split up the middle, billowing in the breeze.

'She wants to swim,' he says.

I describe the rest of it factually, with detachment. Exactly what I saw. I don't want to colour him with my emotions. He shuts his eyes briefly when I describe how she jumped up on Jeff, wrapped her legs around him, clung onto his neck, letting her head fall back in laughter, the dangle of her long curls dancing.

'She's happy,' he says, opening his eyes again, smiling out to the sea.

The noise. Not easy to describe. He probes. Was it a scream? Was it a wail? Was it a song? Was she in pain? Was she afraid? I tell him that I don't know. I have no idea what it was.

'Do it,' he says. 'Make the noise.'

I've heard it so many times since, playing over and over in my mind. I'll have no problem replicating it, even if I'm uneasy doing it, right here at the very spot. I squeeze the pebbles tight in my fists and begin. The lightness of it at first. The crescendo into something else. Until I sound like a banshee. He's nodding.

'She's not distressed,' he says when I've finished. 'It's some sort of a calling.'

'Calling who though?'

'I'm not sure. Go on. What happened next?'

The toughest bit. I say it quickly. Rattle it off, as if this will reduce it somehow. Minimize the blow. A jogger pummels past, directly in front of us, breaking the trance. Conor turns his head in my direction but I keep staring out across the bay. I know what's coming.

'Can we open it now or should we wait for Mum? Nina says she wants us all to be together.'

Ted stands before Jeff, holding a large red envelope with their three names written in black ink. The first letter of each name is in a calligraphic sweep.

'We can go ahead,' Jeff says.

'She said we should light the fire and sit around it.'

'Let's do that, then. You can set it.'

'I can?'

'Yes, just do it like Mum does, firelighters, a few briquettes and a log on top.'

Ted grabs the briquettes from the copper box on the hearth. He makes a tepee around the firelighters and places a small log across the top.

'Can I light it too?'

'Yes, little man.' Jeff hands a box of matches to Ted.

'I think she'd like you doing it,' he says.

'Mum?' Ted asks, striking the match.

'No, Nina. She'd like you being a big boy, helping Daddy.'

'When will Mum be back? Are you sure we shouldn't wait?'

'Mum hasn't said when she'll be back, but she didn't know Nina like we did, so it's okay if we go ahead without her.'

Ted rips at the back of the envelope and yanks out a card. It's a black and white sketch print of Alice in Wonderland, a deck of playing cards flying all around her, her arm up protecting herself from them. He opens it and three white envelopes fall out. One for each of them.

'Can I open mine first?'

'Sure.'

'I can't read this joined writing.'

Jeff takes the page from Ted. The script is carefully crafted, small letters with long stems. He scans it first, just to be sure. Then he reads it out loud.

Dear little Ted,

I'm sorry I had to go. I will miss you. Meeting you changed my life. I am so proud of you. Be good for your Dad and Mum. They are very lucky to have such a sweet, funny, kind little boy and I am very lucky too. Watch lots of great films with Dad and follow your dreams. You are in my heart.

Forever,
Love,
Nina xx

A single tear rolls down Jeff's cheek, stopping just at his mouth.

'What made her die, Dad?'

'Oh, Ted, she had a bad illness.'

'I know, she told me about it.'

'She did? You two got along really well.'

'Are you going to open yours now too?' Ted asks.

The log crackles and spits a spark out onto the rug, singeing it slightly, before Jeff flicks at it with his index finger to limit the damage.

'Yes,' he says, sitting back down, 'but I'm not going to read it out loud.'

Jeff opens his envelope, slowly, stopping halfway, as if he might just not continue. Then he pulls out two pages swiftly, like he's ripping a plaster off quickly to lessen the pain. One is written on thin blue letter paper, both sides, a black sprawl. The other on the same paper as Ted's, thick and cream-coloured. Jeff holds up the blue page first, the handwriting unfamiliar, small, spidery letters, a mixture of Italian and English.

Nina, stellina e la luce dei miei occhi. Nina, little star and the light of my eyes.

A letter to Nina. He scours to the end.

Con tutto il cuore, Mamma. With all my heart, Mum.

He knows and he doesn't know what it contains. He flicks to the cream page. Carefully crafted letters, just like Ted's. He inhales and holds onto his breath while he begins to read.

Dear Jeff,

It was instant. An overpowering pull that I felt the very first time I saw you. Then every time after that. It's an astonishing feat of nature. I didn't know what it was, but it felt electrifying, seeing you, and then each cell tingling inside me when you were close. Every little thing seemed to make sense in life, everything suddenly had a purpose. I was buzzing from that first moment. The smell of you. Blindfolded I'd know you. It's a magnetic thing. I'd march straight up to you. Throw my arms around you. Just as I should. I have never been happier than I am now that I understand.

Jeff releases his breath slowly, his ribs sinking back down.

'Oh, Nina,' he whispers, and he turns his head towards the fire, so that the flames reflect on his glasses, making his eyes seem as if they are burning. Down his right side a terrible ache takes hold, as if he's been running and has developed a stitch. Piercing into him as he begins to know. He glances back at the words on his lap.

I mixed it up with romantic love, this energy lingering between us. I felt it as a powerful urge for intimacy, sensual, sexual or whatever. Primal anyway, I know now. I'll carry that with me, the experience of being in love with you. Lucky, I guess, that you didn't feel the same way?

He stops reading, as she knew he would, he's sure. Was it lucky? Did he feel the same way? That moment in the hotel bathroom as she bent over him, slipped her hands into his, tried to pull him up off the floor. It had felt like pain more than desire. Not a sexual aching but something else. A tear had welled in his left eye, and when it brimmed over and trickled down along the edge of his nose, it was like a drop of burning oil. He was disturbed by it at the time and so he sat there on the floor, waiting for it to die. When he got up, long after Nina had left the bathroom, he studied his face in the mirror expecting to see a red ugly streak stopping just above his lip, from where he had licked the drop away. Perhaps it would be bubbled with blisters too, he had thought, as he steadied himself against the sink and peered. Instead, what he saw staring back at him had disturbed him even more. An image of his father, nodding slowly in the way that he did when he was saying yes to something. A slow, low nod, somehow questioning, somehow disapproving in its assent. It was enough to sober Jeff back up, tipping him as it did into that swampy terrain, the feeling that he'd never be quite good enough. There were other moments too with Nina. Moments where he wasn't quite sure what was taking place as she dazzled him with something she said or some little gesture, the tinkle of her bracelets as she reached for one of her curls and twisted it further. The glint from her lip stud as she spoke rapidly, turquoise eyes shining, so that it was impossible to hear the words or make sense of them at times. Then he'd open his mouth to say something, to encourage her on and she'd be gone.

I've thought, since reading her letter, about asking you if you remember her at all, my mother, Maria. But if I ask and you don't, then I guess I'd be upset. It was the night she lost her virginity, maybe you knew that, maybe you didn't. Does the blood come immediately? I don't even want to know. Not now. My mind spirals when I think of it. There's no real way for me to reconcile it. I wanted you to be the person to take my virginity too.

As confirmation of what he has been dreading begins to assault him, the pain that has been localized, down his right side, travels to his stomach, as if he has been punched and he's now winded. He smiles. This is the least he deserves.

'Little love,' he whispers, and he lies down on the couch on his side, and he pictures her lying on her side on the beach, smiling up at him. He holds the letter out at arm's length.

If we saw a docu-film of this story, you and me together, I know we'd love it. Can you do it? I'd like you to do it. Set it in Positano, my Nonna's village on the Amalfi coast if you can. It's like the coast at Killiney, only a little more dramatic, a little more stunning. This authentic story, mixed with real-life secrets and misunderstandings will fly. I know it will. Do it as a tribute to me if you like. But please just do it.

Hidden in your briefcase is a USB with all I've been working on since we were last in touch. Down in the slim pocket where you should have a pen. I took your notes, to have something of you too. They needed a little updating, which I've done, and they're on the USB as well. I've drafted something fresh — Joycean influences in Fellini films — with a particular focus on Otto e Mezzo, 8 ½. I hope it might be useful for your book. I'm sorry I couldn't respond to your emails after I found out. I had a lot to work through. Anyhow, I think you'll like what you see. I submitted an article to Camera Obscura, under your name outlining the male hysteria concept. I just don't think you'd do it after I'm gone and now that I won't be doing the PhD it can be set free. I hope they'll be in touch with you. Go with it. Make it yours. Get yourself up to the next level if that's what you desire. That seems to be what you desire.

Jeff bends his knees and curls his legs under himself, allowing the enormity of it to pulse through him. Nina is right. That has been his desire. Blinding him from the start.

Knowing that I have a wonderful father and an adorable brother makes me so happy. I allow myself to imagine if things had been different, if Mamma had told me the truth years ago, instead of the story she fabricated about my birth father — an English tourist passing through Positano when she went back to look after Nonna. I wonder what we might have done with that truth. Would you have embraced me, invited me in? Would I have gotten to feel part of a family unit as well as an appendage to my mother's family? I'm not angry with her, she made her choice out of her own free will and thought she was doing the right thing. Which is all any of us can do. I will always wonder if you knew though, if you had an inkling at all about me, if you felt anything of the electric tingling that I felt with you. I knew you were special, that we would be special together. I just didn't understand why. I don't want to ask you about it. It wouldn't change things now to know.

The sitting room door opens and closes quickly, causing a gust of wind to inflame the fire. Jeff sees Ted's shadow stretch across the floorboards, distortedly long and slim, an adult child. His child. Children. *My children*, he whispers. As Ted steps further in towards the hearth, his head is cut off by the cream rug and Jeff sits up abruptly, adrenalin already pumping fiercely in him.

'I got this for you,' Ted says, holding out a small black plate to Jeff. On it lies an assortment of jagged chunks of red Leicester cheese and pimento-stuffed green olives. Jeff feels the full force of his loss, their loss, somehow with this gesture. As he takes the plate from Ted, he can see that he is shaking. The brine from the olives shimmers on the plate and coats the bottom of the cheese, turning it white. Ted must've been at this a while, he thinks.

'You haven't eaten anything and you'll feel better if you do. That's what Nina said to me.'

Jeff doesn't feel like eating, not at all, but he has no choice now and he picks an olive from the plate and pops it into his mouth, sucking the saltiness out of it before chewing down on it. The pimento releases its smoky sweetness and as he swallows, Jeff feels the lump in his throat dissolve.

'Thank you, little man,' he says, and he plucks the pieces of cheese and remaining olives from the plate and tosses them into his mouth. Then he tips the plate and drinks the brine, before handing it back to Ted.

'You're right, both of you. Just what I needed,' he says, and Ted leaves the room again. Jeff wants to call him back, to ask him to sit with him here for a while so that he doesn't have to read on any further. There's one and a half pages left.

I want you to know that Mamma often told me how overjoyed she was when she discovered her pregnancy. She had feared that Nonna would die and she didn't want to lose her without having first brought a child of her own into the world. She wanted her mother to meet her child. She wanted her mother to become a grandmother. I was born and we stayed for my first few years, a beautiful precious time. When Nonna was well in the clear we returned to Ireland, to the family business that my great-grandfather had established here. It was thriving, with shops opening up in the city centre and the suburbs as well as the original one in Bray. When you met me, formally, that first time and you said my surname out loud, perfectly, beautifully, I thought you might ask me then if I was part of the chippy family. Most people ask me. But you didn't. I was happy that you didn't.

My mother never finished her degree. She worked and loved me fiercely instead. Another thing you didn't seem curious about I'd like you to know now. My passion for film. It came from her. As a child and teenager when I was sick a lot and off school we'd watch Italian black and white movies together. She had a Fellini box set. La Strada was her favourite film too. And so it was my mother who led me, inadvertently, to your door.

As the images from Nina's words flood through Jeff, so too the razor wire of regret, circling his torso, digging in. There was so much to know, if only he'd been brave enough to ask.

It hasn't been difficult to make up my mind about the ending. I can see it. Crystal clear. It is to be a beautiful early-morning beach scene. You are to be there. We are to be together. We will swim out. Only you will return to the shore. It will be a show of love from you to be with me. Father-daughter love. It will make me ecstatic to have that connection with you, singing me off. The drug that helps to keep me alive will end my life out in the sea. I like the symbolism of this, and I hope that you will too.

I don't want you to be sad about my decision. I've struggled with my health, with this illness, all my life. It affects me beyond the physical realm, depressing me at times, leaving me feeling stuck. I didn't want to tell you about it, I didn't want it to define me or for you to feel sorry for me. That night in the hotel, it wasn't carbon monoxide poisoning. I hadn't taken proper care of myself, focusing on the work instead, trying to impress you. Do you remember later on in the hotel bathroom when I was checking you for signs of a stroke? That's something Mamma made sure I knew. There's a heightened risk for us. The very next evening she succumbed to this herself and I wasn't there to check her. I was at your cottage, trying to find my way to you. Her death has been excruciating, but it has resulted in this unveiling of the truth and for that I am deeply grateful.

Please know that beyond my resounding shame, I will die happy, with you, my father, beside me.

I hope that you understand that this, my final act, is also for you. Make something from all of this, a thing of beauty. Move up. Soar high. Shout it out. Our story.

Con tutto il curore,
Nina x

Jeff continues to stare at the page in a trance. If he takes his eyes off it, sees Tuppence watching him, needling him with just one look, it will be over. He will be gone. He flicks to the blue paper, sobering him. This is all his doing. Does he remember Maria Ruzza? Of course he does. Not the name. He didn't ever know that. But the description of what took place, in Maria's hand, would be entirely accurate, should he manage to summon up the courage to read it.

She had scared him that night at first, springing up on the

stool beside him in the bar, as if on a dare, saying that she'd like him to help her. He scanned around and couldn't see who had set her up for this. Someone lurking somewhere.

'You speak Italian?' she'd asked, more a statement than a question. Her voice, heavily accented and deep for a girl. A turn on. Her beauty, a shock of dark, straight hair down to her small waist, enormous green eyes glinting at him in a sideways swoop, so that the pureness of the whites of them sent a shudder of pleasure through him and he knew already then. She started to speak to him in Italian, because she did not want to be overheard, she said. He began to act drunker than he was. She wanted it gone. This thing. She was sick of it, how it loomed there, making her feel separate, an outsider, which she supposed she was, she said, and she laughed. A tinkling soft breeze of a laugh, at odds with her deep voice. She spoke of an event that would be taking place in her family and how she wanted to have this out of the way, gone, before then. Could he help her? He wondered if he had a choice, his body already responding, primed, ready to go. He should just say no, suggest she finds someone more her own age who would be delighted to deflower her, and to have a relationship with her. Instead, he turned away from her and walked out of the bar, knowing that she would follow. He reached inside his jacket for a condom, and when he found none he had asked her to wait. He'd go back to the bar to the toilet and get some. *No*, she had said. *I'm prepared for this.*

Her lightness as he picked her up to carry her to the place, down the steps below the restaurant, a little alcove covered from above by the leaves of an elm tree. He murmured into her hair that she should wait, really she should, as she took his hand and placed it up inside her shirt, to cup her small, firm breast and that was it. There was no going back. It was frenzied and fast, as he held her up against the wall, her legs wrapped around him. *Talk to me*, she had said, *I want to hear your voice*, and he pressed into her, eased himself inside, tried and failed to think of words, looked away from her face as she winced, squeezing her eyes tightly shut. For the briefest of moments he stood there and thought that he could, should really stop. Then he pummelled deep, until he came in a convulsive judder, his pleasure twinned quickly thereafter with a tinge of something else.

The words tripped off his tongue, then, as he put her back down, zipped himself up. He doesn't remember what he said, a flood of gibberish in Italian to assuage, but he remembers her smile and her words. Simple and clear.

Hai una voce bellissima. You have a beautiful voice.

They went back up the steps together and she walked off towards the restaurant while he returned to the bar. He thinks she called after him, *Grazie*, but equally he may have decided to hear that. A cushion. He remembers the swift downing of three pints of Guinness and then a whiskey chaser, as he sat alone on the tall stool that she had sat on just minutes before, wondering if this encounter would bring his already faltering career to a complete halt. His arrest and caution for urinating in public, contrary to public decency six months earlier had been reported in the newspapers. If any nugget from this encounter emerged in the ether it would grow and it would spread. It would take on a life of its own. He'd be as good as gone.

He had darted through the campus in the first days and weeks that followed, head down, as if perpetually late or else on the verge of delivering his most important lecture of the year, nervous about it. In truth, he was trying not to run into her. He had no idea where she had sprung from but spring again he was sure she would. He taught like that too, hanging his face into his notes as if he didn't know what they contained all of a sudden. Gripped by a fear of what would happen should he look up and see her there in front of him. Dazzling a redness onto his cheeks, making him falter and stumble over his words or worse still render him mute. Because this encounter was not something that he didn't want to think about again. Quite the reverse. He had found himself obsessively going over every little bit of it. Her lightness as he picked her up an unequal match for her solid determination. Her deep, hoarse voice a mismatch for the tender beauty in her eyes. Her small breast cupped in his hand which seemed oversized suddenly, ugly, long fingers squeezing hard, thumb circling her nipple as she urged him on. The urging. The wincing. The urging through the wincing. Each thought he had about it was accompanied by arousal, and by having to relieve himself during his working day. In the staff toilets. In his room, venetian blinds, slats down. This was all new to him and he wished the encounter hadn't taken place with almost as much fervour as he felt for the fact that it had.

After some weeks of hoping not to catch a glimpse of her he found himself raising his head again and scouring. Searching for her face in the huddled groups dotted about the campus. Listening out for her voice in the restaurant, resonating around. Her laughter. He longed to hear that again. Each class he held, looking never down at his notes now, but up, going systematically through each row of students, willing one of them to be her. Latecomers. Each time the lecture theatre door swung open a little jitter of panic, accompanied by a nauseous regret that he didn't search for her from the beginning, when each time the door refused to render her up to him. She had disappeared as effortlessly as she had appeared. He began to spend more time in the bar in the evenings. If she wanted to find him, she'd know where to look. He revisited their spot beneath the restaurant and waited for her. Drunk, sitting down on the cold paving stones, a numbness travelling from his arse cheeks down to his toes, reimagining the moment, waiting. He no longer cared about the job so much. If she appeared and wanted to be with him, they could go somewhere else. Italy. He fantasized about that. Starting over in a nice little Italian university town. The weeks turned into months and Jeff spent them in a stupor. She never re-emerged, never came looking for him. Until now.

He folds the blue pages back over, not yet able to read Maria's account. Inside him, deep inside, an eagle's claw clenches and twists at his organs, squeezing the oxygen out of them, dumping it uselessly down in his feet. A light-headedness kicks in. This is his fault. Had he done the right thing and searched for Maria in the days and weeks that followed their encounter, he would have known about Nina and none of this would've taken place. He senses Nina in the room with him now, sitting on his knee as she should have been over all the years, laughing at his regret, his melancholy. She has no time for it. She has acted freely throughout, determining her authentic course, her death being her own individual choice. She would like to hand him her baton. To help him to make something more of his life. Something passionate and true. Which he knows now he will do.

The sitting room door opens again, breaking his trance. Cassandra stands there, her shadow looming up to the hearth. Ted jumps up from beside him, grabbing the last envelope from the coffee table. Jeff has been unaware that Ted is back in the room with him.

'Nina asked me to give this to you, Mum,' Ted says. He thrusts the white envelope into his mother's hand as she stares at Jeff, neither of them saying a word.

FRIDAY

CASSANDRA

I push the door gently. The fire is lit and Jeff and Ted are sitting side by side on the two-seater couch. It's like a normal Friday evening, full of the promise of relaxation. Apart from the silence. They are never this quiet together. Even the dog seems a little subdued. Then Ted sees me and a flash of excitement dances in his eyes. He jumps up and thrusts an envelope into my hand.

Two other envelopes and a page have fallen onto the rug and Ted kneels down to gather them. Jeff looks up at me, impassively, without a flicker of recognition, as if I am a fellow commuter on a train. Pages rest on his knee, folded blue and open cream. Handwritten. I tighten the belt on my coat, one notch further in and I take myself over to the chair opposite him, to the other side of the fire.

She has printed my name in ink. She's cut it short, Cass, as if she knows me. The first letter is in a beautiful calligraphic sweep. I don't want to open it, this suicide note from someone who was clearly in love with my husband. Someone I've never even met. Had I met her at all it would have been as a client. Or eventually as my husband's lover. The damage is done. That look from Jeff, a dead-fish-eyed look, tells me the damage is well and truly done.

'We've read ours, Mum. It was nice of her to write to you as well.'

'It was, darling.'

'Why aren't you opening it?'

'Oh, you know, I didn't really know her like you two did. I'm not sure why she's writing to me at all.'

'Read it,' Jeff says, rising up from the couch, folding his papers back into the white envelope and placing it, along with the blue one, in a pocket inside his jacket. He pokes at the log on the fire until a burst of flame surrounds it. Then he leaves the room, calling Tuppence as he goes. Ted follows them. I hear the jingle of the lead and her excited yelps. The front door closes. I look behind at them going down the garden path to the gate. Jeff has left without his stick. I listen for his return. He does not come back for it.

I pour myself a large Baileys and sip at it, allowing it to warm me up on the inside. Then I rip the envelope open and pull the page from it. I skim it at first to see if I should read it at all. Then I see it. The word standing out, standing proud, as if it's the only word worth reading in all the world. *Daughter.* The noise, when it comes, doesn't seem to be mine at all. It's as if she's here with me, the same caterwaul that came from her on the beach, only I can't make it stop. There is no way to make this stop. Tears spring and chase down my cheeks. One falls onto the page, a little pool raising the ink in the word *sorry*, swirling the letters together into a murky soup, bleeding into the other words. I read the rest of it before it gets destroyed. Her words that will ring in me for all my life.

Afterwards, Tuppence skits across the floorboards and jumps up at me, her paws clawing my jeans, demanding to be petted, cooed at. I wipe my face on the sleeve of my coat before the others come in, and I talk to her as she licks my hand, comforting, enthusiastic rhythmic little licks. Her eyes shine with the sheer simplicity of it all. She's here with the people she loves who love her also. Everyone is home. Almost.

Ted comes in, his cheeks a little flushed after the walk. He throws a chew-stick down on the rug for Tuppence. She gives me one last lick before removing her paws from my knee and claiming her reward. I fold up the page and slip it back in the envelope.

'Did you read it?' Ted asks.

'I did. It's very nice, what she says about you, me and Dad.'

'Why are you crying, then?'

Why.

'I'm sad because she is dead now, and I didn't get to know her properly. It would've been really lovely to get to know her. Lovely for us all.'

Ted talks on about Nina but I'm not listening. I think about the only thing that I will ever really think about for god knows how long. Had I acted differently, run down to them on the beach, called an ambulance, maybe, she could be alive and with us now.

Jeff hovers in the doorway, listening to Ted, glancing my way to see if I now know. I nod, just once.

'Can you go to your room and get into your pyjamas, Ted? I'll be along in a minute to read you a story.'

He sits back down opposite me and I see how his face is waxen, his eyes dull, as if he has a colossal hangover. If he opens his mouth to speak to me, he looks as though he might just vomit instead. So I begin.

'Why, Jeff? Why didn't you tell me about her?'

He takes a deep breath and seems to hold it there with no need to release it.

'We tell each other everything, or so I thought,' I continue. 'But you hid her from me. There's a reason you hid her. She says you didn't know about her and she didn't know about you. So what was it then, this need for secrecy?'

He stares into the fire, my words bouncing off him, impervious.

'What was it, Jeff? Were you having an affair with your own daughter?'

When he turns his head and looks up at me, his eyebrows are raised into questions of their own. He shakes his head just once. Then he smiles, his lip curling higher on the right. The same as Ted. When he speaks it comes out slowly. A quiet deliberation.

'You thought that I was capable of killing somebody. You were afraid of me. There's no way back from that for us.'

'Jesus, Jeff, I saw you hold your hand over her face until she collapsed down in a heap. She was found dead. What the hell would you expect me to think?'

'I don't know, Cassandra. Maybe I'd expect you to think, because you love and trust me, that something else, something other than sex and murder, had taken place. If I'd known you had seen, I would have told you all about her there and then. You could have gone down and checked she was okay when I left her.'

'I don't understand why you did what you did, why put your hand on her face at all?'

'I don't have to explain any of it to you, Cassandra. I played no part in her death, much as she wanted me to. She wanted me to be with her, for us to swim out together where what she had taken would kick in. She wanted to die out in the deep sea with me close by.'

My hands are beginning to feel cold, clammy. My mouth dry. I take a slug of Baileys.

'But we got to the beach earlier than usual that morning. I'd already had my swim when she came running up to me. When I saw her I thought, oh god, what is she up to now? She's the most passionate, dramatic, quirky, bright person I've ever known. She leaped onto me and she was naked, on top as you know, but also under her skirt, and I thought great. If Cass sees this, she'll assume I'm having an affair. I wasn't wrong about that, clearly. She begged me to swim with her and I said no. She was gibbering on, rapid speech, laughing with tears in her eyes, not making any sense to me at the time. I thought she was manic or something like it. I released her grasp and put her down. Then she began to screech and scream. It was just too much. I said quiet now, calm, and when she continued to screech I covered her mouth. I didn't want to risk you hearing her. To risk Ted seeing her like this. I held my hand there and her eyes lit up, twinkling at me. I spoke to her in Italian, a few words. She relaxed and loosened and when I took my hand away she was smiling right up at me, beaming, no longer screeching. When she went down onto her knees and then onto her side she was very much alive. I told her I'd see her soon. She had become stuck lately, not answering emails, not turning up for meetings, not producing her usual work. That was it.'

I reimagine the scene as he tells it. What he's missing from his account is the beauty. The haunting beauty of her lithe young body running and jumping into his arms. Of him holding her there, effortlessly, despite his leg. The beauty that stopped me and froze me, because at the time I was engulfed with jealousy. I'd never be able to run into his arms like that. I'm taller than he is and I know that his girl-friends before me were all petite. When he put his hand over her face I was struck with horror, and also, if I'm completely honest, a little bit of glee.

'So now I just wish you had confronted me, roared out from the car, come down onto the beach, like I'd expect you to if you'd seen.' His words are speeding up and his voice is growing louder. He looks across at me for a moment before he turns his head back towards the hearth.

Trying to redirect his anger into the flames, but it rests firmly with me.

'It would've changed everything, for all of us. I didn't know she was my daughter. I didn't know I had another child. Naturally, I would've welcomed that. Now that I know, she's gone.'

He's saying exactly what I'm thinking, but I'm unable to speak. I'll tell him, in time, about the beauty of it, seen from above. In slow motion. I'll tell him it all, if he'll let me.

He lowers his voice again now, back to its usual register, calm and melodic and reassuring. But it's not me he's trying to reassure.

'I need some time away from you to digest everything that's taken place. I'll book into the Royal Marine in Dún Laoghaire for a few nights. I'll be back to take Ted to the funeral whenever that is. We'll get a taxi. No need to change your arrangements.'

He doesn't ask. He tells. I'm no longer worthy of consideration.

'Thanks for letting me know,' I say and I watch as the remark lands, his brow furrowing as the sarcasm registers, his eyes closing for a moment before they ping back open and stare directly at me. His beautiful, deep brown eyes, laced with fury.

'Are you really going to start this now?' he says, standing up.

'You never once let me know that you were bringing Ted to meet a student. In fact you told him to keep it a secret,' I say, and I hear the quiver in my voice as he does, but he doesn't react to it.

'What do you think that was like for him, being asked to keep stuff from me? Did you ever think about that? How it might not be a good idea, how that sort of thing can cause anxiety in children?'

He shakes his head.

'Not everything needs to be pathologized, Cassandra.'

He wants to bow out, for this to be his parting shot. But I have so many questions and I'll fire whatever I can at him. Nothing to lose.

'Why did you pack the codeine in the bag for the hospital, when you knew I was withdrawing? It felt as if you wanted to keep me drugged up.' He takes a deep breath in and releases it slowly.

'I wanted you to have the choice. I didn't like the way you were being treated, infantilized, told what was happening without any say in it. I have more respect for you, for your capacity to decide what's right for you and when it's right. To withdraw at your own pace, if that's what you wish to do.' A shiver darts through me. That's so very Jeff. Why didn't I think of that? My mouth has gone dry. I take another slug of Baileys, draining it, hoping he won't hear my tongue catching when I speak.

'Your girlfriends before me, they were all petite like Nina. I always feared that you'd seek that out again, that I'm too large for you, oversized, so when I saw her, saw the two of you together, it made sense, you know?' He takes his time, pressing his lips together as he does when he's bemused by something, releasing them again slowly.

'No, I don't think I do. You seem to have taken one small part of my past and blown it up in your head to suit your own insecurity, and it doesn't make any sense to me because you're beautiful, inside and out. No matter what I did or said to convince you of how much I loved you, how mad I was about you, how much I craved you, it was never enough. It's as if you always expected me to stray, to abandon you like your father did, and that it would be your fault some-how. Self-sabotaging, that's how I see it. But you'd know more about that than I do. So here we are. And the conse-quences are so very sad.'

He makes his way to the door, unsteadily. From behind, his loss seems more obvious, more resonant. It sings out from his taut raised shoulders, from the flattened silver waves of his hair, from the slight shake of his left hand and the dull glimmer of his wedding ring as he goes for the door handle.

The grief that's coming for him assaults me now too.

I want to get up, reach out to him, embrace.

But I do not.

He stops. It's as if he can sense what I'm thinking. If he steps back towards me, I'll do it. I'll get up and wrap my arms around him, hold him tight in perfect silence.

But he doesn't step back. He speaks without even turning around.

'Nina has asked me to do something for her and as I failed

her in life, I'm going to try to honour her final wish. I'll discuss it with you when I've given it some proper thought. It would involve Ted, so I'd like you to be on board with it.'

I stay stuck to my chair. I hear our drawers opening and closing and then the soft murmuring voices of father and son. A car pulls up outside. I watch Jeff walk down our garden path to the gate, pulling our golden hand-luggage case behind him. He doesn't have his stick. I close my eyes and listen to the car door being pulled shut and the engine revving, taking him away.

I pour myself another Baileys before going to our bedroom to see if he has smoothened down the bed for me.

JULY

TED

Now I know why Nina wanted to leave and come back to her village. The houses are all different colours, white and pink and orange and red, and they're stacked up on a cliff, like a big Lego build. When I'm on the beach I look up and wonder if they could just all tumble down into the sea, and I'm not afraid.

Dad told me a story about how Nina's village got its name. A very long time ago, a ship carrying a picture of the Virgin Mary got stuck off the shore. The captain heard the picture whisper to him, *Posa, posa,* set me down, set me down. He threw the picture into the sea and the ship floated again. Everyone said it was a miracle. I tell Dad that I like this story and he tells me some more. About the little islands. One of them looks just like Dalkey Island and when I say this Dad says, yes you're right, but it's different too. He looks across at the three of them and says they are the islands of sirens. He speaks very slowly, as if he's tired all of a sudden. I'm thinking about police sirens and ambulances, and I don't know why islands are like sirens, but then Dad says that it's from the Greek myths, like the ones he reads to me at bedtime. He says that sirens were dangerous creatures and they would enchant sailors with their music and singing and the sailors would end up shipwrecked on the rocky coast of the islands. I ask Dad what the sirens looked like and he says at first they were a mixture of a woman and a bird and later they just looked like beautiful women. I ask him why they want to shipwreck the sailors and he shakes his head. He looks out at the islands but he doesn't have an answer. I tell Dad that I like how Nina's village has great stories, that it reminds me of her, and he says, *Yes, indeed, and now we have another story to tell*, and he turns away from the sea and walks across the grey and silver pebbles and I think how it's just like Killiney beach. I run after him and ask if I can have a gelato, it's so hot, and he says yes later, after we've done some good work on the film.

They curl her hair and colour her eyes from brown to a sea blue, but she is not like Nina. Not at all. I stick my fingers into her curls and shake my head until Dad says, *Just pretend, Ted. This is what she wanted, for us to do this.* So I try again, waiting for her eyes to sparkle, for her laugh to come, but they don't and it's all wrong.

Nina's granny wants me to call her Nonna, she says it will make her very happy, but she cries when I say Nonna. I got mixed up and called her Nina one time and then I cried instead. She speaks to Stephano and he tells me what she says. She's laughing and nodding when he tells me that Nina sometimes called her Nonnina, which means little granny,

369

and that it doesn't matter if I call her Nonna or Nonnina or even Nina, I'm not to worry about it. She's like Nina, small for a grown-up, smiling with a wet face, eyes shining, speaking quickly in Italian, saying things that I don't understand. Stephano tells me that she loves me and that she's very happy and that sometimes tears are because of happiness and not sadness at all, and I know this anyway because Mum sometimes has tears of happiness too. He doesn't tell me everything that Nonna says because she talks a lot and he says very little. He tells her what I am saying too, back in Italian. It sounds better in Italian. Nonna likes to cook a lot and she tells Stephano that she will tell me all about Nina, what she was like as a little girl when she was my age. I say to Stephano that I will tell her what Nina was like too, and when he says this to her, she laughs and she cries again, so I don't know if I should tell her or not.

Stephano says I was the last person to see Nina before she died and that's very special. *It was meant to be that way*, he says. Then he asks me again what her face was like, what her wave from the beach was like, and I tell him that she was quite far away and I was in a dark tunnel, but I think she was smiling and she waved her hand just once in the shape of a crescent moon. Above her head a large white bird was flying around in circles.

Good, good, he says and then he gives me some spaghetti to eat, even though I'm not hungry. He doesn't ask first, and I try to eat it to be polite. But it's so long, not like the spaghetti Mum makes, and there's no mincemeat or meatballs with it, and it's shiny with little specks of black and green through it. I try to twirl it on my fork like Stephano but it keeps slipping off, so I scoop it and drag it to my mouth and they laugh and nod their heads until I feel like I'm going to cry. Then Stephano says this was Nina's favourite dish when she was my age, and that she ate it the same way as me. *That's why we're laughing, little friend*, he says. *There was no teaching her, was there,* he says, and then something in Italian to Nonna and she shakes her head and laughs some more. When he asks me if I like it too, I know that I should say yes, I want to say yes, but it's too slippery and there's something strong and spicy in it that I don't like very much, so instead of saying yes which would be a lie I ask how he makes it. As he talks I think about why he says there was no teaching Nina when Dad says she was the best student ever. *It's all about the garlic, crushing three cloves and tossing them in the olive oil on a low heat for just fifteen seconds. That's the trick to it, so that a little sweetness is released but the true raw flavour dominates the dish*, he says. *Nina loved garlic*, I say out loud to join in and he stops talking and looks at me and I don't know if it's a cross look or a sad look but then he smiles and says, *Tell me, my friend, what else did Nina say she loved?*

So I tell him about the day when she brought the game along with her. It was one of Dad's days to collect me but she was there at the school instead, waving at me. She said Dad was delayed at work and that she would bring me to the coffee shop where we could play a game until he arrived. She strapped my bag onto the back carrier of her bike along with her one and she pushed the bike with one hand. She was talking quite a lot saying, *Poor Dad, some timetable error, again, but not to worry as we will have some fun*. She was walking very fast and I began to get a stitch but I didn't want to tell her so I held her hand which always slows Mum down and it worked. She stopped walking for a minute, and she smiled down at me, and her eyes were wet from the cold breeze which made her look sad even though she was happy really. She squeezed my hand and the long silver twisty ring on her middle finger was sticking into me a bit but I didn't mind. My best friend Josh is collected every day by his minder and she's young like Nina but not as pretty and not as nice. She's from France and she doesn't hold his hand and she doesn't even smile when she sees him and she doesn't talk very much even though he says she's here for a year to learn English. When Nina collected me I wanted everyone to think that I had a minder too. I slowed down some more and Nina lifted me up onto her saddle and walked the bike with me on it all the way to the coffee shop. It felt really nice.

The game was called 'SSHH! Don't Wake Dad!' and Nina set it up on a table in my favourite corner in Starbucks, with the soft purple seats and the long glass window looking out on the sea so that it feels like it's a boat we're on, a great big cruise liner. I watched her setting the game up and she was so shiny that day. Maybe it was the big window and the sunlight but everything was sparkling. Her hooped earrings and the ring in her lip. Her eyes. The colours in her hair. She was wearing bracelets too and they jingled and tinkled like bells on Santa's sleigh at Christmastime. I didn't really want to play the game because I didn't know it and I didn't want to look silly in front of Nina but then she said it was easy and it would be great fun and that we'd learn lots about each other. *Playing games is the best way to learn*, she said. She shuffled the cards making her bracelets jingle even more and when she dealt them her thumb and fingers moved so fast and I said I wanted her to show me how to do that too. *So, Dad's asleep in bed*, she said and she looked at me for a long minute, as if she was thinking about something else. *And we have to try to get to the chocolate cake in the fridge without waking him.* She put the bed legs into four holes on the board, pressed something and the Dad began to snore which made me laugh, but not Nina. She must play it a lot for it not to be funny any more. *Does your Dad snore like that?* I asked her. She didn't say anything at first but then she said, *I guess.* I told her about Dad's snoring and that Mum says it's like a volcano erupting and that's why she has to sleep in with me or on the couch sometimes. *I didn't know that*, Nina said and she stared out the window all the way across to Howth Head. *You see, learning stuff already*, she said then and turned back to face me. She explained all the rules really fast and then she said, *I hope you get to the chocolate cake first and win because I'm not really allowed to eat it*, and she laughed. I didn't think it was funny that she's not allowed to eat chocolate cake and when I asked her why she said she'd tell me but first she made me promise not to tell anyone else. *Especially Dad*, she said. *Our little secret.*

I asked her why it was a secret and she said that people can be very silly and when they know you have an illness they are different towards you, as if it changes who you are. *They want to talk about it and ask questions and take care of you. I made that mistake once with someone who was going to be a boyfriend and as soon as I said it the magic was gone. He saw me differently and treated me differently and became a great friend, my best friend, but it killed the romance stone dead.* I asked her why she told me then and she said that it was different with children and that children are wiser than adults and know that having an illness doesn't change who you are. And children are good at keeping secrets she said and she winked at me. *Now enough about me, you're the youngest so you begin*, and she told me to choose a piece and put it on the slippers beside the bed, and then to spin the spinner. I spun. I moved my piece to the correct space. I didn't have a matching card so I had to press the alarm clock five times and each time Nina closed her eyes and said, *Don't wake up Dad* and he didn't wake up. Not until it was her turn. She had to press the alarm clock just once and he woke up so she was caught. *Just as I wanted to be, once upon a time*, she said and she put Dad back into sleeping position and we continued to play, until I won and Nina went up to the counter and chose a piece of chocolate cake for me. *From Dad* she said when she gave it to me. *You love chocolate cake but you're not allowed it. What do you love that you are allowed?* I asked and I began to eat it. Nina made her eyes go bigger for a moment. *That's an excellent question, little guy. Allowed. Hmm. I've been thinking a lot about that word recently.*

She was looking at me as if she really wanted to taste the cake so I cut a piece off with my fork and pushed the plate over to her. *Rules are made to be broken, remember?* I said. *Some are indeed,* she said and she popped it in her mouth. A dark crumb got stuck on her lip and as she began to tell me what she loved I watched it, wondering when it would fall off and if it didn't should I tell her about it.

I love garlic and I love pomegranate and I'm allowed both, she said. *But not at the same time,* and she laughed. Then her face changed from happy to sad and she got off the seat. I was scared that the cake had made her feel sick. She knelt down beside me and she whispered. *I love you and I love your Dad but I'm not allowed.* She stood up and the crumb fell off her lip and she was staring out the balcony door when we both heard Dad's stick clicking behind us and like a robot she left without even turning around. She forgot to pack her game and Dad called her but he sounded quite cross and she didn't come back. He was cross with me too. *Never, ever do that again,* he said. *Do what?* I asked, but he didn't answer. He told me to wait exactly where I was and he went after Nina out the door and down the steps. A minute later he was back, panting as if he'd been in a race, his face all red.

Gone, he said. *Disappeared into thin air.* I was happy but tried not to show it.

Don't ever leave the school with anyone like that again. I was on my way, a little delayed that's all.

But you told Nina to collect me.

No Ted, I did not. She sent me a message when you were already here and I was at the school, looking for you, really worried. Look, don't tell Mum about this, little man, okay? She has enough on her plate already.

My head felt like it could burst that night. When Dad was reading me a story I kept thinking that Nina was not right about children, not really. I had to tell someone all the stuff I was supposed to keep secret and so I did. Tuppence kept it all to herself and my head felt better until Nina died.

When I stop talking Stephano is very quiet. He pushes his chair back from the table and takes our plates over to the sink and begins to tell Nonna what I said. Only it doesn't take him so long. Nonna is nodding her head.

I think Nina was trying to tell you something important that day, in her own way. Something she had just found out herself. Now is the time for you to know.

JULY

CASSANDRA

I don't expect them to turn up. Not after everything. But they do. En masse, as it happens. Ian, Alice and Sheena here for a family appointment. Ian nods when I open the door. Just once. As if all that passed between us in April is contained there, in a simple nod. Sheena leads the way in through the hall and up the spiral staircase. Her mother follows. Ian hovers in the doorway, inspecting the new stained-glass side pane. It's not the same as it was, but it's close. If he notices he doesn't say.

'Never got to the bottom of that one. I still have my suspicions,' he says, as I close the door. I haven't given it a thought since. I don't feel endangered any more. The worst has already happened. I follow him, twisting up to the light timbre of mother–daughter banter.

'Great that you could all make it along here today,' I say sitting opposite the three of them. A family. I haven't seen one for a long time. Even with their difficulties they look united as hell in front of me.

'Apologies for having to cancel the last family appointment. Sheena, as you know, has been attending weekly for the last couple of months and we've been working with a specific therapeutic intervention for self-harm called CBT. I know from Sheena's perspective how this has been working for her and I'd just like to begin by asking you, her parents, how you think she's getting on.'

Alice takes the baton and runs. My thoughts match hers, racing along to a different conclusion.

'So we're going to trial it,' she says, and Ian smiles coyly, his eyes darting in my direction before landing firmly on Alice, a fresh red hue to his cheeks.

'Yes,' he says looking back at me now. 'We'd like to consolidate the progress that Sheena has made. I've started to see someone myself too.'

A twinge of something hits me. I try to smile, to encourage him on, but his words grate like fingernails along a blackboard.

'She thinks I've been going around with undiagnosed post-traumatic stress disorder. I was first on the scene of a crash a couple of years back. Multiple fatalities. A child, a little girl, well, I won't go into it now. But months later I wasn't sleeping properly, got irritated really easily, and angry too at the slightest thing. It affected us all, caused our separation I've no doubt now, but I just didn't know.' He reaches across for Alice's hand, and the twinge is now a full-blown abdominal pain, like the start of a contraction that I can't stop.

'So, yes, we'll try again as a family under the one roof.'

I'm nodding and smiling while the pain bores into me. A twisting stab. An impossible family situation resolves in front of me while my own dissolves in my wake.

AUGUST

TED

I want Mum to come back but she's gone home to see the people she has to see to help make them better. Dad says we might just stay for the whole summer or even longer, we'll see, he says, however long it takes to get it right. When I say that I miss Mum and I miss Tuppence and that I like it here but it's too hot and sticky, and I'm getting tired of walking all the steep steps in the village, he says, *Well, there's not much I can do about that,* and he drinks some more grappa and falls asleep in the chair. He was very sad when Stephano told me about Nina. He says that he wanted to tell me after the film was made because now that I know it will change the way that I am with the Nina who is not Nina and that will change the quality of the film and then it won't be the best it can be for Nina. When he says *after* his voice goes low and deep, like a growl, and I think about Nina, how she'd make her funny face to me if she heard him, with her eyes all big and her cheeks blown up, so that I'd be laughing and he wouldn't know why, and he'd look at her in the way that he always does. Like we've just got off a boat and he's still feeling a little dizzy.

He's waiting for me outside Finnegan's, seated at a small silver table. The late-evening sun shines strongly down, filling the two lagers in front of him with an extra-golden hue. He's wearing sunglasses and his face seems different, a smattering of light freckles perhaps. He's not looking for me, not really, but as I get closer to him he looks up, as if he knows by my footfall that it is me. He removes his sunglasses to greet me and asks if it's okay to sit outside, or would I prefer to move inside. A beautifully mannered young man, as I hope Ted will be in time also.

He has asked to meet to run a few things past me about his little sisters, in the main. They've taken the death badly and are showing signs of withdrawing from things, activities they used to love. Some advice please, he said. But when I sit opposite him it is clear that he needs to talk about himself. He pulls something from the pocket of his black jeans and I recognize it, the handwriting, and he tells me how his mother found this, stuffed inside his pillowcase, a week after. How if he had been vigilant about washing his bedclothes, as his mother has taught him, he would've found it before. On the day she left, in fact. The Sunday. Sunday is bedclothes washing day. But he liked the traces of her on his pillow, a white jasmine muskiness, the dent from where her head had lain. He could summon her there beside him in his thoughts, with just one sniff. So he left it. Had he found it on that day, he could've stopped her.

'But she didn't want that, did she? Or did she?' he asks me, and he continues, not waiting for an answer. Knowing there is no answer.

'That message she sent me the night before about the swim . . .'

He pauses to look at me, to see if I remember. I do, of course. Although what she must've meant by it didn't kick in for me until some time later.

'I still like to see it as her making an arrangement with me. It was, I guess though, a last goodbye. The kiss at the end of it – she never did that on a text. And my reply to her went unread.' He sips at his pint, making little impression on it. All around us people are smoking and the scent wafts and lingers in the still hot air.

'Nina loved that, the smell of tobacco in the sun. She was sure she would've been a smoker herself if it wasn't for her diabetes. In pubs and cafés she was drawn to the outside spaces where smokers gather. For the colour and the craic she used to say. This would've been her thing,' he says and he scans around, smiling, as if appreciating it now with her gaze. He slips his hand into the top pocket of his denim jacket and pulls out a packet of cigarettes.

'Something I've taken up myself since. Do you mind if I have one?'

As he lights up I think about how Jeff was a smoker when we met and how much I liked it, the smell of it on his soft tan leather jacket and in his hair especially, until I asked him to stop when I fell pregnant and he did. Conor takes a long drag and blows it slowly out the side of his mouth, away from me.

'She's left instructions for me – what to do with the twins at key moments as their lives unfold, and it's torturous imagining all this future stretching out without her, it's difficult to even breathe at times. She says she hopes I'll get to know her little brother, Ted, too, see here where she's written it?' He taps his white lighter at her words on the page.

'She says he could do with someone like me as a role model, and I don't know, I'd like to do as she asks with all of it, but I don't know if I can, you know?'

Yes, I know. I know exactly.

'Take your time,' I tell him.

'Call me or visit if you feel like it. She's right. About one thing, at least. Ted will love you.'

ACKNOWLEDGEMENTS

My deepest gratitude goes to the following people:

To my father, Pat Gallagher, Emeritus Professor of Spanish, UCD, who unwittingly lit the spark for this book back when I was a child. To my mother, Kristine, for her constant writing encouragement and annual gifts of membership for the Irish Writers Centre. To my big sister Brigid, a former A&E doctor for checking the medical bits in the book and to my little sister Catherine for advising on the Italian. To my brother Stephen who shares the writing bug with me.

To my father-in-law, the late actor and writer Frank Kelly, for encouraging the writing and celebrating early successes and to my mother-in-law, Bairbre, who continues to encourage and celebrate. To the rest of my fun-loving, creative in-laws – Aideen, Fíona, Jayne, Ruth, Steve and the late Rachel, for their interest and support over all the years.

To my late English grandparents, Audrey and Clif, for the wonderful summers – especially the ones that included the canal barge holidays.

To the enriching members of the Dún Laoghaire Writers Group for inviting me in and giving feedback at the earliest stages of this work – Pat Talbot, John Maguire, Paddy

Connolly, Imelda McDonagh, Jane Ryan, Suzanne Cullen and Simon Dowling.

To my former colleague, Liam Roe, family therapist, for all I gleaned from working with adolescents and families in sessions with him. To my current colleagues in the Irish Association for Counselling and Psychotherapy, for the warm, supportive work environment.

To my supervisors and inspirational sociologists, Professor Stephen Mennell and Professor Tom Inglis for noticing the creative elements peeping through and for somehow making doing a PhD seem like fun.

To my superb agent, Ivan Mulcahy, MMB Creative, who took me on when this was only a couple of chapters in and stayed excited, patient and good humoured throughout.

To my excellent editor Florence Hare and all the team at Quercus – for their contagious enthusiasm for this book from the start and for getting it out there.

To my lovely old pals, Hilary, Sheila, Nicola, Gerri and Siobhán for always asking and encouraging me on.

To my darling boys, Charlie, Daniel, Leo, Myles and Felix, for the constant excitement in the house, for inspiring this work in a myriad of ways and for putting up with a mother who can be found at the laptop, with her head in her hands, unresponsive.

Finally, and above all, to Emmet, for his unending belief and stimulating book chats over flat whites and pints. For ultimately turning the spark into a flame and running alongside me, all the way to the end.